W9-CJL-556

"The Raisin series brings the cozy tradition back to life. God bless the Queen!" —*Tulsa World*

"The Miss Marple–like Raisin is a refreshingly sensible, wonderfully eccentric, thoroughly likable heroine. . . . A must for cozy fans." —*Booklist*

"Agatha displays a wit and sharp tongue that will continue to please her many fans." —*Publishers Weekly*

"Agatha Raisin manages to infuriate, amuse, and solicit our deepest sympathies." —*Bookreporter*

Also by M. C. Beaton

AGATHA RAISIN

M.C. Beaton
Devil's Delight

AN AGATHA RAISIN MYSTERY

WITH R.W. GREEN

St. Martin's Paperbacks

Published in the United States by St. Martin's Paperbacks, an imprint of St. Martin's Publishing Group.

DEVIL'S DELIGHT

Copyright © 2022 by M. C. Beaton Limited.
Excerpt from *Dead on Target* copyright © 2023 by M. C. Beaton Limited.

M. C. BEATON® is a registered trademark of M. C. Beaton Limited.

All rights reserved.

For information, address St. Martin's Publishing Group, 120 Broadway, New York, NY 10271.

www.stmartins.com

Library of Congress Catalog Card Number: 2022035598

ISBN: 978-1-250-81618-4

Our books may be purchased in bulk for promotional, educational, or business use. Please contact your local bookseller or the Macmillan Corporate and Premium Sales Department at 1-800-221-7945, ext. 5442, or by email at MacmillanSpecialMarkets @macmillan.com.

Printed in the United States of America

Minotaur hardcover edition published 2022
St. Martin's Paperbacks edition / August 2023

10 9 8 7 6 5 4 3 2 1

Thanks to Krystyna, Rebecca, and the team at Constable, as well as to Sally for talking me through Cavalleria Rusticana!

Foreword

by R.W. Green

Carsely is a lovely village. It could be argued that its nearest neighbour, Ancombe, is prettier but Carsely is slightly bigger—big enough to support a scattering of shops strung along the high street.

There's Harvey's, the post-office-cum-mini-supermarket where Agatha stocks up on frozen meals to nuke in her microwave, the odd bottle of wine and cat food for Boswell and Hodge.

There's a haberdasher selling everything Agatha might need to mend a torn jacket or stitch a split seam. Needless to say, she's not a regular customer—"make do and mend" is not a Raisin motto. "Bin it and buy new" is more Agatha.

There's a butcher from whom Agatha has been known to buy a steak or some pork chops on the rare occasion she's decided to test her culinary skills but, as we've seen so often in the past, Agatha far prefers eating food to preparing it.

There's also a strange little shop that sells lovely, pretty things such as dried flowers, although you have to be very lucky ever to catch it when it's open.

The fourteenth-century Church of St. Jude stands at one end of Carsely High Street and the Red Lion pub— all oak beams and inglenooks—stands at the other.

Of course, Carsely, its shops, church, pub and its little side streets, including Lilac Lane where Agatha lives, doesn't actually exist. The village, along with other nearby places such as Ancombe, Ashton-Le-Walls, Herris Cum Magna and Mircester, were all invented by M. C. Beaton—Marion—as the backdrop to Agatha's adventures. Yet Marion didn't pluck these places from her imagination entirely.

Up to her death at the end of 2019, Marion's home was in the Cotswolds where she visited towns and villages that inspired her fictional creations, cherry-picking elements that fitted story ideas she was considering. Without identifying the precise locations of her fictional towns and villages, Marion managed to wedge them into their Cotswold setting by weaving real places into her stories alongside them. Evesham is a real town that regularly gets a name-check in Agatha's investigations. She visits The Almonry Museum (a real museum) in Evesham with Charles in *Wizard of Evesham* and in *Perfect Paragon*, she meets a real masseur and his wife at a real gift shop called The Honey Pot in Stow-on-the-Wold.

Bringing real places into the stories ensures that

Agatha's beloved Cotswolds, a designated Area of Outstanding Natural Beauty, plays as much of a role in the stories as the regular cast of characters, and *Devil's Delight* is no exception.

One of the places Agatha visits is the Rollright Stones. This is a real monument site south of Long Compton and north of Chipping Norton, straddling a small road off the A44. The standing stones on the site date back more than five thousand years and the stone circle known as the King's Men originally comprised 105 stones. Over the years, some will have collapsed or been hauled away to be used as ditch bridges or in building barns or outhouses, leaving only seventy-seven still in position. In *Devil's Delight*, a fictional missing stone, known as the Lone Warrior, has a starring role, again helping to anchor Agatha's world firmly in the Cotswolds. Given that there must be twenty-eight real "Lone Warriors" somewhere in the area, I don't think that adapting the folklore surrounding the Rollright Stones is stretching the imagination too far.

While real places bring authenticity to Agatha's world, Marion always had a lot of fun with her fictional settings. There are any number of societies, clubs and organisations around Carsely, from the ladies' societies and ramblers' clubs to the Mircester Players' amateur dramatics theatre and a health farm in Ashton-Le-Walls—so why not a Naturist Society?

Knowing Marion's wicked sense of humour, I think she would have loved the idea of Agatha and her friends being involved with a bunch of nudists. I hope you enjoy reading about the predicaments in which they end up as much as I enjoyed leading them there.

Chapter One

He was naked.

Some people are easily shocked. Agatha Raisin would never count herself as one of those people. She was a private detective, after all—no wilting flower, no timid swooner, no feeble faint-heart. She was made of sterner stuff. Yet even she was a little taken aback. She blinked hard, but when she opened her eyes, he was still there, still naked, in the altogether, not a stitch on, in his birthday suit, in the buff—totally nude. It's not the sort of thing Agatha would normally have expected to see as her assistant was driving her along a quiet country lane and, while not admitting, even to herself, that she was shocked, she was certainly . . . perplexed.

"Agatha . . ." Toni said, slowing the car to a halt, "are you seeing what I'm seeing?"

"If you're seeing a naked young man running down

1

the middle of the road towards us," Agatha replied, unable to tear her eyes away from the spectacle, "then, yes—I'm seeing everything."

The man ran to the driver's side of the car and squatted low, presenting his face, rather than anything else, at the window while knocking urgently on the glass.

"What should I do?" Toni asked, turning to Agatha with a look of panic on her face. "I mean, he could be a carjacker or something. There might be more of them."

"A naked carjacking gang?" Agatha raised her eyebrows. "I think that would be a first. Wind down the window, Toni. Let's hear what he has to say."

"I know it looks a bit strange . . ." said the young man as the window slid down.

"Don't be too hard on yourself," said Agatha. "It all looked perfectly fine to me."

"I mean me not having any clothes on," the young man said quickly, still catching his breath from his dash down the road.

"Let me guess," said Agatha. "A bigger boy stole them and ran away?"

"Please let me explain," he said. "I need your help. I just found a dead body up in those woods!"

Agatha stared at him. His clear blue eyes were sharp with fear and the tremble in his voice came from more than just running.

"Get him something to cover himself up with, Toni," said Agatha. "We need to find out what this is all about."

"Really?" said Toni. "What if he's lying?"

"I've been lied to by many men," Agatha said slowly,

"and I pride myself on having learned to tell precisely when a man is lying—especially the naked ones."

"If you say so," Toni said with a sigh, casting around the car for something the young man could use as a cover-up. Her eyes settled on Agatha's hat in the back seat. They were on their way to a wedding—their friends Bill Wong and Alice Peters were tying the knot—and Agatha had agonised over her choice of hat, eventually settling on a deep blue silk skullcap adorned with delicate blue-and-silver silk flowers and surrounded by orbiting swirls of feather-like silk fronds. Toni had gone against Agatha's advice and chosen not to wear a hat.

"No," Agatha said firmly when she saw where Toni was looking. "He's not using my fascinator as some kind of codpiece."

Toni reached under her seat to produce an old, over-sized T-shirt that she used for wiping the windscreen.

"Here," she said, passing it out of the window. "Maybe you can put your legs through the arms and . . . no . . . everything would drop out of the neck . . ."

"Just cover yourself up," Agatha said, a sharp note of impatience in her voice, "and get in. I want to see where you found the body. You can tell us how you ended up in this state on the way."

The young man wrapped, tied and held the T-shirt in place as a makeshift loincloth, then sat nervously in the back of the car. Toni drove on.

"Start from the beginning," said Agatha. "Tell us who you are and what's happened."

"My name is Edward Carstairs," the young man be-

3

gan. "I'm the social convenor of the Mircester Naturist Society. Take the next turning on the right and you'll come to our clubhouse pavilion."

Toni swung the car across the road and through a gate onto a gravel track that snaked through the dappled shade of tall oak and beech trees, opening out into an area that appeared to be a car park. A red hatchback was parked in front of a single-storey wooden building, which, apart from the red-tiled roof, looked like a giant log cabin.

"I came here earlier today to start preparing for our annual barbecue and put our emergency contingency plan in motion," Edward explained.

"Your emergency what?" Toni asked. "What were you all planning?"

"Today's going to be sunny," said Edward. "Tomorrow it's going to rain. I started a phone chain to let people know the barbecue's being brought forward from tomorrow afternoon to this afternoon. I phone two people, they phone two people and so on—all of our members then know within minutes."

"Sounds very efficient," Toni said, "but why not just send an email or text?"

"It's Saturday, so not all of our members will look at an email, and not all of them are comfortable with messaging, but emails and texts were also sent."

"Yes, yes, that all makes perfect sense," Agatha said, turning to face Edward but finding the sight of him clutching a T-shirt around his groin so awkward that she immediately faced forwards again, "but where does a dead body fit in? And where are your clothes?"

4

"My clothes are inside," said Edward, "in the male changing room. I'll go grab my shorts and my phone. I need to call the police."

"I think you should let us have a look . . ." Agatha began, but Edward was already out of the car, bounding bare-buttocked up the pavilion steps, having left Toni's T-shirt on the back seat.

"I take it that's not what you wanted us to have a look at," said Toni, watching Edward's naked form disappearing into the building.

"No, I thought it would be a good idea to make sure that someone wasn't playing some kind of practical joke on him before we called the boys in blue."

"Still, he's not difficult to look at, is he?" Toni commented, stepping out of the car, her eyes still on the front door of the building. "I mean—he's fit, good muscle tone, nice tan. Funny little birthmark on his left hip."

"You had a good look, didn't you?" Agatha commented, walking towards the pavilion with Toni.

"We're detectives," Toni said in her defence. "I was using my observational skills."

"So what colour were his eyes?"

"Um . . ."

"Maybe you should have looked at his face, Toni. Then you'd recognise him with his clothes *on*."

Agatha pushed open one of the large, glass-panelled oak doors and they entered a spacious, square vestibule. To their right was a door marked "Witches" and to their left one marked "Wizards." Toni studied the signs with a puzzled expression but Agatha was more interested in the full-length mirror that took up all of the wall

5

beyond the "Wizards" door. She smoothed her bob of glossy brown hair, checked her lipstick and admired the way that her dress was hanging wrinkle-free, even after sitting in the car.

She was extremely proud of the way her dress fitted, having dieted mercilessly and exercised furiously leading up to the wedding in order to achieve the flattest stomach she'd had in years, when she remembered to suck it in a bit. She did so, turning sideways to watch how the open frill that ran from the calf-length hem up to her hip tousled, then settled. Agatha was of the opinion that only women with a good, shapely figure could wear a dress like this. It was off the shoulder but not cut too low, with a tight bodice and a skirt that flared out from the waist.

She glanced at Toni, who was peeking through the door marked "Witches." She could never get away with this dress. She was beautiful, of course, in that blonde-haired, blue-eyed sort of way, but she was too straight-up-and-down—too skinny. This dress was definitely for the more chic, slightly more mature woman.

"It's off West Carsely Lane," came Edward's voice as he appeared from the "Wizards" door with his phone clamped to his ear and a pair of shorts now covering his magic wand. "Yes, a dead body. I know what I saw! Please hurry!"

"I was hoping you would let us confirm what you'd found before you called the police," Agatha said as Edward rang off. "We have a great deal of experience in these matters and we're on good terms with the local officers. We're actually on our way to the wedding of

Detective Sergeant Bill Wong and Detective Constable Alice Peters. I'm Agatha Raisin, private detective and proprietor of Raisin Investigations. This my colleague, Toni Gilmour."

"Agatha Raisin—yes, of course!" Edward said, recognition dawning on his face. "I've seen you in the *Mircester Telegraph*. You're the one who caught the gang that was selling endangered animals."

"If you know who I am," Agatha said, "then you know that it would be a good idea to let us take a look at the body. Lead on."

They followed Edward through an archway opposite the main doors that led into a bar and function area, where there was a dance floor around which were arranged tables and chairs. French windows then opened onto a patio extending out to a well-tended lawn bordered by flowerbeds bursting with the varied, vibrant summer colours of roses, dahlias and geraniums. To one side of the lawn was a swimming pool and to the other a tennis court.

"I had some time to spare," Edward explained, motioning them to follow him down onto the lawn. Agatha slipped off her high-heeled sandals. She was not fond of walking barefoot, but she knew how easily heels could dig into a lawn. The heels were elegant, but elegance evaporated along with dignity should a heel snap and send you sprawling on your face. "I decided to take a closer look at the Lone Warrior."

"What's the Lone Warrior?" asked Toni.

"It's a huge, ancient stone slab in a clearing in the woods at the far end of our grounds," said Edward.

"They say it was once used for human sacrifices. That's where I saw the body. It was sitting on the stone."

"Just sitting there?" said Agatha, wincing slightly when she stepped off the grass onto a vague path at the edge of the woods where pebbles, twigs, spiky leaves and other forest-floor debris alien to the tender soles of a city girl's feet lay in ambush. Toni was wearing flat shoes and a look of sympathy. Agatha gritted her teeth and marched on, sandals in one hand, clutch bag in the other.

"Not actually sitting," said Edward, "more sort of crouching, all hunched over with his face in his hands. It's just through here and . . ."

They walked into a clearing, the sun streaming down between the treetops to create a brightly lit patch on the forest floor. In the middle of the pool of sunlight stood a weathered grey stone. It was three feet tall and six feet long with a flat top wide enough to lie on . . . but nothing lay there. There was no crouched, hunched body on the stone. It sat empty and still in the glade with only the chattering of chaffinch and blackcap in the treetops subverting the silence.

"It's gone!" Edward gasped, looking around in desperation as he approached the stone. "I swear it was here! You have to believe me!"

"I believe you saw something here," said Agatha, studying the stone, "but in my experience a dead body does not get up and walk away. What exactly did you see here? How close did you get?"

"I saw a man's body, naked, crouching with his face in his hands," Edward replied, continuing to look around as if the body might somehow appear at the base of a

8

tree or in a stand of ferns. "I knew he was dead because the back of his head was all bashed in. There was matted blood in his hair and when I reached out to touch his shoulder, he was stone cold."

"Yet this stone is not cold," Agatha said, laying her hand on the Lone Warrior, "and there's a damp patch in the middle—a little puddle of water."

"Where did that come from?" Toni asked. "It hasn't rained for days."

"It's difficult to make out any footprints among all the leaves and weeds," Agatha noted, examining the area around the stone, "but that looks like it might be a tyre track."

"A single tyre track?" Toni said with a frown. "Maybe a motorbike?"

"I didn't hear any motorbike," Edward said. "The thing that spooked me was when I heard a mobile phone ring just as I touched the body. Obviously it wasn't my own phone . . ."

"No pockets," said Toni.

"No trousers," said Agatha.

". . . and I thought that the killers might be lurking in the trees, so I ran," Edward went on. "I ran in that direction." He pointed. "Through the trees, over a fence and out onto the road."

"Are there any other ways out of here?" Agatha asked.

"I suppose there must be," Edward replied, "but I'm not really sure. I've only been down here a couple of times and I've always gone back to the pavilion from here."

"There are various paths through the woods," said Toni, studying her phone, on which she had called up an aerial view of the area. "They appear to lead to tracks that run down to the road we were on as well as a couple of other minor roads heading in the direction of Mircester."

"So, anyone hiding in the woods watching you," Agatha pondered, scanning the treeline all around the clearing, "could have made off without returning to the pavilion and without us seeing them."

"But if someone had decided to dump a body here," Toni said, frowning, "why would they then take it away again?"

"Maybe they didn't want to dump it here," said Agatha, still peering into the woods. "Maybe they were disturbed by nudie Eddie and hid until he was gone. Then they moved the body to somewhere like . . . over there, where there are thick shrubs under the trees." Agatha pointed to the spot. "That looks like a—"

"Nice place to dump a body?" said Toni, then, returning Agatha and Edward's bemused stares with a shrug, added, "She says it all the time."

"I do *not* say it all the time," argued Agatha.

"Yes, you do," said Toni. "Every time we pass a—"

"Just go take a look." Agatha cut Toni short, then lifted one foot to display immaculately painted toenails. "I had a pedicure yesterday. It's survived this far, but I'm not ruining it scuffling around over there."

Toni and Edward picked their way through the tangle of ferns and brambles to where a clutch of tall rhododendrons stood in the shade of the trees. Toni picked up a stick to prod around in the undergrowth, shining a light from her phone to illuminate the darkest recesses of the dense shrubbery.

"There's nothing there, Agatha," she called, looking back towards the Lone Warrior, on which Agatha had now parked her sandals, then pointing beyond her boss, through the trees towards the swimming pool, "but here comes trouble!"

Agatha turned, catching a glimpse of the unmistakable form of Detective Chief Inspector Wilkes marching down the lawn. He was wearing a suit that was somewhere between brown and grey, matching his greying hair and pallid complexion. It occurred to Agatha that, if he were to lie down on the forest floor, no one would ever notice him. He would merge right in to the decaying debris of sticks and fallen leaves and probably never be seen again. Unfortunately, however, she could see him quite clearly now. He was a tall, thin man and, even on this gloriously sunny day, appeared darkly miserable. His beady eyes glowered from beneath a furrowed brow when he spotted Agatha.

"What are you doing here?" he barked.

"Same as you," said Agatha. "Looking for a corpse."

"This is a police matter," he said, glancing over his shoulder to where two uniformed officers were jogging past the swimming pool towards him. He waved at them to hurry. "One of my officers will take a statement from you, then you can be on your way."

"A statement about what?" Agatha asked. "I can't see that any crime's been committed."

"That's for me to decide, not you," Wilkes said, curtly. "Where is the person who reported finding a body?"

"The young man over there in the shorts," Agatha said, pointing to Edward, who was picking his way back through the brambles with Toni, "but the body he found seems to have gone missing."

"What are you talking about, woman?" Wilkes snapped. "How can a body disappear?"

"I understand it was sitting on this stone slab," Agatha explained, stooping to examine the surface of the stone, "but by the time we got here there was only a little puddle of water. Even that's dried up now."

"Ridiculous!" Wilkes barked. "Bodies do not simply evaporate like water!"

"I know what I saw," said Edward. "There was the body of a man with his head all bashed in. I was startled by a phone ringing in the bushes and ran off to find help."

"You need to cordon off the area and get some forensics people out here," said Agatha. "There will have to be a fingertip search of the surrounding woodland and—"

"There will be no such thing!" Wilkes said, a sweep of his hand drawing a line under the idea. "Do not try to tell me my job, Mrs. Raisin."

"As we've seen so often in the past, Chief Inspector," Agatha said, setting her chin and folding her arms, "apparently someone has to."

"I don't have the manpower to waste on what is clearly some kind of practical joke," Wilkes said, bluntly. "Half the force seems to have taken leave in order to attend the wedding of DS Wong and DC Peters."

"I take it you weren't invited?" Agatha gave Wilkes

a transparently insincere smile and picked up her sandals. "Toni and I are on our way there now."

"It's a lovely day for a wedding," came a low, powerful voice from the direction of the pavilion.

Agatha and Wilkes turned to see a dark-haired man approaching. Agatha judged him to be in his mid-to-late forties. He was not quite as tall as Wilkes but was more powerfully built, with broad shoulders and well-defined muscles. He had piercing blue eyes, tanned skin and a beard styled and clipped with bonsai precision. The hair on the rest of his body was equally well-groomed, artfully trimmed to show off his impressive physique to best advantage. Agatha was able to assess his physical attributes so thoroughly because, like Edward when he had come running down the lane, the newcomer was entirely naked. Unlike young Edward, the bearded man had an aura of calm maturity, radiating confidence in a way that Agatha found beguilingly attractive, despite his beard. Agatha had never liked beards. She had a sudden urge to check her lipstick but settled instead for a little extra abdominal squeeze to hold her tummy taut.

"What do you think you're playing at, man?" Wilkes bellowed. "Put some clothes on at once!"

"I don't feel inclined to dress myself right now," answered the man.

"You don't feel . . . ? Gittins!" Wilkes yelled at one of the uniformed constables, frantically beckoning him closer. "Arrest that man!"

"Er . . . what am I nicking him for, sir?" asked the constable.

"He's to be charged under Section Sixty-six, Sexual

13

Offences Act 2003—exposing his genitals intending to cause alarm or distress," Wilkes stiffly quoted the regulations.

"Are you going to arrest all of them, too?" asked Agatha, nodding towards the lawn where a small crowd of naked men and women of all ages, shapes and sizes was beginning to gather, standing and staring like a throng of fleshy statues. When he spotted the undressed horde, Wilkes's mouth dropped open.

"The thing is, sir," said Constable Gittins, "this here's a naturist club, so everyone's allowed to go around in the altogether."

"Thanks for explaining, Ian," said the bearded man, giving the constable a nod of gratitude.

"You know this man, Gittins?" Wilkes said, frowning at his junior officer.

"Oh, yes, sir," said Gittins. "Everyone knows Jasper Crane. He's our chairman."

"OUR chairman?" Wilkes was flabbergasted. "You mean you're—"

"Exactly, Chief Inspector," Jasper said with a smile. "Ian is one of our members. Will we be seeing you for the barbecue later, Ian?"

"Me and the missus will be here soon as I finish me shift," said Gittins, removing his cap to fan himself while tugging at his bulky, stab-proof utility vest to let some air circulate. "Can't wait for a dip in the pool."

"Well," Wilkes muttered, "I'm glad I won't be here to witness that." Then he raised his voice to talk to Gittins. "Disperse that crowd of . . . your friends up there, Gittins, and you," he pointed to the other constable, "have a good look around for anything suspicious, then take a statement from the person who phoned this in. I'm going back to the office."

"Is that it?" asked Agatha. "You're not going to launch a proper enquiry?"

"Whatever your friend in the shorts saw," said Wilkes, "always assuming he hasn't completely lost his marbles and was hallucinating, was undoubtedly a prank played on him by his nudist chums. If I need any sort of statement from you, Mrs. Raisin, I always know where to find you. I just have to look for trouble and you're never far away."

"And you're even easier to find," Agatha replied, fixing Wilkes with her bear-like eyes. "All I have to do is turn over the nearest rock and out you crawl."

Wilkes gave a "harrumph" and marched off towards the pavilion, breezing past two petite, middle-aged women. Each of the women was wearing a loose-fitting kaftan embroidered with gold astrological symbols. They made for Jasper, one of them offering him a black silk robe.

"We thought you might want this while you talked to the prudes," she said.

"Thank you, ladies," said Jasper, treating them to a warm smile and shrugging on the robe. It was decorated with golden images of fiery suns, glowing planets, twinkling stars and streaking comets. There were no fastenings but the edges met in the middle, covering his nakedness. The women bowed and walked back the way they had come, flinging off their kaftans when they reached the lawn.

"Prudes?" Agatha enquired with a raised eyebrow.

"It's just a little fun term we use when we have clothed visitors at the club." Jasper laughed. "We refer to ourselves as the 'nudes' and clothed people as 'prudes'—too prudish to disrobe, you see."

"Yes, I do see," said Agatha, bristling slightly. "I don't think I've ever been called 'prudish' before."

"Please don't be insulted. You and your friend are more than welcome to join us here any time you like." He swept his left arm towards the clubhouse. The robe had openings for his arms but no sleeves, the silk drifting up to his elbow and wafting open down the middle, allowing Agatha another glimpse of what had previously been covered. In an instant, she realised she was staring and averted her eyes.

"It's all right to look," he said gently. "We all look, we all compare—that's human nature and we are, after all, naturists. What we don't do is judge."

"How very . . . reassuring," Agatha said.

"Agatha, we really need to get going," said Toni, looking at her watch.

"Ah, yes . . . the wedding," Jasper said. "Allow me to walk you to the pavilion."

"I'd like to have a quick word with Edward first," Agatha said, and joined him and Toni on the other side of the Lone Warrior.

"I'm really sorry about all of this, Mrs. Raisin," Edward said, "but I honestly saw a body sitting right here on the stone. I wasn't making it up. Now I feel like I've wasted your time."

"I don't like people playing tricks on me," Agatha

said, tersely, "and if that's what you were doing, I'll make sure you regret it."

Edward looked down at the ground, shuffling his feet like a naughty schoolboy in front of the headmistress.

"But I don't think that's what happened here," Agatha went on. "I think you were telling the truth, yet there doesn't appear to be any evidence of a crime—certainly not a brutal murder. It's a mystery and I hate leaving things unresolved."

"We'll help you find out what it's all about, won't we, Agatha?" Toni offered, eagerly. "We'll help you get to the bottom of it, Edward."

"Well . . . yes, of course," Agatha agreed, slightly taken aback by Toni's unbridled enthusiasm. "When the officer takes your statement, be sure to ask for a copy. We can at least go over it all together at some point."

Edward thanked them for being so understanding, then he and Toni followed as Jasper escorted Agatha back to the pavilion. Even more people had now arrived, turning the garden and pool area into a hive of activity. Keen gardeners wearing nothing more than sturdy gloves were dead-heading the roses, the perimeter hedge was being clipped, bugs and leaves were being fished out of the pool, and the patio was being swept. Agatha had never seen so many naked people. They smiled and waved as she walked by, making her feel completely welcome and yet utterly out of place at the same time.

"We do all of our own maintenance," Jasper explained. "We have people from all walks of life, from plumbers and accountants to doctors and, as you know, police officers."

The two women who had brought Jasper his robe came towards them once more, this time without their kaftans. From their almost identical brown hair and similar figures, Agatha had no doubt that they were sisters.

"The ice cream is in the freezer, Jasper," reported the first sister.

"And the bread is in the oven," the other confirmed. Jasper thanked them both and they bowed once again before heading off to join the gardeners.

"Why do they bow to you like that?" Agatha asked. "You may be the chairman, but bowing's a bit over the top. Quite demeaning, actually."

"They're my handmaidens," Jasper said, then burst out laughing when he saw the scornful look on Agatha's face. "Don't worry, Mrs. Raisin, it's just our little joke— part of a game, in fact. Some of our members take part in a fantasy role-playing game on Wednesday evenings— angels and demons, witches and wizards on a grand quest."

"That explains the signs on the changing-room doors," Agatha said.

"Precisely," Jasper agreed. "I play a kind of demonic master-of-ceremonies and devise a storyline with clues to be solved to find various artefacts. It's all a power battle leading to a spectacular grand finale that promises to be quite an event—a buffet dinner, dancing, fireworks. The Lone Warrior will even play a part. You should come along."

"I've always been the kind of girl who likes to dress up for a party rather than . . . well . . . not dressing at all."

"Then you'll love it." Jasper grinned. "Everyone

plays a character and some of the costumes are truly magnificent. Some," he added, with a twinkle in his eye, "are little more than body paint and glitter, but most put a lot of effort into creating outfits that are out of this world. It's a fun evening—why not join us?"

"I'll think about it," Agatha said, reaching down to ease her right foot into its sandal. Jasper offered her his arm on which she rested the hand holding her clutch bag to help balance while pulling on her left sandal. His arm was strong and steady. She thanked him and offered him a business card from her bag. "Let's keep in touch. Your grand finale evening sounds . . . different."

Agatha waved to Toni, who was talking to Edward and two young women who were carrying tennis racquets and wearing only tennis shoes. Toni said her goodbyes and walked with Agatha to the car park, where most of the parking spaces were now occupied, one by a Ford in police livery.

"That," said Agatha, snapping her seatbelt into place, "was a strange experience."

"A real eye-opener," Toni agreed, manoeuvring the car out onto the road. "Who knew there were naked people hidden away in the woods around here?"

"I was thinking more about the disappearing corpse," Agatha mused. "Something very suspicious was going on there. The Mircester Naturist Society, on the other hand, was . . . very revealing."

"I thought Wilkes was going to burst a blood vessel!" Toni laughed. "I've never seen anyone look so outraged!"

"And yet he doesn't seem to mind nudity," Agatha

pointed out. "We caught him in a strip club not so long ago, remember?"

"Yeah, what a hypocrite! The creep was happy to pay to watch women take their clothes off, but when a man shows up naked, it's a different story . . . and Jasper," she added, pointedly, "was a fine example of a man."

"I had noticed," Agatha said, smiling.

"I know you noticed. I could see you noticing. I also saw you giving him your card. Are you planning on seeing more of Jasper?"

"I think I've seen pretty much all of him already," Agatha said, in a matter-of-fact voice, "and you know I don't like beards. They always smell of—"

"Stale beer and last night's kebab," Toni said, finishing off one of Agatha's more familiar mantras.

"I was going to say 'curry,'" Agatha lied, "but I'm glad you pay attention to the things I say. You may yet learn something. Anyway, you seemed very taken with Edward. I thought you were getting ready to settle down with your policeman, Paul?"

"We're kind of . . . agreeing to stay friends," Toni said with a sigh.

"Oh, dear," Agatha said in a voice she hoped was laden with sympathy. In fact, she was hugely relieved that Toni was no longer in a serious relationship. She was young, but she was hard-working and trustworthy—the only one of her staff whom Agatha could comfortably rely on to run the business when she wasn't around. For purely selfish reasons, Agatha needed Toni available to work long hours and to have her mind focused on the job rather than domestic bliss at home. "Such a shame it didn't work out with him. He seemed nice."

"He was nice. I mean, he *is* nice, but he's got his whole life mapped out. He knows exactly where he is and where he wants to be at each stage. When he's not working, he's studying for his sergeant's exams and he wants to be an inspector within five years. He's running his life to a master plan. I was starting to get the feeling that I was a box to be ticked on his schedule. You know, 'find girl, tick—get married, tick—have children, tick-tick-tick.'"

"I thought that's what you wanted—a reliable husband, house, car, kids and two weeks' holiday in Mallorca every year."

"What would be so wrong with that?" Toni asked, glancing sideways at Agatha, suspecting she was being teased, which she was. "But it has to happen naturally, not as part of some sort of master plan. He also wants to transfer to the Met Police in London, where he can go for bigger and better jobs. He doesn't seem to see that my job is here—my life is here in the Cotswolds. This is my home."

"Of course it is," Agatha agreed. "He'd have to be a fool not to see that. Take it from me—London's overrated."

"And men," Toni said with a firm nod. "Men are also overrated."

"A necessary evil," Agatha concurred, "and not always entirely necessary."

"Ah . . . I take it you and James are—"

"I don't want to talk about whether James and I are

or aren't. We'll see him at the wedding if he's managed to get back from his meeting in London in time but I'm not going to let trouble with men get in the way of enjoying myself today. I've been looking forward to this wedding for too long to let anything spoil it."

"Even a murder? A body that goes missing?"

"That's a real puzzle," Agatha admitted, "but I don't believe that a sensible bloke like Edward was frightened out of his wits by some kind of prank. If he says he saw a dead body, then I believe him. So who was murdered, where is the body now and who is the murderer? I intend to find out."

"Good. I was hoping you'd say that."

"Would that be because you're so keen on Edward by any chance? You were determined to let him know we would help him. I can't quite believe that, with a bunch of naked people milling around, you told a nudist that we would help him 'get to the *bottom* of it.'"

"I couldn't help it," Toni said with an embarrassed laugh, a slight blush colouring her face. "I've never seen so many bottoms!"

"Well, get them out of your mind and concentrate on the driving," Agatha said, flipping down the sun visor and using its mirror to reapply her lipstick. "We've still got a wedding to get to, and we're going to be late."

Chapter Two

Lower Burlip Village was on the other side of Mircester from Agatha's home in Carsely. It wasn't an area that Agatha could recall ever having had cause to visit, yet it was there that Bill and Alice were to be married. When she had called up a map on her phone, at first glance Lower Burlip looked to be only a few minutes' drive away but Agatha had insisted Toni pick her up early as Saturday was one of Mircester's market days and she had seen today's market widely advertised on posters around the town as the "Inaugural Vegan Event." Traffic on market days was usually bad enough, with roads through the town turning to gridlocked purgatory. For the vegan extravaganza, Agatha fully expected it to be even worse, imagining ageing hippies in crumbling Citroëns sharing peace and love with swarms of new-age activists riding unicycles and playing bongo drums.

Added to the delay at the naturist club, she was now convinced that they had no chance of getting to the church on time. To her surprise, she was wrong.

The roads through Mircester were actually no busier than usual, even though the market area near the old cathedral was thronging with people. Clearly the dedicated vegans and curious carnivores had taken advantage of the glorious weather by walking into town. They drove past the town's modern, yet thoroughly dilapidated shopping centre, and on through an area where most of the shops appeared either to be selling burgers or bathroom tiles, or offering to carpet your whole house for less than the price of the dress Agatha was wearing. While she was interested neither in fitted carpets nor ceramic tiles, Agatha had a penitent penchant for fast food. In order to fit into her dress, she had consumed only coffee for breakfast. Her stomach gave a little rumble and she was glad when they passed swiftly beyond the burger joints, out of the grimy commercial zone and into the treelined streets of the suburbs.

Lower Burlip Village was not a typical Cotswolds village. It was not a single street of age-old yellow-stone cottages leaning against each other for support and competing to display the most luxuriant hanging baskets bursting with cascades of begonia, fuchsia and lobelia. Neither was it surrounded by fields, although it certainly gave the impression of being on the edge of the countryside. There were plenty of trees, gardens were well-tended and the houses were of traditional, mellow Cotswold stone, but these were far from being the cottagey former homes of farmworkers. They were large, modern houses fit for business executives, bankers and lawyers. The gleaming new cars sitting in the driveways further confirmed Lower Burlip Village as a comfortable, affluent neighbourhood, albeit a suburban district rather than an actual village.

"I've lived in Mircester all my life," Toni said, looking left and right, "and I've never been up here."

"And 'up' is precisely where we are," said Agatha, craning her neck to see beyond the hedge surrounding a mansion-sized property. "We've been going uphill ever since we left the town centre and we've certainly been going upmarket. If this is Lower Burlip, I wonder if there's an even posher 'Upper' version?"

"If there is, then I've never heard of it. So this is where Alice was brought up?"

"It is—she went to Sunday school at St. Giles's Church, which must be that building just up ahead."

Agatha pointed to a large, stone castle–like tower at the end of the wide, leafy avenue up which they were driving. The road circled round a flat expanse of grass boasting a street sign that simply announced "The Green." To its right stood St. Giles's Church. Like many English churches, the tall, square bell tower, topped with battlements robust enough to stand fast against any battalions Satan could muster, made the building look far older than it really was.

"Wow," Toni said, clearly impressed. "That looks like it's been transported straight from the Middle Ages—you can imagine King Arthur and Sir Lancelot riding past."

"Not quite, Toni. I'd say it was actually less than one

hundred and fifty years old," Agatha said with the firm confidence of someone who had just spotted the year "1879" carved on one of the tower's mighty stone blocks. "The Victorians loved to build things that looked like they belonged in another time."

"Looks like we can park here," Toni said, pulling over to the kerbside in the shade of a chestnut tree. "We'd best be quick, Agatha," she added, looking in her rear-view mirror to see a white Rolls-Royce making stately progress up the hill. "Here comes the bride!"

Taking time only to check her make-up and to insist on Toni checking that her hat was positioned at just the right angle, Agatha rushed into the church, one hand holding her hat in place and the other grasping her clutch bag. Toni trotted alongside her and, immediately inside the main door, a smiling young man in a dark blue, tail-coated morning suit enquired "Bride or groom?" before fulfilling his function as an usher by directing them down the right-hand side of the aisle, where the pews were occupied by Bill's family and friends. Toni slipped into the nearest pew, but Agatha spotted James and skipped down the aisle to stand beside him just as the organist switched from an intricate piece of tinkering that nobody recognised to Wagner's "Bridal Chorus," the congregation all rising to their feet.

"You cut it a bit fine," James said with a frown of disapproval. He was ex-army and a stickler for punctuality.

"Better late than never," Agatha replied, casting a well-practised, patently insincere smile at the jowly woman in front, who had turned to scowl at the noisy latecomer. No amount of scowling, however, could have silenced the murmur of approval that burbled round the church when Alice paced slowly up the aisle on her father's arm. He was wearing the same tail-coat morning suit as the ushers. He was tall and good-looking, his dark hair greying at the sides, and he looked every inch the proud father, but he might as well have been invisible. All eyes were on Alice.

Her glossy waves of black hair were decorated with a simple garland of white flowers and round her neck hung a delicate gold chain displaying a gold flower pendant, which Agatha knew had been a gift from Bill. Her ivory silk dress was an image of divine elegance. Small sleeves capped her shoulders, the neckline falling from the sleeves in a shallow "V" that accentuated the way the tight bodice, overlaid with intricately patterned lace, hugged her torso. From her hips, the silk dropped straight down to pool in a modest, rippling train that trailed along the tiled floor in her wake. The back of the dress plunged lower than the front, but here the wide "V" was partially closed by a scalloped lace insert.

It was not, Agatha decided, the kind of dress that she would ever have considered for either of her own weddings. She had what she liked to think of as a more voluptuous figure than Alice's. Alice didn't have the curves to carry off the designs that best suited Agatha. Alice was, in fact, more like Toni. She turned to see Toni, who mouthed the word "Gorgeous" and wiped a tear from the corner of her eye. Yes, Agatha thought to herself, there was no denying that Alice looked gorgeous and that hungry rumbling in her tummy had now turned to a pang of jealousy. She had admitted, but only ever to herself, a long time ago that she felt a little jealous of Alice. What, after all, was there not to be jealous about? Alice was young, smart and beautiful, and she was marrying Bill who was also young, smart and beautiful. They were a young, smart and beautiful couple. So she felt a bit jealous—that was entirely natural and honest. She also felt enormously happy for them—that was natural and honest, too.

Alice and her father made their graceful procession to where Bill and his best man, both also wearing the blue morning suits, stood facing forwards. Agatha was admiring the way Bill's frame filled the shoulders of his suit so well when Alice reached his side, glanced across at him and beamed a smile that lit up the whole church. He returned the smile in kind and Agatha surprised herself with a little gasp. The happy couple had just exchanged an unmistakeable look of absolute love and, just for a moment, Agatha felt a slight stinging in her eyes, as though a tear might be struggling to make an appearance. The moment passed when a mournful wail echoed from the front pew. Agatha stared forward through a couple of rows of men's heads and ladies' hats to where she could see the backs of Bill's mother and father in the front pew. Ma Wong's shoulders began to shudder. She was a large woman and Agatha estimated that, should the wedding guests need somewhere to congregate prior to the reception, the voluminous yellow dress she was wearing could be pitched on the Green as a sizeable marquee.

Pa Wong reached out an arm to comfort his wife. Unlike his son, he was not tall and well-built. His hand appeared when the overlong sleeve of his blue morning coat slid up his arm. Gently, he patted his wife's shoulder. That, too, thought Agatha, was a gesture of love. They were an odd couple, not because he had been born in Hong Kong and she in the Cotswolds, but because they led a peculiarly insular life. Having estranged themselves from their families when they first got together, Ma and Pa Wong had solidly supported each other over the years, developing a bond that made them mistrustful of others, sometimes to the point of being rude. Yet they doted on their handsome son.

To them, the old adage that the wedding meant "not losing a son, but gaining a daughter" was utter claptrap. They were most definitely losing a son, and it was Agatha who had stepped in on Alice and Bill's behalf to persuade them to let him go. In the process, family rifts had begun to heal and Agatha was delighted to see that Ruby, Bill's cousin, was one of the two bridesmaids who had followed Alice up the aisle. The other she assumed to be one of Alice's relatives.

The ceremony was joyous, uplifting and, to Agatha's mind, mercifully short. When the vicar eventually declared Bill and Alice "husband and wife," there was another sobbing wail, this time higher-pitched, from the front pew, and Ma Wong gently put her arm around the shoulders of her husband—another small gesture that showed the love between them. Agatha looked at James standing tall at her side. Was there any real love binding her and James together?

His face was lightly tanned with just a few characterful wrinkles. He was every bit as handsome as the day she had first met him, when he had moved into the cottage next door to hers in Carsely. He had, at first, been quite aloof—a handsome man living but a stone's throw away, attractive, available, yet unattainable. Agatha had seen him as a challenge, all the more desirable for the fact that he seemed to take no interest in her. She felt that her initial infatuation had blossomed into love, but when they were engaged and she had asked him if he loved her his response was a short, "I'm marrying you, aren't I?"

James hadn't been the sort to, as he put it, "go babbling on about emotions," but they had been through a great deal since those early days, especially when he had become involved in some of her investigations. They had faced danger and even death together, but had taken those major traumas in their stride. It was the little things that had torn them to shreds. Their marriage had crumbled under the weight of petty squabbles and intransigence. Both were set in their ways, with neither willing to change nor compromise. He still lived next door.

Once they were apart, however, they seemed to get on better than ever. James had changed, reacting with unexpected enthusiasm when Agatha had suggested that they may have given up on their marriage too soon and should give it another go. His attempts to rekindle their relationship had left Agatha confused. Why was it that she found him so much more attractive when he had been tantalisingly out of reach? Then, when they had taken a motoring trip through France together, with travel writer James using the trip to research his latest book, he had seemed to revert, to fall back into his old ways, almost as if he had given up on the idea of them being together again. It hadn't taken Agatha very long to lose patience with his moodiness and by the time they arrived back home, the atmosphere in the car was distinctly frosty. Now she was confused all over again about how she felt about James and whether he was still in love with her. Did love ebb and flow like that? Did it blow hot and cold? Did it sometimes evaporate completely?

If he had noticed her looking at him, James didn't react. He was staring straight ahead and Agatha's attention was drawn to the wedding party once again, with Alice and Bill making their way down the aisle together, wearing smiles that looked as though they would never fade.

The wedding reception was held at a local hotel not more than a few minutes' drive from the church. James drove Agatha in his car, while Toni offered a lift to one of the ushers, whom she seemed to know.

"Why were you running so late?" James asked as Agatha clicked her seatbelt into place. "I made it all the way up from London this morning in good time."

"Yes, I know that," Agatha said, slightly irritated by the competitive tone in James's voice, "but we had to deal with a whole bunch of naked people and a dead body."

"Really?" James said, taking his eyes off the road for a second to look Agatha in the face. "Who died?"

"We don't know," she explained. "The body was spirited away, but it seems like it was murder."

During the short drive, she explained the strange incident of the naked man in the road, the disappearing

31

corpse, the sacrificial stone and her encounter with the Mircester naturists.

"I think you may be reading too much into this," James said with a smile. "It all sounds to me like some kind of hoax—a joke that's got out of hand."

"You sound just like Wilkes," Agatha replied, annoyed that she was being patronised and that he wasn't displaying any faith in her judgement.

"Well, maybe the detective chief inspector has got a point this time," he said, pulling into a parking space outside the hotel.

"Actually," Agatha said sharply, "I'd back my instincts over Wilkes's any time. I had hoped that you might do the same. Edward Carstairs was panicked by something far more sinister than a simple practical joke."

They made their way inside where, having been greeted at the entrance to the function suite by the newly minted Mr. and Mrs. Wong, along with the rest of the bridal party, they joined the other guests. Everyone was served champagne and chatted merrily, clustered in small knots on a dance floor that was surrounded by tables laid with white cloths, flowers, a full array of cutlery and bottles of wine.

"Looks like we're in for a fine feast," Agatha said to James, sipping her champagne.

"It does indeed," James agreed. "I'd best go easy on this stuff, though," he added, nodding at his champagne glass. "I need to be up bright and early tomorrow."

"What's so special about tomorrow?"

"Well, last night I had dinner in London with my

publisher and the marketing director of a big cruise line," James explained. This came as no surprise to Agatha, who had known James was coming to the wedding straight from the London train. "We had dinner and stayed the night aboard one of their cruise ships moored at Tilbury."

"Sounds very glamorous."

"It was totally luxurious. I think you would love it. The company is sponsoring a series of books about different cruise routes around the world and the first one is a Scandinavian experience. It visits Copenhagen, Oslo, Bergen and various fjords all the way north to the Barents Sea, with the chance to see the northern lights practically guaranteed."

"Fabulous—that's an amazing journey."

"It is, and I'll be a special guest with a brief to write about the whole experience. Why don't you join me? You'll have the chance to relax and to dress up—formal dinner at the captain's table and all that. The food's always great on these cruises and the facilities on board— pool, gym, spa and so forth—are all top notch."

"Sounds very tempting, James, but I can't possibly leave at such short notice."

"Why not? Do something spontaneous, for goodness' sake. You can let her," he paused and nodded towards Toni, who was chatting with her usher friend, "look after things at the office for twelve days."

"Twelve days? No, that's simply not possible. We have a lot on right now and then there's this murder . . ."

"Don't be silly—you don't even know if there's actually been a murder."

"I am NOT being silly," Agatha growled, her temper rising. "I am never SILLY!"

"All right, calm down . . ."

"Do NOT tell me to calm down! I've worked very hard to build Raisin Investigations into a thriving business. You never seem to appreciate that it's not something that I care to abandon at a moment's notice, and whatever happened today at the nudist club, I DEFINITELY intend to get to . . ." she stalled as she realised what she was about to say, ". . . the bottom of it."

"Have it your own way. I guess you'll please yourself. That's what you usually do."

"What do you mean, I—"

"Enjoying yourselves?" came Bill Wong's voice as he and Alice approached.

"Oh, Bill, yes of course we are." No matter what was going on between her and James, Agatha was genuinely full of joy for her friends, hugging Alice before kissing Bill on the cheek. "Alice, you look amazing!"

James shuffled his feet uncomfortably for a moment, embarrassed at the thought they may have been caught bickering on Alice and Bill's big day. He then awkwardly shook hands with the bride and groom. Bill explained that their names would be on place setting cards on one of the tables and that after the meal there would be the usual round of speeches.

"After that," he said brightly, "we have a band playing for dancing late into the night."

"I'm sorry but I'll have to forego that," James apologised. "I'm afraid I have a very early start tomorrow morning on a foreign trip."

"But I don't," smiled Agatha, flashing a sideways glance at James, "so I will definitely be staying on for the dancing!"

Agatha and James found their allotted places and chatted politely to those around them, if not to each other. The atmosphere between them hung like a lead curtain. Agatha decided to ignore her lack of an entertaining companion by enjoying the food instead. The menu included a selection of appetising vegetarian options, but Agatha chose to sate her hunger by devouring a delightful seafood salad of shrimp, calamari, mussels, octopus and scungilli before launching into a main course consisting of a baby rack of lamb roasted in a herb crust, served with vegetables and a potato croquet, while finishing off with a mouth-watering sticky toffee pudding.

"You seem to have been hungry," James commented, the first time he had spoken to her since they took their seats.

"Mmmm . . ." Agatha said, taking a sip of red wine and reaching for the bottle to study its label. "I need to keep my strength up for all that dancing. The wine is lovely—Primitivo, from Puglia."

"That's in Italy," James said.

"I can see that, James," Agatha said tetchily. "It says so right here on the label."

"Well, I really must be going," came James's brusque response. "I will bid farewell to our hosts and see you in a couple of weeks."

"Enjoy the northern lights," Agatha said without bothering to look up from her increasingly intense perusal of the wine label.

Left with an empty seat beside her as the speeches began, Agatha was treated to a look of sympathy from the woman sitting opposite. She knew that the woman now had an exquisite titbit of wedding gossip in which she would revel for the next week or so. She imagined her telling everyone in her regular morning coffee group, or at the hairdresser, or in the Pilates class about the woman at the wedding whose partner never had a word to say to her all through the meal then got up and left before the speeches had even begun. She gave the woman a look of fierce defiance, fixing her with a withering stare. The woman quickly looked away, suddenly totally absorbed in the conversation going on to her left.

Once the speeches were over, there was a short hiatus before the music began and Agatha, along with a number of other women, took advantage of the pause in proceedings to "powder her nose." She made polite conversation with the other ladies waiting to use the facilities and, on returning to the function suite, she heard the band strike up. There was then a round of applause as Alice and Bill took to the floor alone for their first dance as husband and wife. Agatha smiled. She prided herself on being a good dancer and judged Alice and Bill's self-conscious, shuffling waltz to be charmingly romantic rather than proficient. The happy couple relaxed as others began to join in. Alice's father led Bill's mother onto the floor and Ma Wong waltzed beautifully, showing commendable elegance. Pa Wong then took to the floor with Alice's mother and, again, they proved to be confident dancers, although not, in Agatha's opinion, up to her own standard. Other members of the bridal party gradually joined in and just as Agatha arrived back in her seat, she spotted Toni on the dance floor in the arms of her usher friend. She took a swig of her wine and looked at the woman opposite, whose husband had momentarily abandoned her, standing talking about cricket with a couple of chums. The woman was cradling her wine glass in one hand and drawing invisible circles on the tablecloth with the forefinger of her other. She avoided Agatha's gaze.

It was then that Agatha realised that someone had slipped into the chair vacated by James. She turned to see a man in a well-cut dark grey suit looking straight at her. He had a round, pleasant face, tousled brown hair, dark eyes and an infectious smile. He seemed oddly familiar.

"Mrs. Raisin," he said, just loud enough for her to hear above the music, "I was hoping I might see you here."

"I'm so sorry," Agatha apologised, returning his smile. "I know I should know you, but . . ."

"That's all right," he said, waving aside her apology. "We've met, but never been properly introduced. I'm John Glass." He reached out his right hand and she took it to shake, but he immediately got to his feet, still holding her hand. "Would you care to dance?"

"Actually, John, I'd love to." Standing to follow him onto the floor, she looked down at the woman opposite to make sure she was watching and gave her a victorious wink.

They joined in the waltz, Agatha resting her left hand lightly on his shoulder. He wasn't as tall as James and felt far more solid, but she was relieved to find him refreshingly light on his feet. Clearly she was not to suffer the toe crunching she had endured so many times in the past.

"You dance very well, John Glass," she said, "but I'm still not entirely sure where I . . ."

Then it dawned on her.

"Wait a minute! You arrested me!"

"Actually," he said, his confident smile never wavering, "I slapped the cuffs on your young friend over there." He nodded towards Toni. "It was Wilkes who arrested you, or tried to."

"In that strip club!" Agatha stood still, couples cruising the floor all around them. "You've got a nerve expecting me to dance with—"

"I'm sorry about that," he said. "I'm no more a fan of DCI Wilkes than you are, but I have to work with him from time to time. I'm an inspector, same as Bill. We've been mates for years."

"Bill is a sergeant," Agatha corrected him, resuming the dance.

"Yeah, but he's passed his inspector's exam," John explained. "He'll get a posting soon enough. Then he'll be able to take up the rank properly."

"You mean he might move away?"

"I don't think he wants to go far. He'll wait for something to come up in or around the Cotswolds. He was brought up here. He loves it—so does Alice."

"They make a lovely couple."

"They do," he agreed, "and they told me that you helped settle a family rift that might have meant this wedding never happened. They're very lucky to have someone like you as a friend."

"Well, they've stuck up for me plenty of times in the past. I guess that's what friends do."

"So, setting aside the small matter of the 'arrest,' do you think we might become friends?"

"We might," said Agatha, allowing her hand to drop from his shoulder, the dance having ended, "but I should let you get back to your wife now."

"I'm not married," he said, smiling again. "I'm here on my own."

"In that case," she said, replacing her hand, "I'm keeping you for at least the next dance!"

They enjoyed the dancing, they enjoyed the wine and they enjoyed chatting with other wedding guests, many of whom were police officers John knew, and most of whom knew Agatha either by sight or reputation. If nothing else, Agatha thought to herself, she was making lots of potentially valuable new contacts. Yet there was something else. She was enjoying herself—enjoying herself more than she had done in a long time. She introduced John to Toni, who recognised him immediately.

"You know," she said to him, "I always suspected that you knew Wilkes was messing up our arrest and you let him dig himself into a hole."

"I'm not saying you're right," John said, laughing, "but if there's one thing I've learned over the years, it's that it does me no good to contradict a senior officer when he's busy making an absolute fool of himself!"

"We had another run-in with him this morning," Agatha said.

"So I heard," said John. "The vanishing corpse. To be honest, I don't think I would have been much more help to you there. If there's no evidence of a crime, then there's not much we can do—but I do wish I'd been there to see old Wilkes's face when he was surrounded by nudists!"

John, Agatha decided, was definitely one of the good guys, not an ally of Wilkes. Toni introduced her usher friend, David, whom she knew through Paul and who was Alice's cousin. David was explaining that he worked as a civilian with Mircester Police when there was a commotion near the entrance to the function suite. Bill and Alice were about to embark on their honeymoon and there was an excited throng of young women calling out to Alice.

"We should go wave goodbye to the happy couple," Agatha said, and they walked towards the crowd. She had just turned to say something to Toni when Toni pointed and yelled a warning.

"Agatha—LOOK OUT!"

Agatha faced forward again and was hit in the chest by a bouquet. Her hands shot up to clutch the flowers. There was applause, cheering and laughter. Agatha tensed. She had always hated being treated as a figure of fun. What the hell did they think they were laughing at? She softened when she saw Alice making her way through the crowd. She was no longer wearing her bridal gown, having changed into a deep red silk trouser suit, but she still looked radiant and was still smiling.

"Agatha, I'm so sorry," Alice said, kissing her on the cheek. "I overshot the crowd. You know it's a tradition that—"

"When the bride shuts her eyes and throws her bouquet to the single women at the wedding, the one who catches it is the next to marry," Agatha said, smiling and offering the bouquet to Alice. "Maybe you should try again."

"No, you must keep the flowers. It's only a bit of fun but I'd love you to have them." She gave Agatha a hug, being careful not to crush the bouquet, then she and Bill said their final goodbyes and left. The band played, as Bill had promised, late into the night. When it came time to leave, Toni, having wisely decided to leave her car in the hotel car park and return to collect it the following day, took a taxi with David. Agatha shared another with John.

It was well after midnight when Agatha stepped out of the taxi at the front gate of her cottage in Lilac Lane. She held her trophy bouquet in one hand, along with her clutch bag, and reached for the gate latch with the other. John was there to open the gate for her.

"I've had a fantastic evening," he said, "the most fun I've ever had at a wedding. Thank you."

"No, thank you," she said. "I've had a lovely time."

She put her free hand on his shoulder, just where it had rested as they danced, he stooped towards her and they kissed. Agatha's eyes shot to the curtains at James's bedroom window. She was convinced she'd seen them twitch. Had James witnessed that kiss? What if he had? Would it make him jealous? She hoped it would.

"Should I . . . tell him to go?" John asked, pointing to the taxi.

"Really, sir, I think you presume too much," Agatha said, teasing him. "This was only a first date. In fact, it wasn't even a date and . . ."

"I'm sorry, I didn't mean to take anything for granted, I . . ."

"Don't worry." She reached up and kissed him on the cheek. "I'm a bit tired, but I've really enjoyed being with you. Give me a call—I'd love to see you again."

She took a card from her bag and slipped it into his breast pocket. He smiled and waved goodbye, easing himself back into the taxi. Agatha watched the car's tail lights disappear down the lane. The thought of spending the night in John's arms was enticing, but not this night. The day had been full of bewildering distractions and she wanted time to herself. She made her way indoors where her two cats, Boswell and Hodge, began a purring contest, vying for her attention, winding themselves around her legs.

"Hello, boys," she said softly. "You can't be hungry, can you? I left plenty of food for you."

The two cats stared up at her with big eyes, as though denying all knowledge of any food.

"All right," she said, "you can have a late, late supper, as long as you don't come pestering me again at the crack of dawn. I need my beauty sleep."

She fed the cats, climbed the stairs and was soon curled up in bed, comfortably alone.

Having planned to sleep late on Sunday morning, Agatha was peeved to be woken at what seemed like the crack of dawn. She checked her bedside clock only to confirm that it was, in fact, just after five in the morning. She tutted. She was no longer entirely alone in her bed, Boswell and Hodge having curled up near her feet some time during the night, but it wasn't the cats that had woken her. She had heard a door slamming. Then she heard another.

Tossing aside the duvet, she crossed the room to the window, peering out into the gloomy grey light of an overcast morning. A light drizzle was falling, with dark clouds to the west promising heavier rain to follow. She saw James's car making off down the lane. Those had been the doors—his front door had broken her sleep and his car door had made absolutely sure she was awake. She wondered if he had banged them shut extra hard in order to wake her. Probably not. He wasn't one to indulge in such pettiness. So the slamming of a car door was the last she would hear from him for the next couple of weeks. Maybe he would phone, just to see how she was doing, just to let her know he was all right. On the other hand, James was more likely to assume everything was fine unless he heard differently. In his mind, there would be no need to waste a phone call on idle chit-chat.

In any case, she had more to think about than her ex-husband. She stroked the cats and climbed back into bed, dozing fitfully with misty thoughts drifting in and out of her head. She struggled to organise them in a sensible order. First of all, there was the crouching corpse on the Lone Warrior altar, then came music and dancing with John, followed by Wilkes surrounded by nudists. By the time her thoughts mingled to the point where she was twirling round the floor in the arms of

Jasper, all the other dancers were naked and a nude Wilkes was playing "The Girl from Ipanema" on saxophone, she knew she'd fallen asleep again and gave up the struggle.

She next woke almost four hours later, to the clatter of her letterbox and the emphatic thud of the Sunday papers, complete with hefty supplements, hitting the hall floor. Pulling on a dressing gown, she trudged downstairs, made herself a coffee and popped some bread in the toaster before picking up the papers. Despite their late, late supper, Boswell and Hodge ate a hearty breakfast, then sat at the open back door as though daring each other to go outside. Although steady rain was now falling, Agatha still felt it warm enough to sit at the kitchen table with the door open, sipping coffee and crunching buttered toast while scanning the newspapers.

Neither the nationals nor the local paper made any mention of the incident at the Mircester Naturist Society. She tuned the radio to a local station with regular news bulletins, but there was no report about the disappearing corpse. That, she mused, was pretty much what she had expected. With everyone treating it as some kind of practical joke, there wasn't really anything for the press to get their teeth into. She considered making a few calls and talking to a contact on the *Mircester Telegraph* to try to generate a story that might rattle a few cages and shed some light on the mystery, but decided it would be best to find out more about the Mircester naturists first. Edward Carstairs could certainly help with that, but there was someone else that might be able to shed some light on the society. She picked up her phone and pressed a speed-dial number.

"Barfield House" came the deep voice of Gustav, Sir Charles Fraith's manservant.

"Gustav, it's me," Agatha said. "I need to talk to Charles."

"*Sir* Charles," said Gustav snootily, with heavy emphasis on the "Sir," "is indisposed. If you would care to leave a message . . ."

"Who is it, Gustav?" Agatha heard Charles's voice in the background.

"No idea," Gustav informed him. "She has not had the good manners to identify herself."

"It's Agatha, isn't it? Give me that!" The sound of the phone being snatched from Gustav was followed by Charles in a far clearer voice. "Aggie, it's nice to hear from you!"

Agatha cringed. The pet name had once been acceptable, when they had once been lovers, but it no longer filled her with fondness for him. Still, she reasoned, it's a lot better than "sweetie"—at least she'd avoided "sweetie."

"So how are you, sweetie?"

No—there it was.

"I'm fine, Charles," Agatha said, and got straight to the point. "I'd like to pop over some time to talk about the Mircester Naturist Society."

"Good heavens. Thinking of joining, are you? They're a jolly odd bunch but they seem harmless enough."

"Their clubhouse is on your land, isn't it?"

"That's right. They've got a funny old lease on that patch. A bit peculiar, as I recall. Listen, I'd love to discuss them but I'm about to set off for Cumbria. Spending the night with an old chum. Why don't you come with me?"

"No, thank you, Charles. I'm having some 'me' time today. A nice long bath followed by Sunday lunch at the Red Lion."

"You know I'd love to join you in both of those . . ."

"That ship sailed some time ago, Charles. When will you be back from Cumbria?"

"Tomorrow afternoon, around three, if you'd like to come over then."

"That would be ideal."

"Will you be coming fully clothed, or . . . ?"

Agatha hung up.

Chapter Three

The following morning, the latticed windows of the King Charles were specked with raindrops when Agatha paused outside the old pub. Her reflection was too distorted for her to be able to check her make-up. She noted with satisfaction, however, that the band of pink trimming on her blue umbrella matched both her jacket and her handbag, even if the old window glass was making everything look a sludgy brown.

The pub stood in one of Mircester's most ancient streets, a narrow, winding cobbled lane that led down to Mircester Abbey in the oldest part of town. Opposite was an antiques shop and above that shop was the Raisin Investigations office. As had happened many times before, she now faced her first problem of the day—how best to cross the lane's treacherous cobbles without either catching a high heel in the many gaps and fissures, or skidding on their smooth faces, which the morning rain had turned as slick as polished patent leather. She decided to take off her shoes to pad across the cobbles in her bare feet.

Pausing to bend and replace her shoes, she balanced with her handbag over her umbrella arm and the other shoulder resting against the antiques shop window. An elaborate, gilt-framed mirror stood at one end of the window display, reduced from what Agatha considered an outrageously astronomical price to one that was only stupidly expensive. She saw herself looking in the mirror but also, inside the shop on the opposite side of the display, she spotted the pale, flaccid face of Mr. Tinkler, the shop owner. He was peeking out from behind an old set of enamel signs advertising cigarettes and was, without doubt, staring straight at her bottom. Agatha stood upright, turned round, raised an eyebrow and blew him a kiss. Mr. Tinkler's watery eyes blinked with surprise behind his half-moon glasses, then he produced a feather duster and fussed over flicking imagined specks from the enamel signs.

Agatha trotted up the stairs to the office and, although she always arrived early, she was pleased to see that her staff were, as they always tended to be, in before her.

"Morning, boss!" came the cheery greeting from Simon Black. Agatha had always considered him a strange-looking young man. His thin, hatchet face was too deeply lined for someone in his twenties, but he was never short of female company—or so he liked to tell everyone. While he was prone to complain when he wasn't assigned to the cases he most wanted, Simon had proved himself a

48

valuable asset to the agency and Agatha had grown to like him, although she was always quick to put him in his place when she felt he was getting too big for his boots. She liked to leave no one in any doubt about exactly who was in charge at Raisin Investigations.

Patrick Mulligan looked up from his computer screen and nodded a silent greeting. A retired police officer, he was tall and dark with sunken, brooding features. He spoke only when he felt it necessary, and he was utterly reliable. His police contacts had been invaluable in the past, although Agatha knew she could now add considerably to those after meeting so many officers at Saturday's wedding.

"Good morning, Mrs. Raisin," said Helen Freedman, approaching with an armful of folders just as Agatha furled her umbrella. She offered the folders in exchange for the brolly. "I'll find somewhere for that to drip." Helen was Agatha's secretary and admin angel. She was middle-aged, worked hard and was undoubtedly the most efficient person Agatha had ever met. "There are reports for you to sign off in the pink folders, invoices in the yellow folders and general mail in the blue folders. I'll bring a cup of coffee to your office straight away."

"Thank you, Helen," Agatha said, accepting the folders and looking round the room. "A coffee would be lovely. Where's Toni?"

"We haven't yet seen Miss Gilmour this morning," said Helen.

"Probably still hungover after Bill Wong's bash," Simon said, grinning. "I heard there was quite a knees-up at Lower Burlip."

"It was a beautiful wedding," Agatha said, giving Simon a stern stare, "not a 'bash' and, while Toni enjoyed the dancing—not a 'knees-up'—afterwards, she was perfectly fine when she left. She certainly didn't look like she was heading for a two-day hangover. I'm sure she'll be here shortly. In any case, we'll have the usual catch-up in my office in half an hour."

By the time Agatha had settled down with her coffee, flicked through the various folders Helen had given her and scanned that morning's *Mircester Telegraph*, the others began arriving for the case review meeting. Simon and Patrick shuffled in with chairs, documents and notebooks, finding their usual places between the small office's walls and the edges of Agatha's oversized desk. She had never regretted buying the giant reproduction Georgian desk, which doubled reasonably well as a meeting table—she just wished her office was a little bigger.

"No sign of Toni yet?" she asked, looking from Patrick to Simon. Patrick shook his head and Simon simply shrugged. "Okay, let's get started. Simon, I'll read through your reports on the Sullivan divorce case and the allotment vegetable thief later this morning. In the meantime, what's happening with the pilfering from the Watermill Brewery?"

"The managing director is a Mr. Brown," Simon said, consulting his notes, then grinning and pushing them aside. Clearly, he didn't need any notes to say what he had in mind. "I put it to him that he might expect some of his stock to go missing. Lots of businesses take some losses like that into account. He agreed, but said it had never been a problem until recently."

"How much is being nicked?" asked Patrick.

"It was just a few bottles now and again. Now it's brewing equipment and raw materials as well," Simon explained.

"That's not just pilfering," Agatha commented, "that's robbery. Why hasn't he called in the police?"

"It's a family business," said Simon, "and he wants to deal with this quietly, with a minimum of fuss. I thought we could install security cameras but he already has those, and whoever is doing the thieving is able to dodge them. What we need is someone on the inside to find out what's going on."

"Let me guess," Agatha offered. "You want me to let you go to work in a brewery?"

"Spot on, boss!" Simon made a little hand-clapping, thumb-clicking gesture that left him pointing both hands at Agatha like a pair of cocked pistols. Agatha hated when he did that. It was the kind of thing she might expect from a second-rate gameshow host, not one of her members of staff. Wilting under her scorching stare of disapproval, Simon holstered his pistols.

"And how do you expect to fool people at the brewery—people who actually know what they're doing—into believing that you are joining them as a genuine employee?" she asked.

"I suggested to Mr. Brown," Simon said, his confident grin, never absent for long, coaxing creases onto his face, "he announce to the staff that he's going to start tours of the brewery for the general public and that he's bringing in someone who will act as a tour guide. I will be the potential new guide and will have to learn everything about

51

the brewery. That way I can stick my nose into every department and get to know everyone."

Agatha sat back in her chair and put her fingertips together to make a thinking temple. She pursed her lips and tilted her head slightly to the right, her eyes never leaving Simon. After a few seconds of this silent stare, his grin faltered and he began to shift uncomfortably in his seat. Then, just before his natural confidence evaporated like spilled beer, she made her pronouncement.

"Very well, Simon, I think that's an excellent plan," she said, and the grin snapped back onto his face. "Make sure Mr. Brown understands our fee structure and draw up an agreement accordingly."

"Umm . . . don't you usually handle all that, boss?"

"This is your case and your client. I want you to take responsibility for all of it and I want to see regular progress reports. You're always asking to be given more than just surveillance and you've shown in the past that you can handle bigger jobs, but when you're playing in the big league, you need to take on some of the responsibility that comes with it."

Simon nodded and tried to adopt a serious expression but succeeded only in looking mildly constipated.

"Now, any other new business?" Agatha asked, looking to Patrick, who nodded.

"At ten p.m. yesterday evening, a Mrs. Partridge contacted me through a mutual friend," Patrick reported, sounding as though he was reading from a police officer's notebook, which, in fact, he was. "Her daughter, Sarah, is seventeen and attends Martinbrook Sixth Form College."

"What college?" Simon asked. "I've never heard of it."

"It's a boarding school for girls aged sixteen to nineteen," Patrick explained. "The building is a rambling old manor house on the road to Evesham. Very modern facilities, though. I've taken a look at their prospectus, and the building may be a couple of centuries old but everything in it is bang up to date, from the accommodation and the computers in the classrooms to the science lab, swimming pool and all-weather sports pitches."

"So what is Mrs. Partridge's problem?" Agatha asked.

"On Friday evening," Patrick said, glancing down at his notebook again, "she discovered a quantity of cannabis and a small amount of what she assumes is cocaine in Sarah's bag."

"Where did she get it from?" asked Agatha.

"She says she found it in her dorm at school—she boards during the week and comes home at weekends. According to her, quite a few of the girls use the stuff."

"Again, this should be a matter for the police," Agatha pointed out.

"It sounds like small-scale dealing," Patrick said, "but Mrs. Partridge attended Martinbrook and is good friends with Mrs. Carling, the school's headmistress. They both want to find a way to eradicate any drugs problem without damaging the reputation of the school."

"So we need to find out who's supplying the girls," Simon said, chuckling and rubbing his hands together. "I think we need someone on the inside here and I—"

"Stop right there," said Agatha, holding out a hand to silence him. "Letting you loose in a brewery is one thing, but there's no way I'm sending you anywhere near a school full of young ladies."

"All I meant was . . ." Simon wisely stopped there when Agatha cast him a warning glance. She sighed and looked to Patrick.

"Patrick, can you set up a meeting with Mrs. Partridge and Mrs. Carling, please? We'll try to work out whether this is something we can help them with. Now, if there's nothing else we can—"

"I'm *so* sorry I'm late!" Toni gasped, bursting into the office. "I *hate* being late. Have I missed the whole meeting? I tried so hard to—"

"I think we're finished, gentlemen," Agatha said. "I need to have a word with Toni."

Gathering their chairs and papers, Patrick and Simon manoeuvred their way out of the room, Simon giving Toni a sympathetic grimace that said, *Now you're for it*. Toni tutted at him and rolled her eyes.

"Agatha, I'm really sorry, but—" Toni began, but Agatha swept her apology aside with a wave of her hands.

"You don't make a habit of being late, Toni," she said. "In fact, you're in the office early every day, so there's no need to apologise. What happened this morning?"

Toni looked a little less flustered, although her face was still flushed, clearly from having run to the office and having galloped up the stairs. She wore very little make-up, but her light application of mascara was now smearing its way down her cheeks on a tide of water dripping from her rain-soaked hair. Taking a tissue from her handbag, she wiped the mascara away. She pushed a sweep of blonde hair away from her face and it immediately dropped back again yet, even when she was flustered and slightly bedraggled, having lost her composure, Toni possessed the effortless beauty of youth. Agatha sighed. Had she run from wherever Toni had come and then taken the stairs at full steam, she'd have needed at least twenty minutes in front of the bathroom mirror to make herself look in any way presentable. Toni, she mused, feeling that same twinge of jealousy she felt towards Alice, really didn't know how lucky she was.

"Well, I suppose it was . . . kind of . . . a client meeting," Toni said, scrunching the mascara-stained tissue back into her pocket.

"Which client?"

"It's a new case."

"A new case that you haven't discussed with me," Agatha said, irritated by the way that Toni appeared to be holding something back. "What's it all about?"

"Well, the client thinks he's being followed," said Toni, suddenly more defensive than apologetic, "and he might be in danger because he inadvertently witnessed a murder . . . or at least the aftermath of a murder."

"Another murder? That's really quite . . . wait a minute. The aftermath? He found a body. It's Edward Carstairs, isn't it?"

"Yes," Toni admitted, looking defiantly guilty. "He told me yesterday that someone had been stalking him."

"You saw him yesterday?"

"Yes—in my own time. Surely you can't object to that?"

"No, but I *do* object to you seeing him on *my* time," Agatha snapped, Toni's attitude beginning to fire her temper. "In case you've forgotten, *I'm* the one who decides what cases we take on. This is *my* company and *I'm* in charge."

"Oh, no one could ever forget that!"

"Good!" Agatha shot out a hand to grab a folder from her desk. "Now I have things to do. You, I'm sure, have some *real* work to do as well!"

Toni turned on her heel to storm out of the office, making to slam the door then pausing, raising her eyebrows at Agatha to emphasise how considerate she was being, and closing the door with a soft click. The sound of her restraint fought with the haze of Agatha's temper to fill the room.

She slapped the folder down on the desk. Why had she let Toni rile her like that? She hadn't been upset about the silly girl coming in late. It was the way she had gone on the defensive that had been so annoying. She needed to learn how to stick up for herself. Had that been me, at her age, Agatha mused, I would have lied. I would have said my alarm clock didn't go off, or the bus had broken down, or there was a herd of buffalo blocking the high street—any old excuse would do for a one-off late showing. And why had she been so defensive? Clearly she expected me to lose my temper. Am I really such an ogre?

To avoid becoming annoyed all over again at the thought of Toni expecting her to blow her top, which, in her opinion, she hadn't even come close to doing, Agatha launched into the file of reports, banishing all thoughts of the flare-up.

When Helen Freedman came in to collect some of the folders Agatha had dealt with, she announced that she was popping out for lunch and offered to bring something in for Agatha. Such had been the intensity of her concentration that Agatha had lost all track of time. She thanked Helen, saying she intended to go out herself. A few minutes later, she was heading for the door and paused at Toni's desk. She looked down at her young colleague and smiled.

"I'm heading over to the King Charles," she said. "Fancy joining me?"

"Umm . . . of course." Toni nodded, then pointed to her computer screen. "I just need to finish this email."

"No problem," Agatha replied. "I'll order something for us."

Agatha viewed the creaky wooden floor of the King Charles with suspicion. The occasional gaps and cracks between the floorboards made it almost as perilous as the cobbles outside in the lane. The rain had stopped and the cobbles had dried out, so she had tiptoed the few steps across to the pub. Although she was loath to risk the slim, elegant heels of her shoes on the ramshackle pub floor, she decided that teetering up to the bar on tiptoe like a drunken ballerina was beneath her dignity. Instead, she placed her feet very carefully, treading only on the most solid-looking planks.

"Two glasses of your lovely white burgundy, please, George," she said to the barman, "and two portions of toad in the hole with gravy."

"Mrs. Raisin," George said, with a look of mock horror, pausing his polishing of a beer glass. "White wine with meat?"

"They're sausages, George," Agatha pointed out. "Pork sausages baked in pudding batter. It is perfectly acceptable to have white wine with pork. Even if toad in the hole was made with real toads, they're amphibians, which are practically fish, so white wine would be appropriate."

"I bow to your superior wisdom, Mrs. Raisin." George laughed. "Your usual table by the window's free. I'll bring your drinks over."

The drinks and Toni arrived at the same time. As Toni lowered herself into an overstuffed leather armchair, equally as well-worn and comfortable as the one Agatha sat in, she glanced nervously at her boss.

"I'm sorry we had that little spat this morning," she said.

"The little spat," Agatha said, "is why we're having a glass of wine on a Monday lunchtime—a peace offering." She held her glass out to clink with Toni. "Maybe every cloud really does have a silver lining."

"I was just *so* frustrated," Toni said with a sigh. "Edward was convinced someone was watching him, but when I followed him to work, I couldn't see anyone suspicious tailing him."

"Maybe he was wrong."

"Maybe," Toni agreed, "but he doesn't seem the sort to make things up. You believed him about the body he saw, didn't you?"

"I did—and I'm an excellent judge of character. I don't believe he lied to us, and we *are* going to look into this business of the vanishing corpse."

"I was worried I might have put you off the whole thing."

"Not a bit of it—but we need a plan that we can work on together. I don't want you going solo. If Edward really is in any danger, you won't be much help to him on your own—and you need to keep yourself safe above all else."

"I wouldn't want anything to happen to him," Toni said, looking out of the window, avoiding Agatha's gaze.

"Ah," Agatha slowly intoned, only now realising the full extent of Toni's reticence that morning. "That's what you weren't telling me this morning. You've got a soft spot for Edward. What happened to your handsome young usher . . . David, wasn't it?"

"David's just a friend. We had fun on Saturday, but he's a friend of Paul's and that could get awkward. I can do without the complications, so I'll keep him as a friend."

"Well, it's always good to have a friend on the back burner that you can warm up into something more serious," Agatha said, gently poking fun. Toni pulled a face. "Well," she went on, "I can't say I blame you about Edward. He's a good-looking young man and from what I've seen of him . . ."

"Please don't make any jokes about . . ."

"All I was going to say is that from what I've seen of him, he's very bright and level-headed."

"When he was frightened—running down the road on Saturday—that's not really him. He'd had a shock, that's all."

"I can't think what else anyone would have done. If I'd found a naked corpse with its head bashed in and then realised that the murderers were watching me, I'd have run for my life as well."

"I can't imagine you wandering around outdoors

in the nude," Toni said with a smile just as George arrived with their food. Having heard Toni's comment, he placed the plates carefully on the table and looked towards Agatha, curiosity furrowing his brow.

"Don't tax your imagination too much, George," she said. "Your brain cells will overheat."

"It's not just that Edward thought he was being followed," Toni said, once George was out of earshot. She produced a folded piece of notepaper from her handbag. "Yesterday afternoon, this was pushed through his letterbox."

"But there's nothing on it," Agatha said, unfolding the blank paper and turning it over in her hands. "It's completely blank."

"It is now," Toni explained, "but not when Edward picked it up off his doormat. Then it had writing on it that said, 'Dead men tell no tales.'"

"Disappearing ink," Agatha said, handing the paper back to Toni, "as well as a disappearing corpse. So someone's trying to intimidate poor Edward—frighten him to make sure he keeps his nose out of whatever they're up to."

"That's what I thought, too."

"Well, that makes me even more determined to find out what's going on," Agatha said, jabbing a sausage with her fork. "The Naturist Society is the place to start. We need to know more about what goes on there. As Simon is so fond of saying, we need someone on the inside—someone aside from Edward."

"I think you're right," Toni agreed, "but you can't possibly join a nudist club."

"What do you mean?" Agatha returned the forkful of gravy-laden sausage to her plate, sucking in her stomach and sitting straight-backed in her chair. "I'll have you know I look very attractive naked. Many men have admired my body and commented on how good I look in the nude!"

"Many men . . ." George mumbled, drifting past with plates for another table. "Overheating now . . ."

"Calm down, Agatha," Toni said, smiling. "I wasn't suggesting that you don't have the body for it. All I meant was that, especially after Saturday, everyone at the Naturist Society knows who you are. If you were to join, they would be suspicious, and we would find out nothing. On the other hand, if I were to join, posing as Edward's girlfriend . . ."

"Posing?"

"We'll see where that takes us."

"And you're happy to do the whole . . . undressed thing?"

"I think," Toni said sipping her wine, "it will be a new experience. Definitely something different. It could be fun. . . ." She paused, letting out an uncertain laugh. "Actually, I'm dreading it, but Edward says that after a few minutes it will feel like the most natural thing in the world—so I'll give it a go."

"All right," Agatha said, quietly relieved that she wasn't the one who would be parading around in her birthday suit, "we need to find out more about the members—who they are and if any of them give us grounds for suspicion. I can start by asking John Glass about the constable who was there on Saturday—Gittins,

61

wasn't it? You can report back on anyone at the club you think we should be looking at and we'll run background checks. But this is off the books. We can't expect Edward to pay our fees. This is our own investigation, but that doesn't mean you don't have back-up." She picked up her smartphone off the table and waggled it at Toni. "I want to know where you are all the time, so keep in touch—no flying solo."

"Got it," said Toni.

"This afternoon, I'm going to see Charles. I think the club is on his land and I'm betting he'll be able to tell me all about the place and, for that matter, the Lone Warrior."

"Do you want me to come with you?"

"No, I can handle Charles."

"Okay," said Toni, pointing at Agatha's phone, "but you keep in touch, too. Charles is one thing, but we don't know where else this might take us."

"Agreed," Agatha said. "I can't think of anyone I'd rather have watching my back."

Driving through the ornate black-and-gold gates of Barfield House, Agatha's car was engulfed by the dappled shade lying beneath the long avenue of oak and beech trees leading up to the house. She often thought that this impressively stately welcome to the property was the best thing about Barfield. Charles loved the place. It was his home, but even he admitted that it was a brute of a building—a sprawling mess of uninspired Victorian architecture, designed to look vaguely medieval but succeeding only in looking uninvitingly bleak.

She parked near the steps leading up to entrance doors that would not have looked out of place on a fortress and paused before getting out of the car when her phone rang. It was John Glass.

"Hello, John," she said, adopting a casual tone. "Thanks for ringing back."

"My pleasure," he replied warmly. "I hope this is about us getting together again, but I suspect you had another motive for calling."

"We will spend some time again soon, John, I promise. I'm just a bit snowed under at the moment. The sooner I can get myself sorted out, though, the sooner we can lay some plans for the two of us."

"Why do I feel like I'm about to help get you 'sorted out'?" He laughed. "Come on, then. What do you need?"

"What can you tell me about one of the constables who was with Wilkes this morning—PC Gittins?"

"I can't give you anything that might be confidential, but I can tell you that Gittins is a good man. I wish we had more like him. He involves himself in the local community—charity work and suchlike. He's one of our stalwarts."

"Did you know he and his wife are naturists?"

"Well, there's no law against that, is there? Each to his own, I say. They're also involved with the church down your way—St. Jude's. I seem to remember him saying his wife sang in the choir. They're a respectable couple, Agatha."

"Thank you, John, I've no doubt you're right. Must dash now, but let's speak soon."

She hung up and made for the entrance to Barfield

House. The massive oak doors, peppered with knuckles of black iron studs, swung open as Agatha skipped up the stairs. Ready to greet her, with the smile of a viper, was Gustav. Having worked for Charles's father, Gustav had been part of the fabric of Barfield House for more than thirty years and had played many roles in that time—butler, chauffeur, handyman and cook, to name but four. He was unswervingly loyal to Charles and fiercely protective. Despite a humble background as the immigrant child of a Hungarian father and an English mother, a lifetime in service had left him an utter snob, from his shined black shoes to his shark-black eyes.

"Good afternoon, Gustav!" she called brightly, ignoring the calculated chill of his welcome.

"Mrs. Raisin," Gustav responded. Agatha's on–off love affair with Charles over the years had been met with loathsome disapproval from Gustav, who never believed her to be either a suitable candidate for an aristocratic marriage or a tolerable prospect as a discreet mistress. As far as he was concerned, her pedigree, or lack of it, was entirely unacceptable. He had always resented her presence in the house and she had always despised his interference, yet the two had been occasional allies whenever the one thing they had in common—Sir Charles Fraith—had needed them most. "I believe Sir Charles is expecting you."

"You believe correctly."

"Should I fetch my dustpan and brush?"

Agatha's relationship with Charles had seen many highs and lows, the high points as well as the low points regularly generating debris fields of smashed champagne glasses and broken crockery.

"Always good to have them standing by." Agatha smiled, breezing past Gustav into the hall, heading for the library where she knew Charles, as was his habit, would be working.

"Aggie, how lovely to see you," Charles stood to greet her, hurrying from behind his large oak desk, similar to Agatha's although it did not suffer the ignominy of being "reproduction." "Can I offer you some tea, or perhaps something stronger?"

"Tea would be fine," Agatha said, deciding to accept his open-armed greeting hug, although remaining unresponsive enough to let him know that she wasn't here to rekindle any flames of passion.

"Tea would also be most appreciated by the invisible woman over here," came a reedy voice from a large, wing-backed chair by the French windows.

"Good afternoon, Mrs. Tassy." Agatha nodded to Charles's aged aunt. Mrs. Tassy had lived at Barfield House for as long as anyone could remember. She was tall and thin, with tight curls of silver hair and was dressed in her customary style of a high-necked, long, dark dress. The way the sun fell on the dress, it looked a deep, regal purple rather than black, but it still gave the old widow a Victorian look completely in tune with her surroundings.

"Tea it is, then," said Charles, ringing a small handbell on his desk before immediately rendering the gesture redundant by yelling, "GUSTAV!"

As if he had been listening outside the door, Gustav immediately appeared.

"Tea, I suppose?" he sniffed, then turned on his heel, making for the kitchen.

"So what is it that brings you to our home this time, Mrs. Raisin?" asked Mrs. Tassy.

"Actually, Agatha came to talk to *me*, Aunt," said Charles.

"Oh, well . . . if I'm not wanted . . ." was the old lady's response. She closed the book she was reading and made to haul herself upright.

"No, please stay, Mrs. Tassy," Agatha said. "We're not discussing anything private or intimate." She gave Charles a meaningful look. He smiled, shrugged and glanced out towards the terrace.

"Looks like the sun's coming out," he said. "Let's take tea outdoors."

They moved outside and settled at a table on the terrace, looking down over a vast swathe of impossibly smooth lawn to where birch, oak and ash trees protected the house from the outside world.

"You wanted to talk about the Mircester Naturist Society," Charles said, breathing in the fresh air. He looked across at his aunt, expecting an indignant reaction. There was none.

"Yes," said Agatha. "I know practically nothing about them. The clubhouse seems like it's been there for a while, though. Do you know when it all started?"

"That must have been a very long time ago," said Charles. "I should think it was . . ."

"Nineteen fifty-nine," his aunt declared, moving her chair slightly to put her back to the sun, keeping her face in the shade.

"You seem very certain," Agatha said.

"I am," the old lady replied. "I was one of the founder members."

"You were what?" Charles gasped.

"Don't sound so surprised, Charles," his aunt said, tutting and shaking her head. "We were all young once, you know. I haven't always looked like something out of a Brontë novel. I was twenty-two when we started our little club, and really rather lovely."

"Back then, my grandfather must still have been running the estate," Charles said.

"He was," his aunt confirmed. "He set the whole thing up. He built the original clubhouse and the pool. It wasn't called the Mircester Naturist Society in those days, though. We were just a group of friends—boys and girls—who spent a few summers lazing in the sun, listening to music and drinking wine."

"How many of you were there?" asked Agatha.

"A dozen or so at first," said Mrs. Tassy, "but when word spread, there were plenty of others who wanted to join in. People seem to think that the 'Swinging Sixties' didn't start until women were able to take 'The Pill' but we were having fun long before then."

"And grandfather?" Charles was quite incredulous.

"He was never one for lazing around," she said, "but he liked nothing better than to strip off and do a few lengths of the pool each morning. Other than that, he left the place to us."

"I bet you had lots of admirers, Mrs. Tassy," Agatha said as Gustav arrived with the tea.

"I had my moments." The old lady gave a soft smile.

"Moments?" said Gustav. "When I first started working for the Fraith family, Mrs. Tassy was a legend among the staff. They said she should have been a model. One of the gardeners told me she had titled young gentlemen from half the landed gentry between here and Penzance chasing after her."

"Nonsense," said Mrs. Tassy. "Just pour the tea, please, Gustav."

"I bet it's not nonsense," Agatha said, "yet you chose Mr. Tassy."

"Colonel Tassy is what he became," she replied, "and he was different. One of our original hedonists. We'd known each other since we were children. We were friends our whole lives." She pushed her cup and saucer away. "Do excuse me. I shall go back indoors."

Gustav held the door for her, then followed when she hurried back into the library.

"She's as strong as a horse," Charles said, once his aunt had gone, "until she thinks about my uncle. I truly believe they were what people call soulmates."

"I think you're probably right," said Agatha, taking a sip of tea. "Now what can you tell me about the Lone Warrior?"

"You mean the monolith in the woods near the naturist place?"

"That's the one. I was told it was some kind of altar used for human sacrifices."

"I think whoever told you that was pretty far off the mark. That's the kind of folk tale that people make up when they don't understand what they're looking at. Why are you so interested in that old lump of rock?"

"Because I believe that a murdered man's body was dumped on it a couple of days ago and then spirited away again. I intend to find out what happened, but I'm not about to make up a folk tale—I want to know exactly what I'm looking at. I thought your local knowledge and your history degree might be useful."

"The stone has probably been there for thousands of years. That's a good deal beyond my area of study, but come back into the library," Charles said, standing to lead the way, "there should be something in here that will help."

The library wall opposite the French windows was a mosaic of book spines, row upon row of ancient and modern volumes stacked from floor to ceiling. Charles rolled a wheeled ladder, a kind of miniature spiral staircase, along the wall, positioning it in a precisely chosen spot before locking the wheels and mounting the steps. He was not a tall man, and even with the ladder he had to stretch to reach the book he wanted high on the top shelf. Agatha found herself admiring his lithe form. He was deceptively strong, and an image of them in bed together, his arms holding her close, swam into her mind. It was a hotel room, with the morning sun streaming through the window and the clothes they had worn to dinner the night before scattered on the floor. There had been times, she thought to herself, when being with Charles had made her the happiest woman in the world. The trouble was, he'd always felt compelled to make other women feel that way, too. . . .

"Here it is," he called, making his way back down the stairs. "I knew it was up there somewhere. This was written a hundred years ago by a local historian who made a study of all the sites in the area where standing stones had been found."

He found a passage in the book relating to the Lone Warrior, showed it to Agatha and then read aloud.

"It says here that 'the stone known as the Lone Warrior is of Jurassic oolitic limestone and would originally have stood upright. Its erection on this site almost certainly dates from the Neolithic era, making it over five thousand years old. There are indications that other stones of a similar size formed a small circle at this site, although the rest of the stones have been removed.'"

"Why would anyone remove the stones?" Agatha asked.

"There are any number of practical reasons," Charles explained. "Over thousands of years, the standing stones may have collapsed or broken. Whatever religious or ritual significance they had will have been forgotten and people will have seen them as just a pile of old stones. Local farmers may have hauled them away to use in building a house or bridging a stream."

"Seems sensible—but why is it called the Lone Warrior?"

"That's the really interesting thing about that old stone," Charles said with a gleam in his eye. "It has nothing to do with actual history. It's all legend and folklore. They say, you see, that it is related to the Rollright Stones."

"The what? Sounds like a rock band."

"If you've never seen them, then we should go there." Charles snapped the book shut, grinning enthusiastically.

"Come on, old girl, I'll take you there. It's not far, and if you want to understand the legend behind what you're looking at when you next see the Lone Warrior, then you should see the Rollright Stones."

"I never realised there were so many—" Agatha's phone rang and she fished it out of her handbag, squinting at the caller ID. "Sorry, Charles, but I really should take this . . . Hello, John?" Her face became a study of concentration, her eyes focusing on the floor just ahead of her shoes, but actually seeing nothing. "I see. When was this?"

Charles could hear a man's voice but couldn't make out what he was saying.

"Okay, I'm on my way back," she said, then paused as he responded. "There may not be anything I can do, but I need to be there to see Edward's reaction for myself." There was another short discussion before she bade the caller goodbye and hung up.

"That was a friend of mine," she explained to Charles. "He's a police officer. A body has just been hauled out of the lake in Mircester Park."

"You think it's the one from the Lone Warrior?"

"I do. The vanishing corpse has just reappeared."

Chapter Four

"All I can say at the moment is that the body of an unidentified male believed to have been in his fifties was recovered this afternoon from the lake in Mircester Park." Wilkes's voice somehow managed to be boomingly loud while maintaining the flesh-creepingly nasal overtones of a badly tuned violin.

Agatha walked towards the handful of reporters gathered at the foot of the steps leading up to Mircester police station. Wilkes had positioned himself several steps higher, in order to give the TV cameras the best view of him. The fact that there were no TV cameras, just a few journalists from local newspapers and radio stations, didn't seem to be putting any sort of dent in his sense of occasion. He was an important man conducting an important press call, and Agatha could tell from the way he was standing as well as from the way he was attempting to present what he thought was his best profile, in his pompous little mind there were flash bulbs popping and cameramen jostling for the best vantage point.

In contrast to what was going on in Wilkes's head, the reporters sounded almost bored as they called out the questions they knew their editors would expect them to ask. They did not expect Wilkes to be able to provide the answers. There was definitely a news story with a BODY IN THE LAKE headline, but their colleagues talking to the witnesses who found the body would be the ones grabbing the bylines. Nevertheless, they dutifully held out their recorders to catch what he had to say.

"Did the man drown, Chief Inspector?" one asked.

"Cause of death has yet to be confirmed," said Wilkes.

"Are you treating this as a murder, Chief Inspector?"

"My enquiries are at an early stage," came Wilkes's response.

"When will you release the man's identity?"

"In due course."

"Why do you think the man's underpants were on back to front and his shoes were on the wrong feet, Chief Inspector?"

There was a breathless silence and Agatha looked at the slender young woman with dark-framed glasses who had asked the question, immediately recognising her as Charlotte Clark from the *Mircester Telegraph*. An instant later, the silence was broken by a snort of laughter from one of the male reporters that quickly spread to the rest of the nascent press pack.

"Wh-what?" Wilkes stammered. "What are you talking about?"

"Well, you have to agree that it's a bit weird, isn't it?" Charlotte said. "Why would anyone be dressed like that?"

Questions were fired at Wilkes in quick succession.

"Is it true he was dressed like that?"

"Were any of his clothes missing?"

"Is there a sexual motive to this murder?"

"Is there a sexual predator stalking Mircester Park?"

"Should our readers be worried about a maniac on the loose?"

"Is the park safe, Chief Inspector?"

"Yes, yes, of course Mircester Park is safe," he said, holding up his hands, partly to appeal for calm and partly to protect himself from the barrage.

"How can you be so sure?" asked Charlotte.

"Because the man wasn't murdered in the park, Charlotte," Agatha said, firmly, her steady voice immediately attracting the attention of all the reporters.

"It's Agatha Raisin!" said one and, abandoning Wilkes, they hurried over to her—all except Charlotte. She looked straight at Agatha, smiled and nodded. Agatha gave a slight nod in return. They had dealt with each other in the past and knew each other well. They would speak later. For now, having usurped Wilkes, Agatha was the focus of the press pack's attention.

"How do you know he was murdered, Agatha?"

"Who is the victim?"

"Where did it happen?"

"Do you know who did it?"

"What's your involvement with the case?"

"Mrs. Raisin has no involvement whatsoever!" roared Wilkes, furious at Agatha having stolen the limelight. "This is a police investigation—*my* investigation—and if Mrs. Raisin attempts to interfere in any way, I will arrest her for obstruction!"

"You'll arrest me?" Agatha said, tilting her head slightly and folding her arms. "That didn't work out too well for you last time, did it?"

"Have you arrested Mrs. Raisin before, Chief Inspector?" Charlotte asked, pointing her recorder at Wilkes. "Why was that? What happened?"

"That has no bearing on this enquiry," Wilkes blustered, turning to walk up the stairs. "This press call is over. I have a great deal to do. I'm a very busy man."

By the time he'd taken just one step, Wilkes was talking to himself. The reporters wanted to hear only from Agatha.

"What's your interest in the case, Agatha?"

"I'm interested in getting to the truth. I intend to conduct my own investigation," she explained, "and hope to be able to shed some light on the situation very soon. I can confirm, however, that I do not believe the victim was murdered in Mircester Park. It is my opinion that the body was taken there by his killers and dumped in the lake."

Fending off any further questions, Agatha returned to her car, which was parked nearby with Toni and Edward sitting in the back. She slipped into the driver's seat and started the engine.

"Wilkes was livid," Toni said, with a smile of triumph.

"Wilkes is an idiot," was Agatha's reply. "We're heading into the height of summer and Mircester Park is packed with families every day—parents taking a break and letting their kids play together. They've a right to know that they're safe."

"Do you think you said too much?" Edward asked. "Now the murderers will know that you're looking for them."

"They would know that, anyway, Edward," Agatha said, starting the engine. "This whole affair centres on the naturist club somehow and the fact that we were there with you means that the killers already know I'm taking an interest."

"Won't they be suspicious of Toni joining the society as my girlfriend?" he asked, placing his hand protectively on Toni's.

"Maybe," Agatha agreed, turning left into the high street, "but not nearly as suspicious as they would have been had I joined. Anyway, anyone seeing you two together will believe you've fallen for each other." She glanced at them in the rear-view mirror, teasing them. "You make such a sweet couple!"

"Look, there's Charlotte Clark," Toni said, pointing to the pavement up ahead, where the reporter was watching their car draw near. Agatha pulled over and Charlotte climbed into the passenger seat.

"So where did you get that tip about the underpants and the shoes?" Agatha asked. "Wilkes clearly knew nothing about it."

"I have my sources," Charlotte said, with a secretive

smile. "What makes you think he was murdered—and not in the park?"

"I have my sources, too," Agatha replied.

"Touché!" Charlotte laughed. "Mrs. Raisin, this looks like it might develop into something big pretty quickly. I can let you know if I find out anything else. . . ."

"If I do the same for you," Agatha said. "All right, it's a deal."

"Good," said Charlotte. "Let's keep in touch."

"I take it I'm your source?" asked Edward, once Charlotte had gone.

"You certainly are," Agatha said, pulling away from the kerb. "You've just identified the body in the morgue, after all."

"Not as far as the police are concerned," Toni pointed out. "Edward didn't see the face of the body at the Lone Warrior, so he couldn't make a positive identification when he was shown the dead man's face."

"And I couldn't be sure about the wound on the back of his head, either," Edward admitted, "but the body had been in the water and that would have affected it, wouldn't it? None of that really mattered, though—I knew as soon as I got close that it was the same man. It just *felt* like the same man. Does that sound stupid?"

"Of course not," Agatha assured him. "You need to trust your feelings in that situation. I've been around quite a few dead bodies and each one gives you a certain feeling."

"They just give me the creeps," Toni sighed.

"Well, I think it's instinct," said Agatha, "and it's

really too much of a coincidence for the Lone Warrior body to have a massive head wound and then for the Mircester Lake body to have the same only a couple of days later. The fact that the underpants were on back to front and the shoes were on the wrong feet tells me that our naked corpse was dressed by someone in a hurry before it was dumped in the lake. So I say we go with Edward's instinct and track down our murderer."

Agatha dropped Edward and Toni at his flat in Mircester, from where they planned to make their way to the club for her first proper visit. While they said goodbye to Agatha, Edward pointed out that it was turning into a warm evening and said the pool would be lovely. Toni looked apprehensive.

"I feel like I'm about to jump out of a plane without a parachute," she said.

"Cheer up!" Agatha grinned. "At least you don't have to worry about what to wear!"

Agatha drove out onto the A44, the road climbing gently to give glimpses through gaps in the leafy hedgerows of rolling countryside basking in the early evening sunshine, fields of bright yellow oilseed rape standing in glaring contrast to the dry gold of winter wheat, now almost ready for harvest.

Turning onto the road that led down to where Carsely nestled in a gentle fold in the Cotswold hills, Agatha's headlights flicked on automatically, such was the depth of shade in the foliage tunnel created by the trees lining the road. Over the years that tunnel had come to feel like a welcome arch—Carsely reaching out to bring her home. No matter how stressful her day had been, it was a comforting feeling that banished the tension from her neck and shoulders, the first step in the process of winding down. The second step would be a gin and tonic or a glass of wine. Emerging onto the high street, she cruised past the two long lines of houses, spotting that Harvey's, the post-office-cum-general-store, was still open. She felt the rumblings of hunger again. It had been several hours since she'd devoured her toad in the hole at the King Charles. Realising that she probably had no food in the house, she parked outside her cottage in Lilac Lane and walked swiftly back to the high street, hurrying past the empty spot where James's car would normally be.

Harvey's was one of those stores that might not be open when you expected it to be, occasionally shutting for lunch or on slow afternoons, but the doors were never closed if there was a customer in sight. Agatha made straight for the freezer section and had picked out a chicken curry and a lasagne, one of which she would nuke in the microwave for dinner that evening, when she spotted Doris Simpson, her cleaning lady, squeezing some pears to test their ripeness.

"Hello, Mrs. Raisin!" Doris gave a cheerful greeting. Her white hair was, as always, scraped back in a bun and her grey eyes twinkled merrily behind her pink-framed glasses. "I was in doing your place earlier today. Your boys were looking half starved, so I put some cat-food biscuits in their bowls."

"Thank you, Doris," Agatha replied. "I did feed them

this morning, but they're very good at pretending to be hungry. I'll give them a little less this evening."

"Can't have them getting porky, eh? Need to keep them looking slim and lovely. Speaking of slim and lovely, have you heard about that new choirmaster at the Carsely Choral Society? Giovanni he's called. Apparently he's a right handsome devil. Italian, so they say. Half the women in the choir get the collywobbles when he's around, even them as thought all their hormones curled up and died years ago."

"I'll keep an eye open for him," Agatha said with a laugh, adding a frozen shepherd's pie to her collection. The church choir drew heavily on members of the Carsely Ladies' Society and, having attended a number of their meetings, she could well imagine them having hot flushes over a good-looking Italian. The choir met at St. Jude's, which reminded Agatha that it had been a while since she had spoken to Mrs. Bloxby, the vicar's wife. Margaret Bloxby was a good friend—someone on whom Agatha could rely for a few words of wisdom or just a comforting chat over a glass of sherry. All too often their chats had revolved around James. She had once described him as a "rather cold, self-contained man" and at the height of Agatha's obsession she had warned her that she was allowing James to "live rent-free in your head."

"I see Mr. Lacey's off on his travels again," Doris said, as though Agatha's thoughts of James had somehow leached into her mind.

"He is," Agatha assured her. "It was all a bit last-minute, though. How did you know?"

"He asked if my Bert could do his windows while he

was away," Doris explained. "Well, you know Bert, Mrs. Raisin. He's not one for over-exerting himself but Mr. Lacey was offering good money and it's so difficult to find a window cleaner nowadays."

"It is," Agatha agreed. "If Bert's up for it, Doris, maybe he'd like to do my windows some time, too."

"I'll mention it to him," Doris said, leaving Agatha in no doubt that the "mention" would actually be more of a command.

Agatha strolled home to Lilac Lane, delighting in the lilac bushes that gave the little cul-de-sac its name. There was no street sign but at this time of year, in early summer, anyone looking for Lilac Lane would know they were in the right place. Some of the well-established lilacs in the gardens, including hers and James's, reached around twenty feet high and were heavy with blossoms ranging in colour from a striking dark mauve to a delicate off-white.

In her kitchen, she tucked two of her frozen meals into the freezer, setting one aside for dinner without paying much attention to which it was. She fed Boswell and Hodge then fussed over them for a while, chatting with them in a way that would have left anyone who only knew the no-nonsense, business-orientated Agatha totally bemused. Having blasted her dinner in the microwave, she decided that it was such a warm evening she would sit at the small table in her back garden to eat. The cats joined her.

"What are we going to do about him?" she asked them, looking towards the high hedge that separated her garden from James's. Hodge looked up at her with wide, unblinking green eyes. Boswell curled up on a sun-warmed patio flagstone.

"You're right," she said, agreeing with the cats' silence. "There's not much point in thinking that one round and round in circles. Let's concentrate on our vanishing corpse. We need to find out who the poor bloke was."

She shovelled the last forkful of shepherd's pie into her mouth and, dumping her plate in the kitchen sink to wash up later, decided to take a walk to St. Jude's to see if Margaret Bloxby was around. She was certain to know Mrs. Gittins, the police officer's wife, and to know if any others among the Carsely Ladies were involved with the Naturist Society.

Agatha had always felt something of a connection with the Church of St. Jude, not because she was particularly religious, but because she had been curious enough to want to know who St. Jude had been. When she had looked him up on the internet, she'd found that he was the patron saint of difficult cases—and she had handled plenty of those. Carsely's small, picturesque church dated back as far as the fourteenth century and sat huddled in a churchyard surrounded by trees almost as tall as the building's steeple, which, according to Mrs. Bloxby, had been given "more rebuilds and facelifts than a has-been porn star."

As soon as she set foot on the path winding through the graveyard's display of ancient, crumbling headstones, Agatha heard her friend calling from the midst of a group of middle-aged women.

"Mrs. Raisin! How nice to see you!" Mrs. Bloxby resisted referring to Agatha by her first name, following the tradition of the Carsely Ladies' Society, many of whose members were filing into the church.

"Mrs. Bloxby!" Agatha responded in kind. "I was hoping I might have a word with you."

Having been invited to join those assembling inside, Agatha and Mrs. Bloxby stood together in a discreet corner of the main church hall. Beyond the rows of plain, wooden pews, the last of the evening sunshine cast a colourful glow through the stained glass windows onto the raised area of the chancel.

"Not many men in the Carsely Choral Society, are there?" Agatha noted, scanning the thirty or so choristers.

"There are a surprising number of new female members," Mrs. Bloxby said. She was a petite woman with plain brown hair and her face, which normally wore expressions of kindness and compassion, was animated with a mischievous smile. "Most of them are from the Ladies' Society, and most of them are here to see him . . . Giovanni."

A tall, slim man with lightly tanned skin and lustrous, collar-length black hair strode into the middle of the group. He was wearing jeans and a loose-fitting jacket with an open-necked white shirt that was almost as dazzling as his generous smile. Immediately, all eyes were on him.

"Good evening, everyone, and thank you all for coming a little early this evening," he said, his voice deep, yet soft and alluring, laced with an accent as enticing as warm amaretto. Agatha wanted to hear more.

"Take a careful look at these sheets," he said, handing

83

round sheafs of papers, "and we can start from where we left off last time. We've no musicians tonight, so we'll be using a backing tape . . ."

The more he spoke, the more difficult it became for Agatha to take her eyes off him.

"Quite hypnotic, isn't he?" Mrs. Bloxby chuckled. "Mesmerising, one might say."

"I can certainly see the attraction," Agatha muttered, then felt her friend tugging at her sleeve.

"Let's leave them to it," she said. "How about a glass of sherry at the vicarage?"

They chatted on the short walk to the house, then settled in comfortable garden chairs by the open French doors outside the dining room. Agatha barely had time to admire the roses before Mrs. Bloxby returned with two glasses of Amontillado.

"So what is it that has you seeking me out?" she asked. "Man trouble?"

"Men are always trouble," Agatha sighed, "one way or another."

"Is it Charles?" Had anyone else asked that question, Agatha's immediate response would have been to tell them to mind their own business—in a few short, direct words. Mrs. Bloxby, however, was different. She exuded a goodness and understanding that made Agatha feel quite humble—not a feeling to which she was in any way accustomed.

"Not really," Agatha said, with a sigh. "I'm glad that I can have Charles as a friend, but I don't want him to be more than that."

"That's good. Keep him as a friend if you can, but

84

he's the sort of man who'll be difficult to hold at arm's length. He will see that as a challenge. He will pursue you simply for the challenge—the thrill of the chase."

"That's always been the problem with Charles. When it comes to women, he's always looking for his next conquest."

"I think that he's always put you at the top of the list."

"But I don't want to be on a list. I don't want there to be a list."

"Neither should there be. You are special, but if you don't think you're special, no one else will."

"James seemed to think I was special, but we just annoy each other when we spend too much time together."

"Why do you think that is?"

"I think we're both used to doing things our own way. Neither of us likes to compromise."

"Life and relationships are full of compromises—you know that."

"I suppose so . . . but I didn't come to see you just to talk about men. I wanted to ask you about the ladies over in the hall. I believe Mrs. Gittins is part of the choir."

"That's right. She's been involved for years."

"Did you know she was also a member of the Mircester Naturist Society?"

"Yes, I knew about that."

"I seem to be the only one around here who hadn't heard of them."

"Well, I don't think they really advertise their activities," Mrs. Bloxby said, laughing. "They tend to keep themselves to themselves."

"Are there any other naturists in the choir or the Ladies Society?"

"It's no secret that Mrs. Rayner is. Why do you ask?"

"There's something odd going on there. Something that I believe led to a murder."

"Really? Do tell!"

Agatha explained about the disappearing corpse and the body in the lake. Mrs. Bloxby listened intently, then suggested that they return to the church where she would find some pretence to introduce Agatha to the two women.

"Maybe I should introduce you to the lovely Giovanni as well?" she asked, raising an eyebrow.

"Why not, but may I use your bathroom first?" Agatha said, pointing to the lipstick marks around the mouth of her glass. "I have some repair work to do. A girl needs to look her best when she's meeting a handsome Italian!"

Back at the church, the choir was taking a short break from their rehearsal and the first person they bumped into was someone Agatha recognised straight away from Saturday's incident at the naturist club—one of Jasper's handmaidens.

"Hello," she said, switching on her professional smile and holding out a hand to shake. "Nice to see you again. What a coincidence."

"Mrs. Raisin," said the woman, taking Agatha's hand and holding on to it while she stared up into her face. Her smile held no warmth but her green eyes were filled with curiosity or, thought Agatha, was it suspicion? "We were never really introduced. I'm Ulrika Rayner. Jasper said we might see you again, although I think he hoped it would be at our club, not in a church."

"I'm surprised to see you in a church," Agatha said, still smiling brightly. "It's hardly the sort of place you'd expect to find a handmaiden to a demon master!" She gave a short laugh to show she was joking. Mrs. Rayner failed to crack a smile.

"I believe your young friend has decided to join us," she said.

"Toni? Ah, yes. I think she's rather fallen for that handsome young man, Edward."

"Well, if you'll excuse me, I was just on my way to . . ." She nodded towards the ladies' lavatory.

"Not exactly a bundle of fun, is she?" Agatha said, once Mrs. Rayner was gone.

"Don't be too harsh on her," said Mrs. Bloxby. "She's had her troubles. Her husband emptied their bank account and ran off with another woman not so long ago."

Agatha attempted to look suitably abject. Mrs. Bloxby hailed another of the choristers, introducing her to Agatha as Mrs. Gittins.

"My husband told me all about seeing you at the club," said Mrs. Gittins. She had a high-pitched, wailing laugh. If Boswell or Hodge could laugh, Agatha thought to herself, that's what they'd sound like. "The body that never was—and old Wilkes ordering Jasper to put some clothes on! It was the talk of the barbecue."

"I'll bet it was," Agatha said, her professional smile on full beam. "Did anyone at the barbecue have any idea what on earth poor Edward actually saw?"

"If it were one of them other youngsters," Mrs. Gittins

said, "we might have thought they'd been on the wacky baccy, but not young Edward. He's not one for that sort of thing. Whatever he saw is a mystery—but I hear you're on the track of a murderer."

"You hear right," said Agatha, deciding not to give too much away, "but as you say, at the moment it's all a mystery."

Mrs. Gittins made a strangling gesture with her hands at her neck, announced she was parched and that she needed a cup of tea before the rehearsal resumed. She joined a group of women gathered around a small table, serving themselves from a tea urn.

"Excuse me, Mrs. Bloxby," Giovanni's velvety voice oozed from behind them. They turned to find him standing with his smartphone at the ready. "I was wondering if we can book another couple of rehearsal sessions here before the big performance?"

"That should be fine," said Mrs. Bloxby, introducing Agatha. "If you'll both excuse me, I'll fetch my diary from the house."

"Have you come to join the choir, Mrs. Raisin?" asked Giovanni.

"No, no . . . not me, no," Agatha said, slightly taken aback by the nervous twinge she felt when he looked directly into her eyes, then reprimanding herself for acting like a silly schoolgirl. "I'm just visiting my friend, Mrs. Bloxby. I'm not sure I've a good-enough singing voice for the choir."

"Really? But I have heard of you. You are the detective, yes? You seem to me like the sort of woman who can do whatever she puts her mind to—a woman who likes to get whatever she wants."

"I do?" Agatha coughed to take the squeak out of her voice. "I mean, I do but I . . ."

"Giovanni, can we have a word, please?" Two of the ladies from the choir approached. Agatha judged both to be in their late forties. One was taller, with steadfastly permed brown hair while the other had a heavier figure but what Agatha thought to be a pretty face in need of more effective make-up.

"We really need to know what you've decided," said the taller one.

"You promised you would let us know this week," said the other.

"Ladies, ladies, you must have patience," he said, holding his hands with the palms towards them in a calming gesture. "All in good time. All will soon be clear. Now, if you will excuse me, I am talking to Mrs. Raisin."

The taller one sniffed, turned on her heel and stalked off. The other let out a heavy sigh and followed her.

"What was that about?" Agatha asked. "They seemed upset."

"They are squabbling over who will play which part. We are to perform a choral version of Mascagni's *Cavalleria Rusticana*. One of them will play Lola and one Santuzza but, of course, they both want to play Santuzza."

"I see," Agatha said, sounding slightly confused.

"You don't know the story of this opera?" Giovanni

raised his eyebrows, giving her a playfully incredulous look. "But you must! It is a story of great drama—great passion. You must allow me to explain it all to you. Have dinner with me tonight."

"Actually, I've already eaten." Agatha cursed herself for being so limp. What did that matter? She could eat two dinners! Why hadn't she jumped at the offer?

"Ah, and I am getting carried away—I will be here until late, so tonight is not so good. Tomorrow is also not possible."

"I'm er . . . free on Wednesday night," Agatha offered, hopefully.

"Fantastic! So am I! I work with other choirs here and there, and when I am in this vicinity, I like to stay at the Royal Oak on the road to Evesham. It is a very nice hotel with an excellent restaurant—do you know it?"

"I do," Agatha said. She and Charles had stayed there on a number of occasions, having gone for dinner and stayed for afters.

"Then meet me there on Wednesday evening at seven-thirty. You will come, yes? Please say you will. I shall explain everything about *Cavalleria Rusticana* and we will have a wonderful meal together."

"Then I will come," Agatha said, and handed him her card.

"Until Wednesday," Giovanni slipped the card into his pocket, reached down to take Agatha's hand, then stooped to kiss it before striding back to where the ladies of the choir were watching in awed silence. What had they just seen? Had that Raisin woman really managed to snare the heart-stoppingly gorgeous Giovanni?

Agatha stared back at them, giving them a smug smile and a slow wink before turning to leave.

Although the evening cooled with nightfall, it was still warm enough for Agatha to be lying awake on her bed, unable to sleep, with her windows open wide. Boswell and Hodge were curled up at her feet, snoring disgracefully, even though that was what they'd been doing for most of the day. Each flexed an occasional claw or suffered the indignity of having their paws judder into stilted running motion, joining in a dream that involved far more exercise than either of them was accustomed to while awake.

Agatha, on the other hand, had more on her mind than chasing blue tits or squirrels. She thought she had exhausted herself by trying on a dozen different dresses before going to bed, still leaving herself undecided over what to wear for dinner with Giovanni at the Royal Oak, yet she couldn't get to sleep. When she forced herself to push Giovanni out of her mind, thoughts of the disappearing corpse came flooding in. She was in no doubt that the body in the lake and the Lone Warrior corpse were one and the same, but who was the dead man, and who was his killer?

The answers, she was sure, would come from the naturist club. She had thought Ulrika Rayner odd enough when she had seen her as one of Jasper's handmaidens, but her strange demeanour at the church had been even more baffling. Your husband running off with another woman and your life savings was certainly no joke, but

Agatha had the distinct impression that Ulrika's weirdness ran deeper than the break-up of her marriage. She may have missed him, she may have missed the money even more, but there was something else in her eyes that concerned Agatha. She'd have Patrick run a background check on Ulrika first thing in the morning.

She picked up a book from her bedside table to try to banish all other thoughts. It was one of her favourite Agatha Christie novels, *The Sittaford Mystery*. She loved the Emily Trefusis character—a smart, resourceful woman determined to solve a despicable murder. Every time she dipped into the book she saw herself playing Emily and, drawn into the role once more, she had almost lost herself on a snowy Dartmoor when her phone rang. Was it Giovanni? It had to be him, didn't it? She felt a thrill of exhilaration spinning her stomach. Snapping the book shut, she snatched up her phone. It was Charles.

"Aggie, sweetie! Didn't wake you, did I, old girl?"

"Charles, do *not* call me Aggie, or sweetie," Agatha snapped, "and I am certainly neither old nor a girl!"

"Well, of course. I didn't mean . . ." The enthusiasm drained from Charles's voice momentarily, then effortlessly gathered momentum again. "Anyway, I've been looking into the Rollright Stones and it's all jolly interesting. As a matter of fact, the whole story's absolutely fascinating. It's been years since I saw the things, so why not let me take you there tomorrow afternoon? It will be fun—just like old—"

"Charles, I don't know how long it's going to take

you to realise that things will never again be 'just like old times.' I will, however, come to see those damned stones with you. Right now, however, I'm tired, so goodnight."

She hung up and placed the phone on the bedside cabinet. Maybe she'd been a bit short with Charles but he was behaving like an overexcited puppy and he had to learn that he was no longer the centre of her world, if he ever really had been. Suddenly, the phone rang again. This time it had to be Giovanni! It had to be! She grabbed the phone. It was Toni.

"Toni, what is it?"

"You said to keep in touch."

"Yes, of course I did." Agatha set aside the disappointment of not having Giovanni crooning in her ear and concentrated on Toni. "How did it go this evening?"

"It was a bit strange at first, but you soon get used to it."

"Get used to what?"

"Being naked in front of so many other people, of course! Actually, because they were all naked, I think I'd have felt more awkward if I'd had my clothes on. After a while, being nude just seemed perfectly natural and I—"

"All right, Toni, so you're a born-again nudie, but what were people saying about the murder?"

"All the kinds of gossip and speculation you would expect but nothing of any value. There was one woman I found really weird, though. Her name is Ursula Danieli. She has a sister called Ulrika Rayner and they're the ones who were . . ."

"Jasper's handmaidens." Agatha finished Toni's sentence for her. "I met Ulrika this evening. She gave me a very disturbing look."

"Ursula was the same. She made me feel like she was trying to see inside my head."

"What does Edward think of those two?"

"He steers well clear of them. Says he finds them really odd. Ursula is married to an Italian called Antonio. He's in the ice-cream business."

Agatha asked Toni to work with Patrick in the morning to dig up whatever they could on the two sisters, then told her to get some rest and hung up. She was intrigued that Toni had the same feeling about Ursula that she had about Ulrika. The sisters were strange but that didn't make them murderers. Neither, however, did it rule them out as suspects. Background checks might give her something to go on. She'd also ask Patrick to use his contacts to check on recent missing persons reports. Wilkes would be doing that as well, trying to match the body with no name to a name with no body. Maybe John Glass could help with that, too. Ah, John—he was sweet but he was no Giovanni. Giovanni was . . . the phone rang yet again. Surely it was him this time! She put the phone to her ear but instead of Giovanni's soft Italian accent, she heard a harsh, metallic, electronically disguised voice.

"Keep your nose out of our affairs, or you will be the next to die!"

The phone went dead and a chill ran down Agatha's spine. She slipped out of bed and closed her bedroom windows before flitting downstairs to check that all the other windows and doors were locked and bolted. In the kitchen, she picked up a heavy cast-iron saucepan—part of a set that she'd bought when she'd thought about learning to cook but now kept for show. She tested its weight in her hand. Anybody coming after her would get more than they bargained for. She had been frightened, but now she was angry and more determined than ever to find the murderer.

I've been threatened before, she thought to herself, setting her jaw. I've been held at knifepoint and I've stared down the barrel of a gun. I will *not* be scared off with a silly voice on the telephone!

"Snakes and bastards!" she snarled. "No one threatens Agatha Raisin and gets away with it!

Chapter Five

Agatha was woken by the early morning sun streaming through her bedroom windows. She could hear muted birdsong and, for a moment, wondered why the room felt a bit stuffy and then why the windows were fully closed. Then her eyes caught the cast-iron pot on her bedside table and the ugly metallic voice filled her head. She tutted, determined not to be intimidated by a voice on the phone, and crossed the floor to open the windows.

The room was immediately flooded with cool morning air and the high-volume trill of a blackbird, cheerfully reminding the whole village that it was time to rise and shine. Agatha looked down onto the gardens in Lilac Lane and the fields beyond. All was peaceful. There was nothing threatening out there, just the gentle beginning of another bucolic morning in Carsely.

Agatha showered and sat at her small dressing table, running through her morning routine, checking for new wrinkles, applying her make-up and finishing off with a lipstick she was confident would suit the outfit she had in mind for work that day. She looked over to the chair in the corner of the room, stacked with the dresses she had been considering for her liaison with Giovanni tomorrow evening. She smiled. Deciding what to wear was a conundrum she would embrace later in the day. Right now, the insistent wide eyes of Boswell and Hodge persuaded her it was time to feed the cats again.

She shrugged on a light dressing gown then, halfway down the stairs, drew it tighter when it billowed open. Why am I bothering? she asked herself. There's no one in the house but me and the cats—no one to see me. Toni, after all, bared all in front of a bunch of complete strangers last night. Why should I be such a . . . prude?

Having fed the cats, she stood sipping her first coffee of the day in the open kitchen doorway, looking out over her small back garden. The house cast a shadow over the narrow, flagstone patio but the lawn, surrounded by tall hedges of privet and yew as well as borders bursting with outrageously colourful dahlias and geraniums, was warming in the sun. She wondered what it must have been like for Toni in the garden at the Mircester Naturist Society. What was it like to wander about naked outdoors?

"Our garden's not overlooked by anyone, is it, boys?" she said to the two cats. Boswell carried on eating, but Hodge glanced up from his bowl, giving her a mystified look. He was good at that. "You can see over the hedge from James's back bedroom, but he's not there, is he?"

She set her coffee mug down on the kitchen table, stood facing the garden and slipped her dressing gown off her shoulders, letting it fall to the floor. Then she took a deep breath and stepped out of the kitchen onto the patio, completely naked. The flagstones were cold beneath her feet but a couple of paces took her out of the shade. She felt the sun first on her shoulders, then on her back, then its gentle warmth caressed her buttocks. Strolling up the garden, she smiled, delighting in the feeling of fresh air all around her.

Agatha thought of all the glamorous beaches she had visited around the Mediterranean. She wasn't one for sitting on the beach. Lipstick started to feel like the bottom of a budgie's cage once the sea breeze had coated it with salt and sand. Aside from relaxing by a pool, however, strolling along a beach was the best way to show off the latest bikini on which she had spent a small fortune and dieted and exercised for weeks to fit into. She'd seen other women going topless, even naked, on beaches, but had always thought that took all the joy out of modelling your most fabulous swimwear. Now she was beginning to understand why people liked to feel the sun on their bodies uncluttered by cloth, ties, clasps or sequins.

Holding her arms out wide, she closed her eyes as she turned and held her face up to the sun. She had always avoided too much harsh sunlight, worrying about patchy skin, liver spots and wrinkles, but this gentle morning sun simply felt delightful.

"Morning, Mrs. Raisin!"

Agatha's eyes popped open and she froze. Bert Simpson was up a ladder cleaning James's windows.

"Lovely morning for it!" Bert called, cheerfully.

Dignity, Agatha thought. Poise, elegance and dignity.

"Good morning, Bert," she said calmly. "Yes, it is a lovely morning, isn't it?"

Head high and shoulders back, she walked slowly back to the kitchen while Bert returned to smearing the windows with a damp rag.

Once out of sight, she grabbed her dressing gown and scuttled through the kitchen towards the stairs where she caught sight of herself in the hall mirror and thought, "Thank God I'd done my make-up!"

When Agatha arrived at work that morning, the first thing she noticed was a schoolgirl sitting on a chair just inside the entrance to the main office. She was a pretty young thing with long curls of light-brown hair and had the truculent, hooded-eye expression of youth. She appeared to be multi-tasking by rapidly thumb-typing a message on her phone while also chewing gum.

The next thing she noticed was Simon, staring at her with a smugly confident smile that Agatha found instantly irritating. Clearly he was looking for some sort of reaction.

"Morning, boss," he called, the smile widening to a grin.

"What are you doing here?" she said curtly. "Why aren't you at the brewery?"

"I needed to have a quick word with you before I went."

"In my office."

Agatha marched into her own office, waving aside Helen Freeman. She placed her phone on her desk and dropped her handbag into a desk drawer. She took her seat and Simon stood facing her.

"I assume that girl out there is something to do with you?" she asked.

"She is," he responded. "She's my suggestion for a way to get someone inside Martinbrook. She can go in, posing as a new pupil."

"Are you mad? We can't possibly use a child in that way! And certainly not in a case that involves drugs!"

"Please, boss, just hear me out." Simon put his hands together in a gesture that appeared to be part pleading and part prayer. "Let me bring her in to talk to you."

Agatha sighed and waved her hand, ushering him out to fetch the girl. As he exited, Helen entered, delivering a cup of coffee, a pile of folders and some mail to Agatha's desk. She hurried out again without a word, clearly anxious not to become involved in whatever was going on.

"This is Paula," Simon said, introducing the girl. "She's a friend of mine."

"Really?" Agatha replied. The girl had stopped chewing and her phone was nowhere in sight, although she was now carrying a document wallet. Although she wasn't quite as tall as Simon, she had long legs, accentuated by what was, in Agatha's opinion, an indecently short skirt. The white blouse beneath her dark blue blazer was a little too tight, which, combined with the short skirt, seemed to be the fashion from what Agatha had seen of girls on their way to school in the morning. "I'd say she was way too young, Simon, either to be your friend or for us to employ in any capacity."

"Would you tell Agatha, please, Paula?" Simon said.

"My name is Paula Wallace," the girl announced, opening the document wallet and placing several items on the desk for Agatha to examine. There was a driving licence, a passport and a birth certificate. "I'm twenty-three years old and I have a degree in maths and economics."

"Paula looks about sixteen," Simon explained. "She always has to carry proof of age to get into clubs or to get served in pubs."

"So, Miss Wallace, you are Simon's . . . girlfriend?"

"He should be so lucky!" The girl laughed, revealing perfect white teeth, but the laugh showed no wrinkles on her face. Agatha noted that she was wearing not a scrap of make-up, but her skin was smooth and flawless. One day, young Paula might have to resort to the torture regimes of concealing, tweezing and using face-hair removal creams, but she had years of effortless beauty ahead of her. Not for the first time Agatha lamented the cruelty of age, and the ghosts of recently plucked hairs on her upper lip bristled at the injustice of it all.

Simon feigned offence at Paula's remark, then chuckled. "Paula and I grew up together," he explained. "She was the girl next door. We've always been like . . . best mates."

Paula nodded in agreement, smiling and slipping her hand through Simon's arm.

"Where did you park your gum?" Agatha asked.

"There was no gum," Paula answered. "I hate the stuff. That was just an act. I thought it would help me to look the part."

"Do you have a regular job?"

"I've got a few irons in the fire, but I'm at a loose end right now," Paula explained. "Simon wouldn't tell me everything but this sounded like it might be interesting, so I'd like to help. I won't work for nothing, of course. I'll expect a fee."

"All right, Miss Wallace," Agatha said, sitting back and resting her hands on the arms of her chair, "I have a meeting with the headmistress of Martinbrook Sixth Form College and a concerned parent in an hour, so let's talk."

"Who was *she*?" Toni asked, snittily, dragging her chair into Agatha's office.

"A friend of Simon's," Agatha replied, amused by the way that Toni's eyes were casting jealous daggers at Paula's back as she left the main office with Simon. "She might be useful on the Martinbrook case. Now, do you have anything more on our nudie friends?"

"Not much more than I told you last night, but I have addresses for Ursula and Ulrika. I think our first instincts about them were absolutely right. They are very strange ladies."

"Being strange doesn't make them murderers but, without even knowing it, we seem to be getting under someone's skin."

Agatha told Toni about the previous evening's threatening phone call. She had checked her incoming calls and the number had been withheld. The caller was untraceable.

"Anyone can buy one of those voice-distortion gadgets. There was even a boy at our school who could do the electronic voice without a gadget. Are you sure the phone call is to do with the murder?" Toni asked. "I mean, we're sticking our noses into all sorts of things all the time—divorces are usually top of our list."

"True," Agatha agreed, "but the voice very specifically said 'our affairs.' There's always more than one person involved in a divorce, of course, but I don't think that's what it meant. Whoever we've upset is working with a team, or a partner . . . or a sister."

"As far as the murder's concerned, I suppose the only people who would think we were sticking our noses in are those at the Naturist Society. We've both been there, caused a fuss with the police, then you announced to the press that you were investigating a murder, and now I'm back. They might think I'm snooping around."

"No doubt," Agatha agreed. "Posing as Edward's girlfriend wasn't the strongest cover story, even if you weren't exactly . . . posing?"

Toni looked at her blankly, on this occasion refusing to be baited on her private life.

"So what should we do?" she asked.

"If we're having an effect," Agatha said, "we have to keep up the pressure. We need to get closer to the weirdo sisters."

"Apparently Ulrika is involved in organising the

role-playing game that some of the members play. I could tell her that I'd like to try it, too. I can pay her a visit later today."

"Good idea. I'll find a way to get to Ursula. Keep your wits about you, though, Toni. We have to take that phone call threat seriously."

"I will. There's one more thing. Patrick came up with this on Jasper." She pushed a sheet of notes across the desk. "No criminal record. He used to do a stage act as an amateur magician—charity events, that sort of thing. He's now an accountant, a partner in Crane & Maclean. His office is in Mircester, not far from here."

"In that case," Agatha said, scanning the sheet, "I shall arrange to 'bump into him' and have a little chat."

Mrs. Carling and Mrs. Partridge arrived punctually together and Patrick introduced them to Agatha in her office, having already arranged seats. Helen provided coffee and biscuits.

Mrs. Carling was in her sixties, slim and fit with a blonde perm and a blue business suit, the hem of the skirt just below the knee. She had the aura of a woman bursting with energy—the sort of person who gave you the impression that she desperately needed to be somewhere else, doing something terribly urgent. Then she made you feel important by giving you her time instead.

Agatha gauged Mrs. Partridge to be in her mid-forties. Her dark hair was pushed back from her face and Agatha admired the skill that had gone into the application of her make-up, keeping the telltale signs of age at bay.

They discussed what Mrs. Partridge had discovered in her daughter's possession and Agatha asked if Sarah had ever shown signs of using drugs before.

"Never," said Mrs. Partridge. "Sarah's a good girl, although things have been tough for her since her father and I split up."

"Who is her father?" Agatha asked, making notes.

"His name is Jim Sullivan. We divorced five years ago. I've since remarried and run an events management business with my current husband. That can take us all over the country—all over Europe, in fact, so it worked out best for Sarah to board at Martinbrook. We live further north, just outside Warwick, and I try to be at home to spend time with Sarah at the weekends."

"Does she spend time with Mr. Sullivan?"

"Jim visits her at least once a week to take her out to dinner."

"What does Mr. Sullivan do?"

"He owns an ice-cream company."

"Really?" Agatha sounded surprised. "That's a coincidence—the second time I've heard ice-cream companies mentioned today."

"That's all very well, Mrs. Raisin," said Mrs. Carling, with a touch of impatience, "but what can you do to help us with this problem?"

"Someone is clearly supplying drugs to the girls," Agatha said, "and in order to put a stop to it, we need to find out who that is."

"That much is obvious," the headmistress pointed out impatiently. "How are you going to do that?"

"What Mrs. Raisin would like to propose," said Patrick, joining in the discussion for the first time in an attempt to placate Mrs. Carling before she could trigger Agatha's temper, "is a two-pronged investigation."

"Indeed," Agatha agreed. "I would like to get to know your staff. According to your prospectus, you teach business studies at the college. We don't want anyone to think that we are carrying out an investigation, so I will give a talk to the girls about working in business—I used to run a successful PR operation in London."

"I trust my staff implicitly," said Mrs. Carling.

"I'm sure you do," Agatha said, "but I don't. We'll need you to give us their details so that Patrick can run background checks."

"That information is strictly confidential," Mrs. Carling pointed out.

"Everything we do is strictly confidential, Mrs. Carling," Agatha assured her.

"The second part of the plan is to enroll this young woman at the college," said Patrick, passing a photograph of Paula to Mrs. Carling and explaining who she was and how her job would be to find out which of the girls might be distributing the stuff.

"I must say that I abhor all this subterfuge," Mrs. Carling said, tutting.

"If the police were to become involved," Agatha pointed out, "their approach wouldn't be nearly as subtle and all of this would come out in the open."

"That's something we all want to avoid," said Mrs.

Partridge. "I am prepared to make a substantial donation to the school that will cover your fees, Mrs. Raisin."

"When can you start?" asked Mrs. Carling.

"We're already on it," Agatha said with a smile. "Help us get Paula kitted out with her Martinbrook uniform today and Patrick, posing as her grandfather, will deliver her to you tomorrow morning."

This, Agatha told herself, is the essence of sleuthing. She was loitering, watching, taking care neither to attract attention nor to be seen by her target. This was how a private investigator operated in the field.

Having called to speak to Jasper Crane and been told that he'd popped out for lunch and was expected back in a few minutes, Agatha was staking out the building where Crane & Maclean had their offices. Then she spotted him. He was wearing a very conventional dark suit with an open-necked shirt—not the sort of outfit you'd expect to find a demon master wearing. His neatly coiffured hair and beard, however, were unmistakable. He was carrying a large take-away coffee cup and a sandwich bag. Agatha moved to intercept him.

"Jasper!" she said with a beaming smile. "What a coincidence! I almost didn't recognise you!"

"You're not going to use that old line 'I didn't recognise you with your clothes on,' are you, Mrs. Raisin?" He laughed.

"I wouldn't dream of it," Agatha lied—those had been the next words on her lips. "And you must call me Agatha. I'm so glad to have bumped into you. I really wanted to have a chat with you about the Naturist Society."

"Thinking of joining, I hope. I know that your friend has."

"Yes, Toni seems to love it but . . . well . . . I think I still need persuading."

"Then I'm your man." He grinned. "I'm a bit pushed for time right now but . . . why don't you come up to my office? Share this coffee with me—it's the best in town but there's always too much for me to finish."

"Why not?" Agatha made a pretence at checking her watch. "I can spare a few minutes."

Jasper led her up to his office and set two china mugs on his desk, dividing the coffee between them. Around the walls were framed photographs and items of memorabilia—a cloak, a magic wand and a top hat among them—from his time as a stage magician.

"It was a hobby," he said, watching her taking it all in, "that became an obsession, although I raised quite a bit for local charities."

"And what are those?" She pointed to two sinister daggers lying to one side of his desk. They had identically decorated black-and-gold handles and long, gleaming steel blades.

"More magic," he grinned, picking one up. He jabbed the point into a notebook and the blade disappeared, as though straight into his desk. "On this one the blade retracts into the hilt while this one," he tested the other dagger as before, "is the real thing. It always looked very dramatic when I demonstrated this one on stage then appeared to plunge it into my own chest!"

"I always thought these things worked with a little trigger to make the blade disappear," Agatha said.

"They can, but I never liked the idea of the trigger failing!" He laughed and placed both knives on the desk in front of him. "In any case, it was easy for me to substitute one for the other."

He passed his hands in circles over the daggers, then picked up one—but the other had disappeared from the desk.

"Very impressive," Agatha said, awarding him a small round of applause. "I've no idea how you did that—right in front of my eyes!"

"It just takes practice," he said, modestly, "but you didn't want to talk to me about magic, did you?"

"No. I've become intrigued about the whole naturist thing. I tried it this morning, you see."

"Tried what? Going without clothes?"

"Yes, in my back garden."

"I take it your garden is quite secluded."

"Yes—there was no one to see me . . . except next door's window cleaner. I'll be the talk of the Red Lion by the time I get home this evening."

"I bet all of the window cleaner's drinking chums will be jealous!"

"It's nice of you to say so," said Agatha, feeling genuinely flattered.

"Well, you're a very attractive woman. You've every right to feel at ease in your own skin."

"Actually, I enjoyed being outside like that. It felt . . . natural."

"That's just how it should feel," Jasper assured her,

taking a gulp of coffee. "Look, I have a client meeting shortly, but you know where to find me now. Let me know if you want to give the club a try."

"I do," Agatha said, "and you have my card, so you know where to find me, too."

On her way back to her office, Agatha replayed her meeting with Jasper in her head. When they had met at the club, she had thought he was distinctly odd, but today he had been completely charming and . . . utterly normal. He had made her feel remarkably relaxed and he did have the most lovely blue eyes . . . but that beard! She stopped walking, as though to reset her thoughts. She had to stop thinking about him as though she'd just been on a date. She was supposed to be evaluating him as a murder suspect. She prided herself on being an excellent judge of character, especially when it came to men—apart from the one she had first married, and the one she'd become engaged to after meeting him at the airport, and that vet . . . In any case, Jasper did not strike her as being a vicious murderer, and she quickened her pace, her heels clicking on the pavement with metronomic precision.

Toni drove down a treelined street on the outskirts of Mircester where the houses were solid, respectable semi-detached buildings—a far cry from the grandeur of Lower Burlip. She turned left onto a smaller street that dropped down and curved right, ending in a T-junction. Beyond the road lay a wildflower meadow, the white and purple heads of wild carrot mixing with red poppies and the blue of cornflowers. Dense woodland bordered the meadow.

She pulled in to park and checked the map on her phone. Ulrika's cottage was just to the left after the junction. She drove on, turned right and took the car far enough away from the cottage to be out of sight. Then she parked and stepped out. She was wearing walking boots, shorts and carrying a small rucksack, looking like a rambler out for a day's hike in the countryside. Crossing the road, she entered the meadow and walked a long loop. If she was seen approaching the cottage, it would look like she had crossed the meadow from the woods.

She was standing at Ulrika's garden gate, gazing at the flowerbeds packed with blooms when she heard a voice.

"Can I help you?" Ulrika emerged from the side of the house, a flower pot and trowel in her hands.

"I was just admiring your beautiful garden," Toni said, grateful that Ulrika made things easy for her by initiating the encounter. "I've seen you before, haven't I? It's Ulrika from the club, isn't it? I'm Toni, Edward's girlfriend."

"Yes." Ulrika eyed her suspiciously. "I recognise you now. What brings you to this part of Mircester, Toni?"

"I was walking and, well, I don't know this area very well and got a bit lost in the woods up there."

"You poor thing," Ulrika said, forcing a smile. "You must be parched, my love. Come into the back garden and I'll make you a nice cup of herbal tea."

"Thank you, Ulrika. That would be great."

Toni followed her up the side of the cottage into the

small back garden that was bursting with a huge variety of plants, most of which Toni didn't recognise. Along a south-facing wall there was a glasshouse where she could see some of the more exotic specimens thriving.

"Your garden is amazing," Toni said, taking a seat, as directed by Ulrika, at a small metal table.

"I like to feel at one with nature," Ulrika said, "but you know that already, of course." She hurried inside to boil the kettle and Toni sat in the sunshine, trying to spot a plant or flower she could actually identify. When Ulrika returned, carrying two dainty tea cups in saucers, Toni pointed to a plant with wide, crinkly green leaves and delicate, white cross-shaped flowers.

"This is very pretty," she said, "but I've no idea what it is."

Ulrika put the tea on the table, reached down and plucked one of the leaves, crushing it in her hand.

"Most folks rip it out as a weed," she said, cupping her hands around the leaf. "Here, take a sniff. What can you smell?"

"It's a bit like garlic," Toni said, "but there's something else as well."

"Well done," Ulrika congratulated her. "They call it Jack-by-the-hedge because that's where it normally grows, but it's garlic mustard. It's not strong but you can use it much like any other herb."

"Do you grow lots of herbs?"

"Oh, yes," Ulrika said, and began pointing out plants around the garden that could be used in all sorts of ways, from spicing up a stew to dissolving warts. Toni listened intently, fascinated by the depth of Ulrika's knowledge, but also wondering if she and Agatha could really justify putting Ulrika at the top of their suspect list. The woman was, without doubt, a little eccentric but seemed perfectly harmless. She listened to Ulrika explaining how dried marigold flowers could be turned into a concoction that cured measles, sipped her tea and began to feel quite relaxed, enjoying the sunshine and the fragrances of the garden.

Agatha had time to clear some paperwork from her desk before Charles arrived, breezing into the office full of enthusiasm for their visit to the Rollright Stones.

"Come along, old girl," he called, then gave an apologetic smile when Agatha scowled at him. "Your carriage awaits—it's blocking the lane outside, actually. You're not wearing those shoes, are you?"

Agatha looked down at her pale blue court shoes, sighed and produced a pair of walking shoes from a drawer in her desk.

"Let's go," she said. "I'll change shoes in the car and you can explain why these old stones are so special."

From Mircester, they took the road towards Carsely but bypassed the village, heading for Moreton-in-Marsh, then on in the direction of Chipping Norton.

"The area around the stones," Charles explained, "is actually an ancient burial ground. There are a number of burial mounds nearby and one section of the stones is known to be part of a burial chamber."

"Sounds a bit like Stonehenge," Agatha said, breathlessly, her tight skirt making it a real effort to reach down to change her shoes. She gave up, deciding it would be easier when they stopped.

"It is rather," Charles agreed, "but on a smaller scale. That doesn't mean it's any less interesting. Parts of Rollright may be older than Stonehenge. The stones that formed the portal to the burial chamber have been there for well over five thousand years."

Near Little Compton, Charles turned left onto a smaller road and, a couple of miles further on, he pulled into a layby.

"Is this it?" Agatha asked, looking left and right. "There's nothing here."

"Ah, but there is, my dear." Charles grinned. "Here we are surrounded by history, myth and legend. Come along, I'll show you."

Agatha quickly changed her shoes and Charles led her to the entrance to a field, where he shoved a folded twenty-pound note into an "honesty box."

"The place is maintained by a trust," he explained, "but there's seldom anyone here to collect an entrance fee. We've overpaid, but they're worth it."

In the field, protruding from the grass like bad teeth, was a wide circle of weathered stones, some standing taller than others, and one that appeared to have collapsed completely. Their shapes were gnarled and irregular, with lichen scarring their faces.

"These are known as the King's Men," Charles explained. "Originally there would have been one hundred and five stones, all standing shoulder-to-shoulder, with the entrance to the circle near that collapsed stone, opposite the tallest of the standing stones."

"Why was it built?" Agatha asked.

"We can't be absolutely certain exactly what it was used for," Charles said, "but it will have had some form of religious significance to the people of the time and was probably used for ceremonial rituals."

"Like a church," Agatha suggested.

"I think that's a reasonable analogy," Charles agreed.

"I can see why people came to think of them as stone men," Agatha said, peering closely at one of the stones. "The way they've weathered, you can sort of see faces in the stone. What kind of stone is it?"

"It's the same stuff that was used to build your cottage, but these have been here far longer. They've had the elements nibbling away at them for four and a half thousand years."

They wandered round the circle, inspecting the stones before Charles took Agatha on a short walk along a grassy path to where a cluster of large stones leaned haphazardly together, surrounded by a protective metal railing.

"These are called the Whispering Knights," Charles said. "This is the oldest monument on the site."

"The burial chamber?"

"Yes. Evidence of human remains has been found here. Not something for you to investigate though," Charles said, laughing. "The bone fragments were almost four thousand years old!"

Retracing their steps to the entrance, they crossed the road to visit another field where a solitary stone stood at the top of a grassy embankment. Like the Whispering Knights, it was surrounded by a railing but in all other respects it was different. The stone looked deformed, contorted as though it was bending like a tree under the onslaught of a mighty gale.

"The King Stone," Charles announced. "I'm told it's such an odd shape because, would you believe, before the Victorians put the railing in place, people would chip bits off it to take home as souvenirs. This was probably erected to impress ancient visitors and let them know that this was the resting place of important ancestors."

"So how are these connected to our Lone Warrior? It's miles away from here."

"The legend is what connects them," Charles said. "Even though the stones here were erected thousands of years apart, folklore gathers them together in the same period."

"Tabloid journalists always say you should never let the facts get in the way of a good story," Agatha said, smiling. "So what's the story?"

"At one time England was divided into many different kingdoms, each with its own king, and there were countless wars and squabbles. Legend has it that one king was passing through this area with his army, on a mission to unite the whole country. Not everyone thought this was a good idea, of course, and, unknown to the king, some of his knights were conspiring against him."

"The Whispering Knights," Agatha guessed.

"The very same," said Charles. "The knights made a pact with the Devil to stop the king and the Devil sent a witch, who appeared in front of the king right where we're standing.

"The witch told the king that she would guarantee

the success of his mission if he could take seven paces and see the village of Long Compton. If he couldn't, he would be deemed unworthy to rule England and be turned to stone.

"Long Compton is in that direction," Charles pointed towards a low ridge that obscured the horizon, "and the king could see it plainly. He took six paces towards it but before he could walk another step, the witch caused that ridge to spring up, obscuring the view. The king was turned to stone, as were his men and, because you can never trust a witch in league with the Devil, so were the traitorous knights."

"And the Lone Warrior?" Agatha asked.

"It's said that he was one of the king's men, off watering the horses. When he saw what had happened, he fled, pursued by the witch. He came to a cottage in the woods where a beautiful young woman lived. He begged her to hide him from the witch and she agreed on the condition that he would marry her. He agreed and she hid him under her bed.

"The witch passed by outside and the girl told the soldier to come out. He now had to keep his part of the bargain but, before his eyes the woman turned into a wizened, ugly old hag—the sister of the witch who was hunting him. He refused to marry her and she betrayed him to her sister, who immediately turned him to stone—the Lone Warrior."

"It's a good story," Agatha said, "but it doesn't explain why someone would dump a naked corpse on the stone."

"That sounds like it might be more to do with the nonsense about the Lone Warrior having been used in ritual sacrifice."

"Maybe. It's all tied up with the naturists in some way—I'm sure of it."

"Do you have a suspect there?"

"Not really, but we're looking at a woman called Ursula Danieli and her sister, Ulrika Rayner."

"Ursula Danieli? Antonio's wife?"

"You know her?"

"I know Antonio. He's a jolly decent chap. Whenever there's one of those charity fetes at Barfield, he brings along a couple of his ice-cream vans and donates all the profits."

"I need to find an excuse to talk to her."

"No problem. I've been meaning to pay Antonio a visit. I can take you there now. His place is on the outskirts of Mircester. Once we've had a chat there, I can drop you off in Carsely. In return . . ." he paused, grinning, ". . . you must have dinner with me at the Red Lion."

"The Red Lion?" Agatha knew exactly how the whispers would fly between the regulars when she walked into her local pub. Bert Simpson would have been trading his story for free beer all afternoon. Oh, well—she had to face up to them sometime. "Fine, it's a deal. But dinner only—no afters."

"Are you enjoying becoming part of our little society?" Ulrika asked Toni, clearing their empty tea cups from the table.

"Very much," Toni replied, "but I'm intrigued by the fantasy game you play. Edward says it's fun and I'd love to get involved."

"The game has almost run its course," Ulrika told her, taking the cups into the kitchen. "The quests and challenges have been completed. But there may still be a way for you to play a part in the grand finale."

"That would be great," Toni said, with genuine enthusiasm, "but I've taken enough of your time. I really should be on my way."

Ulrika walked Toni to the front gate where they said their goodbyes and Toni trudged off across the meadow again. Following the same loop, she arrived back at her car feeling slightly out of breath. She set off and turned right onto a road that would take her back into town. For some reason, the windscreen seemed to mist over and she switched on the wipers. When they had no effect, she reached forward to wipe the screen inside, only to realise it was her eyes that were misting, not the glass. Suddenly her mouth felt dry, her head felt like it was stuffed with cotton wool and she lost all strength in her arms. She collapsed forward onto the steering wheel and the car veered across the road, slamming into a tree with a horrendous crunch of metal.

Toni sat slumped across the steering wheel's collapsed airbag, unmoving, her eyes closed, and the peace of the suburban street shattered by the blare of the car's horn.

Chapter Six

The legend above the office window said simply "Antonio's" with illustrations of ice-cream cones either side of the name. The office itself was built on the side of a large house and the area behind the office, which had clearly once been the house's garden, was now a yard enclosed by a high wall. A wide gate, also bearing the "Antonio's" logo, gave access to the yard from a side street. Charles parked in the side street and they walked round to the office entrance, where they found Ursula behind the reception desk.

"Good afternoon, Ursula," he said cheerily. "Is Antonio in? I was hoping for a quick word."

"I'm afraid not, Sir Charles," Ursula said, staring straight at Agatha. "He's in Italy—has been since last Thursday. He's trying to do a deal with his cousins to import some new kind of gelato."

"I thought you made all your own produce on the premises," Charles said.

"We generally do, but he wants something new to keep one step ahead of the competition." Her eyes flitted from Agatha to Charles, then straight back to Agatha again. "What brings you here, Mrs. Raisin?"

"Charles and I were visiting some old friends," Agatha lied, "and we were passing by on my way home."

"I wish I had time for visiting friends," Ursula said, coolly, "but as you can see, apart from the kitchen staff, I'm holding the fort on my own."

"What's happened to your usual receptionist?" Charles asked. "Awfully nice young woman—Theresa, isn't it?"

"She's on holiday," Ursula shrugged, "so there's just me."

"I saw a mutual friend of ours earlier today," Agatha said, glancing around walls decorated with photographs of the man she assumed was Antonio beaming proudly while shaking hands with local celebrities, footballers, politicians, rock stars and minor royalty. "Jasper Crane. I didn't realise that his office was so close to my own."

"Is that so?" Ursula's green eyes were as unblinking as Boswell's or Hodge's. "I expect he was trying to recruit you to the society. He seemed to like you."

"Actually, it was the other way round," Agatha said. "I wanted to talk to him about possibly joining."

"I'm not sure it would be to your taste, Mrs. Raisin—no matter how much Jasper might want to see you there."

"I'm a woman of varied tastes," Agatha purred. "I

121

find that being somewhat . . . unpredictable . . . makes life more interesting."

"When it comes to attracting the interest of men, I'm sure you have many skills, Mrs. Raisin."

"Is that a touch of jealousy I hear?" Agatha's voice took on a hard edge. "Really, Mrs. Danieli, you needn't feel your position with Jasper is under any kind of threat from me. I wouldn't want to be anyone's handmaiden."

"Well, well, old girl!" Charles said, awkwardly, feeling the tension between the two women drawing as tight as their smiles. "Racked up another admirer, have you? Goes to show you've still got it, eh?"

Agatha turned to Charles with a look of bewilderment swelling into annoyance.

"'Still got it,' Charles? Whatever made you think I might have lost it?"

"Oh, that's not what I meant at all and . . . goodness me, is that the time?" He tapped his wristwatch. "We really must be going, Agatha."

Back in the car, Agatha snapped on her seatbelt and frowned at Charles.

"What on earth got into you back there, Charles?" she said tetchily. "It's not like you to start blithering like that."

"It's not what got into me that was the problem—it was you two. It felt like one almighty cat fight was about to break out and I wanted to leave before the fur started flying."

Suddenly one of the rear doors was wrenched open and the car rocked as someone dived onto the back seat.

"Don't look round!" hissed a woman's panicked voice. "Just drive! Please get me out of here—just drive!"

Charles drove off and Agatha, startled by the intruder, remained frozen for a few seconds before risking a glance into the back of the car.

"Who are you?" she demanded, trying to talk surreptitiously without moving her lips, then deciding that was pointless. Who could really see her in a car driving along a road? "What the hell are you playing at?"

"I'm sorry." The woman was fighting back tears. "I promise I'll explain everything. Please just drive for now—and make sure you're not being followed!"

Charles did as instructed, driving in silence for a few minutes with Agatha becoming increasingly irritated in the passenger seat. He headed out of town onto the A44 and, with a long, clear stretch of road behind him showing that no one was tailing them, he swung into the car park of the Greedy Goose restaurant. Switching off the engine, he turned to take a look at their passenger.

"Theresa!" he gasped. "What on earth is going on?"

"They mustn't find me," she stammered. "They see things. They know things. I have to keep moving, that way they'll never find me."

"Theresa?" Agatha asked. "Antonio's receptionist?"

"Yes, but Antonio . . ." She began to sob. "I don't know about Antonio . . ."

"What do you mean?" asked Charles. "He's in Italy, talking to his cousins."

"Antonio's not in Italy." Theresa sniffed, pulling an envelope out of her handbag. "He was supposed to be in Spain, with me." She showed them her and Antonio's passports and flight tickets. "We were having an affair. We were going on holiday together, then he simply disappeared. That witch of a wife of his is behind it, I know she is—her and her sister! I just wish I knew where he's gone!"

"Wait here," Agatha said, stepping out of the car with her phone in her hand. She hit a speed-dial number and spoke quickly. "John . . . yes, it's Agatha. Listen, I think I may have a lead on the body in the lake. Can you send me a photo of the man in the morgue? Yes . . . yes, I know it's not strictly by the book but I might be able to give you his name. Right—send the photo to my phone and stay on the line."

A few seconds later, her phone pinged and she retrieved the picture. The image was a far cry from the upbeat photos on the walls of the office, but she had absolutely no doubt that it was Antonio Danieli. She gave the news to John, then climbed back into the car.

"Theresa, I'm sorry to have to tell you, but Antonio . . ."

"He's dead, isn't he?"

"I'm afraid so."

"It was them." Theresa burst into tears. "The sisters. They're after me, too!"

"Why do you think it was them?" Agatha asked.

"Because they've done this before!" Theresa gasped, choking back sobs. "They're evil, Mrs. Raisin! Pure evil!"

"If you're so frightened of them, why were you hanging around outside Antonio's?" asked Charles.

"I was sure Mrs. Raisin would come here eventually," Theresa said. "It said in the paper she was going to investigate. You have to get them locked up, Mrs. Raisin—otherwise they'll do for me, too!"

"The best way to do that is for you to go to the police," Agatha said. "The passport and tickets are evidence. We can take you there. I know officers we can talk to."

"And then what?" Theresa wiped a tear from her face with a trembling hand. "The police can't protect me while they try to make a case against those two. They'll be watching for me to do that. I told you—they can *see* things. And these," she put the envelope back in her handbag, "are my insurance. They might just keep me alive. I know a shortcut to the railway station at Kingham. I'll go to the police, but not here—maybe in London."

She got out of the car and was looking nervously around when Agatha leapt out and grabbed her by the wrist.

"You're making a big mistake!" she said. "Let us help you."

"The only way you can help me is by getting those two put away," Theresa replied, tugging her wrist free.

"At least take this." Agatha gave her a business card. "Call me anytime. Stay in touch. Let me know you're safe."

Theresa took the card, nodded and hurried off, disappearing through a gap in a hedge.

"What do we do now?" asked Charles, having joined Agatha in time to see Theresa disappear. "We could try to head her off at Kingham and talk some sense into her."

"She's so frightened," Agatha said quietly, "and what did she mean when she said, 'they've done this before'?"

Agatha's phone rang and she put it to her ear, listening intently, her face taking on a growing look of alarm.

"Get back in the car, Charles! Mircester Hospital—hurry! Toni's been in an accident!"

The first person Agatha saw when Charles pulled up outside the entrance to the hospital's Accident and Emergency department was Edward Carstairs. She jumped out of the car and hurried through the automatic doors to catch up with him while Charles sought out a space in the car park.

"Edward!" she called above the click of her heels on the polished linoleum floor. "How is she? What happened to her?"

"I'm not sure," Edward said, barely breaking his stride as Agatha fell in beside him. "All I was told is that she asked for someone to call me."

"Me, too," Agatha said, and they turned a corner to see a uniformed police officer standing near a series of curtained booths.

"Paul," Agatha called to him, recognising PC Paul Hastings. "Where's Toni? Is she okay?"

"It looks like she's going to be okay," Paul said. "A doctor is with her now."

"Paul, I'm Edward. Toni and I are . . ."

"Ah yes," said Paul. "This is a bit awkward. Toni and I used to be . . ."

"Will you two pack it in!" Agatha raged. "Nobody cares, okay? I just want to see Toni! What happened to her?"

"I was one of the officers who attended the scene," Paul explained. "She had been unconscious but was responsive when I spoke to her and she didn't appear to have sustained any serious injuries. No other vehicles were involved and no one else was hurt."

A doctor and a nurse appeared from behind one of the curtains.

"Are you here to see Miss Gilmour?" asked the doctor.

"Yes, I am," Agatha said, brushing Paul and Edward aside. "How is she, doctor?"

"It appears she passed out while driving. Fortunately the car wasn't travelling very fast and she has just minor bruising, but the fact that she passed out is concerning. She doesn't appear to have been drinking or to be under the influence of drugs but we're running tests now. I would like to keep her in overnight for observation."

"Can I see her now?" Agatha asked.

"Don't tire her out," said the doctor. "She needs to rest."

Agatha swept back the curtain and Toni beamed a huge smile at her before bursting into tears.

"Oh, Agatha," she sniffed and Agatha handed her a tissue, taking a seat at the bedside. "I made such a mess—the car's a wreck."

"Don't worry about the car, for goodness' sake." Agatha attempted to be sympathetic and reassuring but suspected that she had simply sounded stern. She took Toni's hand. "The car doesn't matter. The main thing is that you're okay. Can you remember what happened?"

"I was heading back to the office when I suddenly felt all woozy and passed out," Toni explained. She gently touched a graze on her cheek. "The next thing I knew there were people all round the car, checking on me, and then I heard Paul."

Agatha assured her that both Paul and Edward were outside, waiting to see her.

"I don't understand why I fainted," Toni insisted. "It's not like I had been drinking, or . . ."

"Or what?" Agatha asked when Toni paused. "Had you had anything you don't normally eat or drink?"

"Only herbal tea, at Ulrika's place," Toni said. "Do you think that could have something to do with it—some kind of allergic reaction?"

"No . . . no, I shouldn't think so." Agatha patted Toni's hand. "Try to get some rest. We'll talk again tomorrow, but I don't want you back at work until you're absolutely one hundred per cent. I'd best let Edward in. He's desperate to see you."

Agatha ushered Edward into the cubicle and met Charles chatting with Paul.

"So glad she's all right," he said, walking out to the car park with Agatha. "What do you think caused her to black out like that?"

"I can't be sure," Agatha admitted, "but she had some kind of herbal tea concoction at Ulrika's cottage. I think the demon master's handmaidens just came close to claiming another victim!"

Charles reluctantly agreed that it really wasn't the best night for dinner at the Red Lion and dropped Agatha in Lilac Lane where she tended to her cats and nuked another frozen meal in the microwave. She opened a bottle of Primitivo and sipped her wine while waiting for the "ping" that would tell her the lasagne was ready. She was pretty sure it was lasagne she had put in there. Her mind really wasn't focusing on food. She was entirely preoccupied with Ulrika and Ursula. The handmaidens were up to their elbows in Antonio's murder—she was in no doubt about that. She needed to know more about those women.

Once she had finished eating, she picked up her phone and called Margaret Bloxby. Agatha exhausted her repertoire of polite small talk in no time and was bursting with impatience when her friend put her out of her misery.

"Come on, Agatha," she said, dropping the formality of the Ladies Society and using Agatha's first name for this private chat, "you didn't call to talk about the weather. What can I help you with?"

"There hasn't been a formal announcement yet," Agatha explained, relieved to be able to get to the point, "but the body in the lake is Antonio, Ursula Danieli's husband."

"Really?" Agatha most certainly now had Mrs. Bloxby's full attention. "Do you know who did it? How did he end up in the lake?"

"We're not entirely sure who bumped him off yet, but I'm convinced he was killed elsewhere and dumped in the lake. It was Antonio who Edward saw on the Lone Warrior in the woods at the Naturist Society, although the police won't accept that."

"I take it you're ploughing ahead with your own investigation?"

"I can't let it go. We're already tangled up in it."

"Be careful, Agatha. You have a stubborn streak that gets you into these things, but when it comes to people who are prepared to commit murder, being single-minded won't protect you."

"No," Agatha agreed, slightly piqued by her friend's lack of faith, "but knowledge will. Information is always my best protection and the best weapon in my armoury. I need to know everything I can about the people who are involved. That's why I want to talk to you about Ulrika."

"I see . . . is she a suspect?"

"Ulrika and her sister are obviously involved in some way—it's Ursula's husband that's been murdered, after all. What can you tell me about Ulrika's ex?"

"I only met him a few times," Mrs. Bloxby said slowly, clearly racking her brains. "His name was Dennis—Dennis Rayner. He was a member of the Naturist Society. It must have been almost three years since he vanished. The woman he ran off with was another naturist—Felicity Kemp. I never met her. I only remember her name because I used to have an aunt called Felicity.

"Do you know if they kept in touch with their friends? I mean, does anyone know where they went?"

"As far as I know, they were never heard from again, but you'd have to check with their naturist chums."

"Thank you, Margaret, I'll do that."

That night, Agatha took special care locking up. In the past, she'd had intruders break in and had installed the best locks and a state-of-the-art alarm system. She was suddenly aware that James was not next door, ready to come to her aid. She thought of Theresa. The poor woman had been convinced that the handmaidens would be able to find her, and would kill her if they did. Maybe she was right. Edward was convinced he was being stalked. Toni may have been drugged . . . and Agatha herself had received that threatening phone call.

She began thinking about the best way forward with the murder case, then reminded herself that she had Paula undercover at Martinbrook and Simon at the brewery. She had a lot to do tomorrow but tried to cheer herself up before going to bed by looking again at what to wear for dinner with Giovanni. She settled on a green satin cocktail dress with spaghetti straps supporting a wrap-over top and a skirt that flared from the waist to just below the knee. That, she thought, would be ideal . . . but by the time she fell asleep she had already changed her mind.

In the office the following morning, Patrick, Simon and Helen were waiting for Agatha when she walked in.

"What's this?" she said, scanning their sombre faces. "An ambush?"

"We heard Toni was in hospital," said Simon.

"How did you hear that?" Agatha asked.

"We're detectives," Simon said, without cracking a smile.

"What's happened to her?" Helen asked, with eyes full of concern.

"She had a little car accident," Agatha explained,

"and they've kept her in overnight for observation. I spoke to her earlier, and she's fine. She can't wait to get out of the place. Now, we have lots we need to talk about, so let's get down to it straight away. Helen . . ."

"Coffee?" said Helen. "Coming right up, Mrs. Raisin."

Patrick and Simon sat with Agatha in her office as she reassured them that Toni was doing fine but that she would be taking a couple of days off to recover.

"In the meantime," she said, "I may need your help on our murder enquiry. First, update me on where you are with Martinbrook, Patrick. How's Paula doing?"

"Settling in," said Patrick. "I spoke to her last night and she's sent me a couple of text messages. She's starting to get to know the girls. Some are friendly, some a bit stand-offish, but there's been no mention of any drugs."

"She'll need time for them to accept her before the ringleaders dare to start letting their guard down," Agatha said.

"Of course," Patrick agreed, "but she's confident that no one knows who she is. Mrs. Carling has told no one on the staff and Mrs. Partridge didn't tell Sarah anything either, so Paula's cover is intact. The one thing that does bother me, though, is Sarah's father."

"Why's that?" asked Simon. "He only sees her once a week, doesn't he? He's not likely to know about the drugs Sarah's mum found on her, or about Paula."

"My one slight worry is what he might do if he does find out," Patrick said. "I thought his name rang a bell, so I checked him out. Jim Sullivan runs an ice-cream business but he's got a history. He used to be a professional boxer and he's been known to throw his weight around. He's been done a couple of times for assault."

"You're worried about what he might do to someone pushing drugs to his daughter?" Agatha asked.

"Exactly," said Patrick. "If he gets wind of it and tries to take the law into his own hands, our operation is sunk. Mrs. Partridge says Sarah is sworn to secrecy about the stuff that was in her possession, but what she does or doesn't say to her father is out of our control."

"For the moment, we proceed according to plan," said Agatha. "I'm going in on Friday to give a talk, so let's hope young Sarah doesn't blab to daddy. Simon, how are things at the brewery?"

"I've now been round the whole place," Simon reported, "and have a good understanding of what they do and how they do it. I've made a list of questions to ask in each department when I go in today—how much of that do you use in a year, how long does it take for this process, and so forth—the sort of thing a guide might include in a tour commentary. Asking questions gives me a chance to keep visiting people and get to know them all better."

"Have any of them so far struck you as the sort to be robbing the company?" Agatha asked.

"Not really," Simon said. "They all seem to love their jobs—even the guys in the dispatch department who just load and unload trucks. The only one who's never happy to see me is Janet, the woman who runs the accounts department, and Mr. Brown doesn't think I should be in there anyway. He says accounts are never going to figure on a tour, so why would I need to know how they work? I don't think he's entirely sure about that side of the business himself. He's into making beer and running the plant. He leaves all the financials to Janet, although he understands enough about it to know that stuff's going missing—his stock inventories don't tally."

"Use your famous charm on Janet, Simon. I can't imagine she's walking out the door with her handbag clinking with beer bottles or sacks of hops stuffed up her cardigan, but she might be able to point you in the right direction even if she doesn't realise it."

"I'll keep on it, boss. I need to get back there now."

Simon left and Agatha turned to Patrick.

"I need to know the whereabouts of Dennis Rayner and Felicity Kemp as a matter of urgency," she said.

"Are they suspects in the murder?"

"No, but Dennis was married to a woman called Ulrika and all three were members of the Mircester Naturists."

Agatha explained about Ulrika and her sister, also filling Patrick in on how she and Charles had an unexpected passenger.

"So this Theresa woman said they've done this before?" Patrick said slowly, reading through the notes he'd made. "You think Rayner and Kemp were murdered?"

"It's a possibility," Agatha said. "Apparently no one has heard anything from them since they ran off."

"I'll make some checks and call in some favours," Patrick said. "If they're alive, we'll find them."

As soon as Patrick left her office, Agatha put in a phone call to Charlotte Clark at the *Mircester Telegraph*.

A girl after her own heart, Charlotte swiftly dispensed with any pleasantries.

"What are you after, Mrs. Raisin?" she asked.

"I need whatever background you might have in your cuttings files on Antonio Danieli," Agatha explained.

"I know him. He's the ice-cream man, isn't he? I've had to do a few pieces on charity things he's been involved with. What's your interest in him?"

"Probably not the charity stuff, but I'll take a look at any pieces you have for interest. I'm looking for anything out of the ordinary."

"I'll take a look for you. What do you think old Antonio's been up to, then?"

"That's the scoop I have for you in return. It hasn't been announced yet, but they must have gone through the formal identification by now. Antonio is the body in the lake."

"Wow!" Charlotte sounded animated for the first time since she'd picked up the phone. "I'll get back to you by email within the hour."

Agatha thumbed the button to end the call only for the phone to ring immediately. It was John Glass.

"I heard about Toni," he said. "Is she okay?"

"She had a real fright, John, but she's fine. I'd really like to talk to you about what happened, though."

"I actually came off shift at seven this morning, but I'm still here trying to catch up on paperwork. I'll be finished in an hour, if you want to pop over to the station then."

"I will do. Thanks, John."

Agatha attended to some paperwork of her own, then looked down at the lipstick marks on her coffee cup and retired to the bathroom to make repairs prior to meeting John. She might have other irons in the fire—the hottest iron being dinner with Giovanni that evening—but John was a good-looking bloke and there was no way she could ever contemplate turning up to meet a man like him without making sure she looked her best.

She slid her hands down her waist onto her hips, smoothing the "little black dress" she was wearing. She would have preferred a light, summery colour for a sunny day like today, but her skin was still a bit too pale. Maybe, she thought, smiling at herself in the mirror, she needed a few more early morning strolls around the garden! She treated herself to a little perfume—wasn't it Coco Chanel who said, "A woman who doesn't wear perfume has no future"? She also said you should apply it wherever you wanted to be kissed.

"Well," she said out loud, smiling again, "maybe later."

Judging herself ready to face the world and whatever Mircester police station could throw at her, she popped back into her office to pick up her phone just in time to see an email from Charlotte arrive on her computer. She read it while standing to avoid creating any new crumples in her dress. The email read:

> Most of the stuff on Antonio isn't very interesting.
> I'll send it through later anyway. This is different.
> It's from five years ago.

An image of a newspaper cutting was attached. Agatha opened the image and read the report:

ICE CREAM VANS TORCHED IN TURF WAR

At least two ice-cream vans have been attacked, wrecked and set alight by rival companies fighting over territory.

A van belonging to Antonio Danieli, who runs the "Antonio's" ice-cream company, was destroyed on Friday at a picnic area near Dembley. Terrified witnesses say a gang of at least six men arrived in an unmarked white van. They frightened customers away and smashed up the ice-cream van with sledgehammers before dousing it in petrol and torching it. The ice-cream man escaped with minor injuries.

On Monday a similar incident occurred near Ancombe where a van belonging to Jim Sullivan of "Uncle Jim's Ices" was destroyed.

There was a photograph of a burning ice-cream van alongside one of a worried-looking Antonio and another picture of a grim, heavy-set man with close-cropped hair—Jim Sullivan. The report went on to give colourful accounts from eyewitnesses and a final few reassuring words from Detective Chief Inspector Wilkes who said that the police were "vigorously pursuing enquiries," that these were "isolated incidents," and that "speculation about some kind of gang war was unfounded and unhelpful."

Agatha knew that was classic Wilkes floundering but

her eye was drawn once again to the name of Antonio's rival—Jim Sullivan. His name was starting to crop up a little too often for her not to be suspicious. Could he be involved in Antonio's murder? It was something else she could discuss with John.

Mircester police station was only a few minutes' walk away but, unlike the cathedral quarter down the lane from Raisin Investigations, there were no delightful old stone buildings in its vicinity. The police headquarters was very much part of the 1960s building boom when Mircester, like so many towns and cities across the country, had fallen victim to developers who were far more interested in making money than they were in preserving architectural heritage. Like most of the area surrounding it, the police station was a dull, grey, slab-sided monument to the period's love affair with concrete.

"Hello, Agatha." John grinned. "You're looking as gorgeous as ever!" He leaned to greet her with a kiss and she presented him with her cheek.

"And you look shattered." Agatha gave him a look that she hoped was sympathetic. "It must have been a long night."

"It was, but I'm off now—back on at midnight. I'd say let's have dinner later but, given that I've got to sleep at some point, it would be more like breakfast for me!"

"I couldn't tonight. Let's wait until we're both better able to enjoy it."

"Sounds good to me. Now, what was it you wanted

to tell me about Toni? I heard she passed out behind the wheel—no drink or drugs involved. How did that happen? Has she been ill?"

"No, John, but I think that, unknown to Toni, there was some kind of drug involved."

"I was told there was nothing in her system."

"Maybe there was nothing they'd normally be looking for, but I still think she was drugged."

Agatha explained about Theresa, her affair with Antonio, the handmaidens, and Toni drinking herbal tea.

"You really think his wife and her sister bumped off Antonio?" John shoved his hands in his pockets and stared off into space, deep in thought. We've already had Ursula Danieli in to identify the body."

"Did she seem upset?"

"Not as much as some, but people react to these things in different ways."

"Has she been questioned?"

"Yes, we ran through all the usual stuff. Ursula has an alibi for just about any time you can think of, although it's been difficult to give an exact time of death. They reckon he was probably killed about three days ago—probably Sunday morning."

"Yet he's been missing since last Thursday and Theresa had the tickets for their flights that day."

"That doesn't make sense, but it doesn't make Ursula and her sister murderers, either. In fact, it makes me more suspicious of Theresa. Maybe they were together, but he tried to end it so they fell out and she clobbered him."

"Could be. She seemed to me like she was scared to

death of the sisters, but I suppose that could have been an act. Maybe we should consider her a suspect as well."

"We . . . ? Agatha, you need to leave this to us now . . ."

"Then there's Jim Sullivan," Agatha went on. "He and Antonio were deadly rivals at one time."

"I remember that, but they settled their differences years ago."

"Maybe they unsettled them. Ursula was talking about him wanting to stay ahead of the competition. Jim Sullivan is the competition."

"Listen, Agatha, you need to stay clear of Big Jim. He can be a nasty piece of work and—"

"Aha! This explains everything!" Wilkes's whining voice echoed down the stairs. He was standing at the entrance to the building holding the early lunchtime edition of the local evening paper.

"That's handy," Agatha said. "You're a man who often needs things explained to him. What's finally been explained? Not the birds and the bees, is it?"

"I warned you that I'd do you for obstruction if you meddled in police business again, Mrs. Raisin, and now I find that the local rag has the identity of our murder victim before I have released the information! How did that happen, eh? Have you two been blabbing to the press? Did you tell her about Antonio Danieli, Inspector?"

"No, sir, of course not. In fact—"

"But you found out somehow, didn't you, Mrs. Raisin? And you gave the name to the press! Now why would you do that, I wonder? Was there a few quid in it for you? A little payment to bring a smile to your face?"

"How about I bring *this* to *your* face?" Agatha drew back a fist to take a swing at Wilkes, but John moved quickly, grabbing her wrist. "Don't you dare judge me by your own grubby standards!" she roared at Wilkes, shaking her wrist free. "I'm not interested in money—I'm interested in finding the truth! You wouldn't know the truth if you picked it out your nose!"

"Did you see that, Inspector?" Wilkes blurted. "That woman just tried to assault me! Assaulting a police officer is a serious offence! Arrest her immediately!"

"You're the one who should be arrested!" Agatha snarled. "Unfortunately, having shit for brains isn't a crime!"

"I think you both need to calm down," John said, stepping between them. "Sir, Mrs. Raisin may have some good leads that could help us clear up this murder quickly. That would certainly help boost your monthly crime figures."

"The crime figures . . ." Agatha watched Wilkes's face twitch, the only sign that a brain was operating somewhere in his head. "Very well, but we will be pursuing the theory that this is a robbery gone wrong. The man was found with no wallet, and the gold Rolex watch and jewellery he normally wore were also missing."

"Oh, for goodness' sake," Agatha said, struggling to bring her temper under control. "This wasn't a robbery. Look at the timeline for his disappearance. Look at the evidence."

"Evidence? What evidence are you talking about?" Wilkes eyed her suspiciously. "If I find that you have been withholding evidence vital to a murder case . . ."

"Sir, why don't you leave me to deal with Mrs. Raisin?" John suggested. "That way we can avoid any . . . clash of personalities."

"There's no clash," Agatha said, with a cold smile. "He hasn't got a personality for me to clash with."

"You deal with her, Inspector Glass," Wilkes growled. "I haven't the time. Just keep her out of my sight."

Wilkes stalked off up the stairs and John spoke softly to Agatha.

"Let's take some time to cool down," he said. "I agree that we may now have four potential suspects—Ulrika and Ursula, Theresa and Big Jim Sullivan."

"I'm not entirely convinced about Theresa as a suspect," Agatha said. "She didn't seem like a murderer to me."

"I respect your instincts," John said, rubbing a hand across his eyes, "but we need to keep an open mind. I'm really tired now, Agatha. Can we talk about this later?"

"Yes, we should," Agatha agreed. "If Wilkes has your lot rounding up a long list of known muggers to investigate, then I'll feel free to do my own thing."

Agatha was making her way back to her office when a now-familiar figure approached. Jasper Crane gave her a cheery greeting.

"Hello, Agatha—we meet again!"

"Jasper," she said, dragging her thoughts away from Wilkes and how much she would love to have landed that punch. "What a surprise!"

"It shouldn't be, really." He gave her a friendly smile.

"Our offices are just round the corner from each other, after all."

"So, are you . . . out for your coffee and sandwiches?"

"No, not today. Actually, I'm on my way down to Antonio's, the ice-cream place. Did you hear that it was poor Antonio they dragged out of the lake?"

"I did. Why are you going to his place? I'd have thought Ursula would have closed the office today."

"She has, but she insisted that I pop down there to pick up some tutti-frutti. I've been friends with Antonio and Ursula for years—I'm the company's accountant. Ursula knows I'm practically addicted to their tutti-frutti and she set some aside for me. Why don't you come with me? There won't be anyone around, so I can give you a tour of the place."

"Well, I . . ." Agatha paused to think. She didn't like unexpected meetings like this. She didn't like not having everything under control. Then she heard James's voice in her head telling her to "Do something spontaneous, for goodness' sake" and she nodded to Jasper. "Yes, I'd like that very much."

They collected Jasper's car from the car park behind his office and drove to Antonio's, chatting on the way about the dreadful tragedy, Jasper confessing to being totally shocked by the murder. Parking at the side of the building, just as Agatha had done with Charles, they walked round to the entrance, Jasper producing a bunch of keys. It was then that they saw a large, black Mercedes parked in front of the building. Jasper's office keys were unnecessary—the front door was standing open.

Walking into the reception area, they were confronted

143

by Ursula Danieli, who was standing talking to a broad-shouldered man with brutally short hair.

"Mrs. Raisin," Ursula said. "We weren't expecting any visitors today. Let me introduce an old friend of ours—Jim Sullivan."

Chapter Seven

Jasper reached out a hand to shake Sullivan's, introducing himself and Agatha. Sullivan's massive paw engulfed Jasper's hand. He grunted a greeting then stared straight at Agatha, cold grey eyes examining her from beneath a heavy brow. Agatha brought her professional smile into play.

"Nice to meet you, Mr. Sullivan," she said. He did not offer his hand, but slowly nodded an acknowledgement. "I was sorry to hear about your husband, Mrs. Danieli. You must be devastated."

"I'm coping," Ursula said quietly, then repeated, "coping . . ."

"I thought you were closing the office today," Jasper said to Ursula. "You've had a terrible shock. You need to take care of yourself."

"Taking care of business is more important," Sullivan said in a low, rumbling voice.

"You're very kind, Jasper," Ursula said, "but I knew you'd be coming in to pick up your tutti-frutti. I wasn't expecting Mrs. Raisin, of course."

"I bumped into Agatha outside my office," Jasper explained. "As you were going to be closed today, I offered her a quick tour of the operation."

"Are you interested in ice cream, Mrs. Raisin?" Ursula said, turning to Agatha.

Agatha could see no grief on Ursula's face, none of the despair a distraught widow ought to show, just the same disturbing, haunting gaze that she had experienced before.

"Who isn't?" Agatha responded cheerfully. "I love the stuff. That's why I was keen to come and see how it's made."

"You're welcome to take a tour with Jasper," Ursula said, "but I need to talk to him first. Jasper, I want to take a look through the accounts covering the last five years."

"Today? Are you sure?" Jasper sounded concerned but Ursula waved aside his sympathy.

"Mr. Sullivan is right," she said. "Taking care of business is important. Come through to my office, Jasper, and show me how to print out what I need from the computer."

They left Agatha alone in the reception area with Sullivan and after a few seconds of awkward silence, Agatha could stand it no longer.

"This seems like an odd day to be having a business

meeting," she said. "I mean, that poor woman has only just found out that her husband has been murdered."

Sullivan looked straight into her eyes and Agatha held his stare without flinching.

"You need to move fast in this business," he said. "No point in hanging around. Ursula knows that. Old Antonio's as cold as a snowman's arse now and she needs to get on with the rest of her life."

"She's looking at accounts going back five years," Agatha said. "Does that mean you're thinking about buying the business?"

A sinister smile pushed apart Sullivan's beefy cheeks and he clenched a mighty fist, holding it between his chest and Agatha's face.

"You keep your nose out of our affairs," he said, and Agatha froze. That was exactly the phrase the electronic voice had used to threaten her on the phone. Agatha took a step back, the colour draining from her face. Sullivan looked pleased with the effect he'd had on her but lowered his fist when he heard Jasper returning.

"Right," Jasper said, "I've started those documents and spreadsheets printing. Ursula has some coffee ready for you in her office, Mr. Sullivan, and I can show you round, Agatha."

"Yes," Agatha said, unable to take her eyes off Sullivan. "I'd like that."

Jasper first took Agatha to the kitchen, which was a sparkling shrine to stainless steel with pristine work surfaces, tall storage cabinets and fridges as well as large ice-cream churns. It looked as much like a factory production line as it did a kitchen.

"These are really for the speciality flavours that the company supplies to commercial customers—restaurants and hotels. The vans carry a supply of Antonio's specials, but they also make their own soft ice cream on board from a liquid mix."

Agatha was only half-listening to what Jasper was saying. Her mind was racing through all of the new possibilities thrown up by the involvement of Sullivan with the sisters. He was clearly keen to take over the business, but was he in league with them over Antonio's murder as well? If it was him who made that phone call, then he had to be, didn't he?

"The little office kitchen's through here," Jasper said, leading her along a corridor. "My tutti-frutti should be in the freezer there, so you'll have to try a taste."

After the commercial kitchen, the office kitchen came as something of a disappointment. It was no bigger than a kitchen Agatha might have expected to find in a small apartment. Jasper fetched two spoons from a drawer and a tub of ice cream from the freezer. He popped the lid off and handed her a spoon.

Despite having been in the freezer, the ice cream was soft enough for the spoon to sink in when Agatha dragged it across the pink surface, revealing an array of colourful candied fruit chunks mixed with pieces of fresh fruit.

"It's delicious!" Agatha cooed, all thoughts of murder banished by the effect the ice cream was having on her taste buds.

"They use different fresh fruit from time to time depending on what's in season," Jasper said, licking his lips.

"It always makes it slightly different and very special. The most amazing version is made with chilli peppers."

"Ice cream with hot chillies?" Agatha asked, surprised.

"Yes, they call that one the Devil's Delight. The story goes that at the beginning of the twentieth century a family called Bandoni lived in a small Italian village. They were ice-cream makers, as were lots of other families in the area, and once a year they would all meet up at a place called Devil's Bridge. They'd exchange recipes and try each other's ice cream. The Bandoni family made one flavour that used chilli peppers.

"Young men would show off for the girls by competing to see who could eat most of the Bandonis' speciality spicy chilli ice cream without breaking into a sweat. The ones who couldn't stand the heat ended up jumping off the bridge into the water to cool down.

"Antonio's Devil's Delight version is simply amazing. I'll let you know next time they make a batch. If you like spicy food, you'll love it."

He put the ice cream back in the freezer, rinsed their spoons and took Agatha outside to the yard, where a fleet of ice-cream vans bearing the "Antonio's" logo was parked in neat rows.

"This yard is usually home to a dozen vans," Jasper explained, "but there's another yard nearby where there are a dozen more. At the risk of sounding like an accountant, when a van is parked at a good pitch—a popular tourist spot—it can generate a turnover in excess of five thousand pounds a day."

"That's a lot of money," Agatha said, doing mental

arithmetic. "Working five days a week, that could be over a hundred thousand a month—from one van."

"Except they work seven days a week," Jasper pointed out. "Not today, obviously. The vans have stayed here out of respect. It wouldn't be right for their cheery chimes to be ringing out when we've just discovered that the man whose name is on the side is . . . well, you know."

"Yet this is big business," Agatha pondered, "which is why Sullivan wants to move quickly and get the cash flowing again."

"Ah, yes," Jasper said, sounding a little embarrassed. "I'd appreciate it if you could keep the fact that he was here to yourself. It's commercially sensitive and . . ."

"I understand. What's over there?" She pointed to a large outbuilding taking up one corner of the yard.

"Those are the freezers," Jasper explained. "Each is the size of a small room—one to keep cold drinks chilled, the other to keep frozen goods frozen. The vans are all diesel and we can't have their engines running all night to keep unsold produce frozen. Some can be plugged in for their on-board freezers to work off mains electricity, but for the most part the frozen items are unloaded into the big freezers."

"Haven't some places banned vans from running diesel engines, churning out fumes where kids are queueing up?"

"They have, and vans are gradually being converted to run the freezers on battery power. In the not-too-distant future, they'll be all-electric—no more diesel."

Jasper retrieved his ice cream from the small kitchen and they left Ursula and Sullivan deep in conversation in her office before driving back into town. Agatha tried to maintain polite conversation, feigning an ongoing interest in the Naturist Society to prevent Jasper from realising that far darker thoughts were running through her mind. She needed to talk to someone about the Sullivan situation and was silently praying that Patrick would be in the office when she got back. She was aware of Jasper asking a polite question and mumbled a response.

"Um . . . yes, that sounds fine," she said.

"Wonderful!" he replied, pulling over outside Agatha's office. "I can't tell you how delighted I am."

"Delighted?" Agatha asked, the conversation finally grabbing her full attention.

"Yes, I'm so glad you'll give it a go. You won't regret it, I promise. I'll pick you up on Saturday afternoon and introduce you to some of the other members."

"Members . . ." Agatha repeated, realisation clanging in her head like St. Jude's bells on a Sunday morning. "At the Naturist Society."

"Don't sound so worried, Agatha. You already know Toni and Edward—and me, of course. You can have a swim and relax in the sunshine with a gin and tonic."

"Of course," Agatha said, stepping out of the car. "Gin and tonic. Lovely. See you on Saturday. . . ."

What on earth have I got myself into now? She scolded herself as she trudged up the stairs to her office. *Toni was supposed to do the nudie thing, not me!* She took a deep breath and muttered, "Best make that G and T a double!"

"Did you say something, Mrs. Raisin?" Helen asked. "Good heavens, you look white as a sheet. You haven't eaten, have you? I'll pop out and get you a sandwich."

Agatha thanked Helen and had just settled at her desk when Patrick came in.

"I'm getting nowhere with tracing Rayner and Kemp," he said with a frustrated frown. "You know, you can find most people in this country just by looking them up in the phone book, or the electronic equivalent. I found three Dennis Rayners and two Felicity Kemps, but none of them were our pair."

"Some people are ex-directory," Agatha commented. "They make sure their names don't appear, especially people who've left broken marriages behind them."

"That's true, but I've spoken to a couple of contacts and had them run unofficial checks via social security, income tax and various other sources. Still nothing. It's as if they no longer exist."

"They could have changed their names."

"They would have to have done that officially, and that still leaves a trail we would have picked up. The only way they could disappear like this in this country would be if they were in some kind of government witness protection programme."

"What if they've gone abroad?"

"That's a possibility, but we're not able to check if their passports have been used to leave the country. The police could, but none of my contacts can do that without attracting attention."

"So they've either fled abroad or . . ."

"Or they're dead," Patrick said gravely.

"Big Jim Sullivan has cropped up again. John warned me to steer clear of him—said he was a nasty piece of work—and then I bumped into him at Antonio's office. Looks like Ursula Danieli is planning to sell the business to him."

"They didn't waste any time, did they? She's only just found out that her old man's been murdered."

"Unless she already knew," Agatha said, sitting back and folding her arms, "because she's the one who killed him."

"It could make things difficult for us at Martinbrook if Sullivan's also involved in the murder," Patrick said, thinking through the potential consequences. "If he's charged, the press will look into his background. They'll want photos of his family—especially his daughter at a posh school—and they'll flock to Martinbrook. That will scare off anyone supplying drugs and scupper our investigation."

"Well, there's not much we can do about that," Agatha said, "but I'm certainly going to do something about Sullivan. He threatened me—possibly twice—and I'm going to make that something he'll regret for the rest of his life!"

Agatha devoured the chicken salad sandwich supplied by Helen while surfing the internet for anything on Big Jim Sullivan's days as a professional fighter. She found a number of reports, none of them flattering towards Sullivan. It appeared he had not been a top-tier boxer but could boast a few short years in the fight game, surviving on power, aggression and savagery rather than skill or talent.

Having come to the conclusion that Sullivan was a thug and then wondering why Sarah's mother had married him, she called Mrs. Partridge to find out more. Once they had dispensed with the pleasantries, Agatha informed her that she had met her ex-husband earlier that day.

"He was meeting with Ursula Danieli, who found out only this morning that her husband had been murdered," Agatha explained, once again ignoring the fact that Jasper had asked her not to talk about it. "It all seemed a bit distasteful and inappropriate to me."

"That wouldn't bother Jim in the slightest," Mrs. Partridge said. "He goes at everything head on—doesn't let anything or anyone get in his way."

"How did you meet him?"

"You mean, 'How did you end up married to a scumbag like him?'"

"I wouldn't have put it quite like—"

"He wasn't always like that. I grew up with him, Mrs. Raisin. We were raised on the same council estate. We hung around in the same gang."

"I wouldn't have thought—"

"I know what you're thinking, Mrs. Raisin. You can't believe that a girl from a council estate went to a top-drawer sixth form college like Martinbrook. Well, it's not that different from a girl brought up in a high-rise council block in Birmingham creating her own PR agency in London, really, is it?"

For a moment, Agatha was knocked off balance. Mrs.

Partridge had given a very accurate description of Agatha's own background.

"So how did you end up at Martinbrook?" she asked.

"When my father left us, my uncle took pity on me and paid my fees. I loved it there—it was a different world from the one I had grown up in. Unlike you, however, I couldn't leave my old life behind. I kept drifting back and, when Jim was making a bit of a name for himself as a boxer, it all seemed quite glamorous for a while.

"By the time I came to my senses and cottoned on to his womanising, we were married and I had Sarah to look after. I left him, got myself a job, eventually started my own business."

"Thank you for being so frank," Agatha said. "I wanted to know who I was dealing with in case he should ever find out about the situation at Martinbrook."

"Very wise, Mrs. Raisin," Mrs. Partridge congratulated her. "It's what we do, isn't it? Women like us need to know as much about whoever we're dealing with as we can. That way we don't make silly mistakes. That's why I took the time to check you out."

"Had I been in your shoes, I'd have done the same thing. If you're footing the bill, you want to know where your money's going," Agatha said. "We have a lot in common, Mrs. Partridge."

"Please call me Kathleen. I think we can drop all that painful formality."

"Very well, Kathleen, and you must call me Agatha."

Agatha decided that Mrs. Partridge, now Kathleen to her, was a woman to whom she could relate and by the time they had finished their chat they had agreed to meet up once the Martinbrook case was resolved and share a bottle of wine. That, Agatha thought, will be an interesting evening.

She checked in with Toni, who was out of hospital and back home, wading through a morass of online form-filling to deal with her car insurance. The sound of her frustration persuaded Agatha that she should allow Toni back to work the following morning.

Simon was her next call. He had made no progress with Janet in the Watermill Brewery's accounts department but claimed to have a plan for later that day. He had to rush into a meeting before Agatha could extract from him exactly what he had in mind. She had her own plans for that evening, of course, and left the office thinking only of the delicious food at the Royal Oak and the delicious Giovanni waiting for her there.

Agatha liked to think that her preparations for a dinner date were always executed with military precision but, while she followed a well-tried routine, her schedule never seemed to work quite the way she intended. Running a little late, she assured herself, was a woman's prerogative. Showing up to meet a man bang on time made you look a bit too keen.

She started by spending too long under the shower, washing her hair and enjoying the scent of a citrus-infused bodywash. That encouraged her thoughts to drift back years to a holiday on Italy's Amalfi Coast, strolling through a lemon grove hand in hand with a charming restaurateur from Positano. He had been a handsome devil, but not in the same league as Giovanni.

Wrapping her hair in a towel, she examined her legs before leaving the bathroom. They were, Agatha had always thought, her best feature, long yet shapely, and they easily passed her most assiduous inspection with no unsightly hairs or evidence of stubble.

She carefully dried and styled her hair into her customary sleek, glossy bob, then stared at herself in her dressing-table mirror. She'd been told many times that she could pass for a woman at least ten years younger. Boswell and Hodge lolled on her bedroom floor, watching her every move.

"Ten years?" she asked them and then, without waiting for an answer, she reached for her make-up. "Let's make that fifteen, with a touch of glamour. . . ."

By the time she'd added jewellery, and checked her watch, she realised that she was now very short of time. She decided that the green satin dress she had picked out previously had actually been a good choice, not least because she could wear it with a pair of leather sandals that had a heel high enough to show her legs off to their best advantage. Once she'd chosen the right handbag, she checked herself out in a full-length mirror, declared herself ready to go and turned to the cats.

"Don't wait up, boys. I didn't go to all this trouble to come home early."

The Royal Oak was an eighteenth-century coaching inn built, Agatha was fairly sure, using traditional, mellow

Cotswold stone. Her uncertainty was due to the fact that the entire front of the building was cloaked in vivid green ivy, trimmed around the main entrance and the many windows as precisely as Jasper Crane's beard.

Agatha parked in a bay near the front entrance, and walked into the reception area where the old part of the building was dominated by an age-darkened oak stair-case and wall panelling. The lovingly polished wood was warm and welcoming, looking so soft that Agatha felt her fingers might sink in should she dare to touch it.

She asked for Giovanni at reception and he appeared moments later, wearing a cream linen suit. Most men attempting to wear linen ended up looking like a crumpled hankie, but Giovanni had the style to pull it off, the few wrinkles on the arms of the jacket and behind the knees of his trousers giving him the air of a man confident in his appearance.

"Agatha, you look amazing!" he greeted her with open arms that he wrapped around her in a gentle hug, planting a light kiss on both of her cheeks. "Come through to the terrace. We can have cocktails there before dinner."

"Thank you, Giovanni," Agatha said, allowing him to take her hand and lead her through the opulently furnished lounge towards the rear of the hotel. "A cocktail sounds like a lovely idea."

Sitting at a table looking out across a lush lawn that rolled down towards a stream Agatha knew would eventually wind its way to Mircester, they sipped cocktails and chatted. When the evening began to cool, they adjourned to the conservatory where they ordered dinner. Agatha decided on a cheese soufflé followed by fillet steak, and Giovanni went for a starter of roast duck salad with lobster linguine as his main course.

"You must allow me to order the wine, Agatha," Giovanni insisted. "They have a Barolo from La Morra here that is exquisite. Naturally, all of this will be on my bill, I will have it no other way."

"That's very generous of you," Agatha said. The last time she had eaten at the Royal Oak had been with Charles, who had been going through one of his impecunious periods and managed "accidentally" to leave his wallet at Barfield House. "Now, you were going to tell me all about *Cavalleria Rusticana*."

"Ah, Mascagni's masterpiece." Giovanni grinned, clearly enthused by the subject. "It is a powerful tale of love and passion and jealousy and even . . . sex."

"Throw in a murder and it sounds like my kind of story," Agatha laughed.

"Then this is very much a story for you, Agatha. You need to know that it takes place in a small village in Sicily maybe two hundred years ago. It is a story in the *verismo* tradition, where Mascagni could make his music about real life, about ordinary people."

"A bit like a TV soap opera?" Agatha asked.

"If you say so," Giovanni laughed, "but I have not seen so many of your soap operas. If they have drama and passion, then you are right."

"I guess some of them do." Agatha smiled.

"Good." Giovanni clapped his hands as though to snap his thoughts back to order. He resumed the story as their starters arrived. "So, a young man from the village, Turiddu, had gone off to be a soldier and returns from the wars one day to find that his fiancée, Lola, has married someone else—a carter named Alfio.

"Turiddu is distraught and plans to win back his beloved Lola. He wants to make her jealous, so he seduces another village girl, Santuzza, and Lola cannot bear the thought of Turiddu with this other woman. Unknown to her husband, she begins an affair with Turiddu."

"Well, it sounds much like a TV soap so far," Agatha smiled, sipping her wine, "and you were right about the Barolo—it is beautiful."

"But of course," Giovanni agreed, "and wine plays its part in this story, too. Santuzza, who has slept with Turiddu but believes he is seeing Lola, comes to the wine shop run by Lucia, who is Turiddu's mother. She asks if Turiddu is home but Lucia tells her he has gone to another village to bring more wine supplies. Santuzza knows that is not true and tells her that Turiddu has been seen in the village.

"Then Alfio shows up with his wagon, singing about his beautiful wife, Lola. He wants to buy Lucia's finest wine—this is Sicily, so it would not have been as fine as our Barolo, of course. Lucia tells him she has run out of wine and Turiddu has gone to fetch more, but Alfio says he has seen Turiddu near his home earlier that day. Lucia is about to say something but Santuzza signals her to remain silent.

"It is Easter and when all the other villagers go to church, Lucia and Santuzza are left outside. Lucia asks Santuzza why she stopped her from saying anything. Santuzza tells Lucia that she has slept with her son but that Turiddu is having an affair with Lola. She feels too ashamed to go into the church but she asks Lucia to pray for her.

"Then Turiddu arrives and Santuzza pleads with him to leave Lola and come back to her. She is on her knees, clutching his arm, begging him when Lola appears. She makes fun of Santuzza and strolls into the church. Turiddu frees himself from Santuzza's grip, throwing her to the ground, and follows Lola into the church.

"Alfio then returns in search of Lola and Santuzza tells him all about the affair. Alfio swears revenge on Turiddu and Santuzza immediately regrets having said anything, begging Alfio not to harm Turiddu.

"Later, Turiddu is with Lola and a crowd of his friends who gather round him at the wine shop, drinking and singing. Turiddu even offers Alfio a drink but Alfio will not drink with him. They argue and Alfio challenges Turiddu to fight—a knife fight. As is the tradition, they then embrace to show the challenge is accepted but as they do, Turiddu bites Alfio's ear, drawing blood, which can only mean one thing—a fight to the death.

"Before he leaves for the fight with Alfio, Turiddu asks his mother to look after Santuzza should he not return and Lucia is distraught, pacing the square until Santuzza arrives and they embrace, crying together.

"It is then that they both hear a cry in the distance—a woman's voice wailing that Turiddu has been murdered."

"That's quite a tale," Agatha said.

"Yes, but the story is nothing without the music,

Agatha." Giovanni's hands and arms, seldom still for a moment as he related the Sicilian tragedy, flew out to each side and dropped, as though exhausted. He laughed. "You must come to the performance. Then you will understand."

"What was it that those two women who spoke to you in St. Jude's were so upset about?"

"They each want to play the part of Santuzza," Giovanni sighed, "but it is a part for a soprano."

"And a soprano has to be able to hit the high notes," Agatha commented. She had been to the opera in London's Covent Garden a few times with clients when she ran her PR agency and had always been impressed by the sopranos. She'd also always been a bit peeved that everything was in Italian but, since everyone else always seemed to know every detail of the story, she sat back and tried to enjoy the music rather than admitting that she didn't have a clue what was going on.

"Exactly," Giovanni agreed. "One of them may play Lola, which is a mezzosoprano role, but neither of them has the range for Santuzza. I will have to bring in a friend from another choir to sing Santuzza's part. You know, I'm betting you can sing very well, Agatha."

"Me?" Agatha gave him a quizzical look. Was he making fun of her? Her steak arrived and she stabbed it with her fork. She didn't like anyone making fun of her, even someone with a voice as rich and smooth as Barolo. "Are you taking the—"

"Not at all," he said, his hands spread in innocence. "I believe everyone has a voice. Not everyone is a soprano—everyone is different but everyone has their own talent, even if they don't realise it."

"Well, I think my talents lie . . . elsewhere," she said, relaxing.

"But it is always good to try something new," he said, twisting some linguine onto his fork. "Don't you agree?"

"I do." Agatha smiled at the thought of the new experience awaiting her on Saturday afternoon. "No one could accuse me of never trying anything new."

They chatted through their main course and a cheese course with more Barolo. Giovanni quizzed Agatha about her work and her time in London, commending the drive and determination it had taken to build her PR business and then to start again with a new venture in the Cotswolds. They compared notes about Mediterranean cities and beaches they had visited and he crooned like a poet over the hills in Piedmont where he had been born—also the home of the Barolo he loved so much. Then they strolled out onto the terrace cradling crystal brandy balloons.

"I have enjoyed this evening very much, Agatha," he said, looking out towards the stream where the lawn and the trees were now grey in the moonlight.

"I have too, Giovanni—another thing we have in common!" She laughed and then shivered slightly in the night air. He put his arm around her and she looked up into his eyes.

"It's late," she said. "I should order a cab. Pick my car up tomorrow."

"You should," he said gently, leaning towards her. She

put her hand on his shoulder and they kissed. "Don't go," he said when their lips parted. "Stay here with me tonight."

She smiled, nodded and they carried their brandy back indoors.

When Agatha woke the next morning her first thought was, "Where the hell am I?" Then she felt Giovanni in the bed next to her and had a surge of panic. She hadn't taken off her make-up last night. What must it look like now? Half of it would be on the pillow and the other half smeared round to her ears. She eased herself out of bed and crept to the bathroom, grabbing her handbag from a side table on the way past.

The bathroom mirror confirmed her worst fears—she looked a fright. Her hair was like some kind of clown's wig. It was not yet six in the morning. There was still time to fix this before he woke up. She locked the bathroom door and turned on the shower.

Half an hour later, with the help of her handbag's make-up supply and the hotel hair dryer, she decided that she looked presentable enough to face the world. She shrugged on one of the hotel's complimentary white towelling robes and went back out into the bedroom. Giovanni was starting to stir. He rolled over, hair tousled, rubbing bleary eyes.

"Wow—good morning!" he said, his eyes half closed. "How do you manage to look so good first thing in the morning?"

"Like you said last night," Agatha laughed, "everyone has their own talent."

She picked her dress up from a chair and gave it a shake to straighten the skirt.

"What are you doing?" he asked, sitting up. He was bare chested and his olive skin against the white sheets looked smooth and warm. "Come back to bed," he pleaded, yawning.

"Steady, tiger," she chided. "Today is a working day for me . . . for you as well, I take it."

"Yes, yes, of course, but I must have coffee before I can function."

The coffee machine in the room provided two reasonably good cups of macchiato and they sat in their robes on the room's small balcony, enjoying the morning sunshine and the same view they had from the terrace the night before. They sipped their coffee in a silence that made Agatha start to feel a little uncomfortable. She reasoned that Giovanni was probably feeling hungover, not yet having benefitted from the restorative power of the shower.

"We should do this again some time," Giovanni suggested, without much enthusiasm.

"I would like that," Agatha said, "but maybe not midweek. The working day always seems to stretch on for ages when you've had a late night."

Agatha's phone rang and she went back inside to retrieve it from the bedside table. It was John.

"I left it as late as I dared before phoning," he said, "but I need you to come down to the station."

"Why?" she asked. "What's happened?"

"Simon Black was arrested at four o'clock this morning."

"Arrested? What for?"

165

"Burglary—at the Watermill Brewery."

"Good grief!" Agatha groaned. "Where is he now?"

"In a cell in the custody suite," John said. "He's refusing to answer any questions until he's spoken to you and the Watermill's MD."

"How long can you keep him there?"

"We can hold him for twenty-four hours before we have to charge him, but I can't help thinking that it would be a good idea to sort this out before Wilkes gets wind of it."

"You're right, John. Wilkes will throw the book at Simon just to get at me. I'll talk to the MD, Mr. Brown, and be there by . . ." In her head Agatha ran through how long it would take to get home, feed the cats, change her clothes and then get to Mircester. "Nine. I'll make sure Mr. Brown is there, too."

"A problem?" Giovanni asked without moving from the position he had adopted, head tilted back with his face in the sun.

"It could be," she answered, flinging her robe on the bed and wriggling into her dress, glad he wasn't witnessing her contortions. "I have to go."

What was Simon thinking about? Agatha thundered down the stairs into the reception area and across the hall to the front door, scowling at the raised eyebrow of the concierge. To him, a woman in a cocktail dress at that time of the morning could only mean one thing—she'd had far more fun last night than he had. She stuck her tongue out at him and hurried past. She had more to worry about than keeping up appearances right now.

If Simon really had done something crazy and bro-

166

ken into the brewery, it put her in a very difficult position. Should Mr. Brown insist on pressing charges and decide to prosecute him, she would have no choice. She would have to sack Simon.

Chapter Eight

Agatha parked in front of her cottage and paused before getting out of the car, staring at the empty space in front of her where James's car would normally be. She felt suddenly sorry for him. He might be enjoying some of life's most desirable luxuries, eating gourmet food and drinking fine wine while cruising the Scandinavian coast in grand style, but he had no idea what was happening here at home.

She had a pang of guilt about last night, then told herself not to be so lily-livered. After all, it wasn't as if James and she were in any kind of proper relationship. In fact, they were barely on speaking terms—and who was to say that he hadn't hooked up with some glamorous rich widow on that "love boat"? She tutted, annoyed at herself for allowing such a pointless distraction to fill her head when she had other things to think about.

She hurried into the house, fed the cats and fussed over them for a few minutes. She excused that distraction as necessary because Boswell and Hodge needed to know that she cared about them. If she was honest, and occasionally she was honest with herself, she enjoyed their affection. Before the cats, she had never had any pets and had always considered herself to be too selfish, too wrapped up in everything she was doing to ever spare time for pointless pets. Now, however, she saw the point completely. She loved the way they purred and rubbed themselves against her legs with their tails as straight as flagpoles. Then she realised that this was the only affection she had enjoyed that morning. Giovanni had been hopeless. Hopelessly hungover, probably, but he hadn't even said goodbye. No doubt she'd hear from him later.

Trotting upstairs, she congratulated herself on having got out of bed so early. All that she needed was a little retouch and refining of her make-up before she chose a nicely tailored but otherwise plain dark blue dress. It was sleeveless but covered her shoulders and had a modest neckline—ideal for a serious meeting. She cursed Simon for having caused such a mess and promised herself she would control her temper while she was at the police station, no matter what. Her resolve wavered slightly at the thought of Wilkes becoming involved, but hopefully John would keep him out of it.

She phoned Mr. Brown, explained the situation and, just before nine o'clock, she met him on the steps outside Mircester police station.

"Really, Mrs. Raisin," he said, his brow furrowed, "this is exactly what I was trying to avoid. I don't want a police investigation causing upset at the brewery. We have a wonderful team spirit there and I can't have anything ruining that."

"I understand, Mr. Brown," Agatha assured him, then, in spite of her anger at Simon, she rallied to his defence. "Believe me, this is as much of a shock to me as it is to you. I'm sure Simon will have a perfectly good explanation. He's a valued employee and I've never had any cause to doubt his integrity. Let's go in and sort it out."

John was waiting for them inside, taking them through security doors along a dull grey corridor to the custody area. He turned to them before going in.

"The custody sergeant is an old friend," he explained. "This is his domain and he is responsible for what happens in there. He'll release Simon to me so that we can take him to an interview room, but the lad needs to be on his best behaviour—no funny business."

"He'll behave." Agatha's guarantee came with a stern expression. "Or serving jail time will be the least of his worries."

John introduced Agatha and Mr. Brown to the custody sergeant, then left them in a small, bare room that contained only a table and four hard chairs. He returned a moment later, leading Simon by the arm.

"Good to see you, boss," he said, looking tired and lacking his trademark grin. He was wearing a black sweater and black jeans. "Sorry about all this, Mr. Brown."

"What on earth were you up to last night?" Agatha asked, barely suppressing the rage that was tightening her stomach. "You look like a second-rate burglar!"

"You were supposed to be on the lookout for whoever's been robbing me," Mr. Brown spluttered, "not robbing my brewery yourself."

"I didn't steal anything, Mr. Brown," Simon said. "I would never do something like that."

"So why, in the middle of the night, did you break in?" demanded Agatha.

"I didn't exactly break in . . ." Simon hesitated, glancing from Agatha to John and back to Agatha.

"Okay," John said, realising that his presence was holding things up. "I can step outside and give you a couple of minutes."

"I didn't need to break in," Simon said, once John had gone. "I have keys to the Watermill and I know the alarm codes for all the different areas, so I didn't trigger any alarms. No one saw me going in—but someone called the police to report an intruder. The call was anonymous and from what I've heard them discussing, the police haven't been able to trace it—but I know who it was."

"How?" Agatha asked. "And why haven't you told the police?"

"Because Mr. Brown wanted all of this sorted out quietly, without any fuss. I think we can still do that. You know that Janet in Accounts hasn't wanted me anywhere near her department, Mr. Brown? Well, yesterday I followed her at lunchtime. She left the office and went straight to the betting shop. I saw her spend a lot of money in there, gambling on the horses, and when she left, I put a few bets on as well . . . um . . . that will have to go on expenses, boss."

"Just this once—best make sure you win next time,"

Agatha said, giving Simon a hard stare. For the first time, a grin creased his face.

"Anyway," Simon went on, "I got talking to the girl at the cash desk and it seems Janet is in there almost every day. She's losing anything from fifty quid to two hundred quid a day. The lady has a gambling problem."

"Janet can't afford that on her wages," Mr. Brown said, sighing. "Do you think she's in league with the thieves who've been stealing from the brewery?"

"Physically, nothing has actually been stolen," Simon explained. "There has been no stock or equipment taken from the premises." He reached down and plucked a small square of plastic from his sock. "I had to turn out my pockets when they brought me in and they took my phone, my belt, my wallet, even my shoelaces, but I managed to hold onto this SD card—take it, boss."

He swiftly slipped the card into Agatha's palm and she popped it into her handbag.

"That little card can hold masses of data," Simon explained. "Last night I let myself into your accounts department, Mr. Brown. I switched on Janet's computer. It took me a few minutes to figure out her password but I had her date of birth from the personnel files and a few combinations of her initials and—"

"Simon, just get on with it," Agatha hissed, impatiently. "We don't have all day."

"Right, well, as soon as I got into the computer," Simon went on, "I saw a little notification in the corner of the screen and I knew that the camera at the top of the screen had been turned on. Someone was watching me and that could only be Janet. She had rigged her computer so that if anyone turned it on when she wasn't there, it would send a message to her phone, or maybe a laptop—probably both.

"I knew I was now in a race to copy the accounts before she could change or delete anything, which she almost certainly has done by now. I copied everything onto that little card I just gave you, boss, then watched the screen as she changed things."

"So she was able to meddle with the accounts remotely—presumably from home?" Agatha asked.

"Yeah, it's fairly common for people to be able to connect to their office systems from home," Simon said. "I guessed she would have called the police, and she probably thought I would have scarpered when I realised I had been rumbled, but I stayed and watched what she was doing. I saw what she was trying to cover up.

"For the last year, a company called Mircester Brewery Supplies has been invoicing the Watermill Brewery for a whole range of things—from bottles and cleaning products to grain and copper piping. Only Mircester Brewery Supplies doesn't actually exist, and neither does any of the stuff they are supposed to have supplied. Janet was paying their invoices, but she must control their bank account—Janet *is* Mircester Brewery Supplies. She set up a bogus company. She was paying herself. She then issued receipts and falsified the inventory to make it look like the stuff had been delivered."

"So no goods were stolen?" Mr. Brown sounded relieved. "Only money."

"It's still theft, Mr. Brown," Agatha said. "Janet has been defrauding the company."

"I know, and I will deal with her—persuade her to leave quietly rather than fire her, I think," Mr. Brown said, stroking his chin, deep in thought. "The main thing is that all of the brewery staff are in the clear. You see, I like to think of them as a kind of . . . family. It was very upsetting for me to think that one of them might have been stealing from us and—"

"How are things going in here?" John came back into the room.

"We're done, John," Agatha said. "Simon's explained everything."

"You mustn't charge this young man, Inspector Glass," said Mr. Brown. "It's all been a dreadful misunderstanding. He had my permission to be on the premises last night."

"At four in the morning?" John seemed incredulous but knew from the blank looks of the others that he would receive no further explanation. He laughed. "Okay, Agatha, you and Mr. Brown had best make yourselves scarce. I'll get Simon booked out."

Agatha made her way to Raisin Investigations, where she was glad to see Toni looking fully recovered. She sat down with Toni and Patrick in her office, filling Toni in on her encounter with Theresa, meeting Jim Sullivan and the disappearance of Dennis Rayner and Felicity Kemp.

"Are we saying that we think Ulrika and Ursula murdered Rayner and Kemp as well as Antonio?" Toni asked.

"Maybe it's how they deal with cheating husbands," Patrick said grimly.

"But why would they then take Antonio's body to the Lone Warrior?" wondered Toni. "In fact, *how* would they have done that? Both of them are quite small. They couldn't have lugged a body around. They'd have had the same problem with Rayner and Kemp."

"We don't know for sure that Rayner and Kemp are actually dead," Patrick pointed out.

"No, and perhaps we shouldn't let that distract us," Agatha said. "Let's concentrate on Antonio. If they were moving the body around, they must have had help. Could that be where Jim Sullivan comes in?"

"It could be," Toni said, "but we mustn't dismiss Theresa as a suspect. She has a motive, after all. You said she was acting scared, but if she bumped off Antonio because he ended their affair, she may just have been scared of getting caught. She might have been pointing the finger at the sisters to pin the blame on them."

"We've got the same problem with Theresa, though," Patrick said. "Why would she take the body to the Lone Warrior and how did she manage it? Come to that, how and why did any of those women then dump the body in the lake?"

"Sullivan also has a motive," Agatha said. "With Antonio dead, he can take over the business, and there's a lot of money involved. Money is always a powerful motive for murder."

At that moment Simon arrived, giving everyone a cheery greeting.

"You've got a lot of paperwork to get through now,

Simon," Agatha said, adopting a serious tone, "after your little escapade last night." She handed him the data card. "I haven't had a chance to look at this, but you need to include the relevant accounts in your report and highlight the false payments. You will still be able to find them all, won't you?"

"No problem, boss. It's all in here." He tapped his head. "I'll do it straight away before it goes cold."

"Good. Don't make a habit of getting arrested, Simon. That was all a little awkward this morning."

"Sorry, boss. I'll try to stay out of jail in future." Simon looked shamefaced. He turned to go to his desk.

"And Simon . . ." Agatha's tone hadn't changed. "Well done for wrapping up the Watermill case. That was good work."

"Thanks, boss!" The grin was back and Simon suddenly looked about six inches taller.

"Now," Agatha said, turning back to Toni and Patrick, "let's pick up that train of thought again before, as Simon said, it goes cold. I think that it was Sullivan who made the threatening phone call and . . . cold . . ." Agatha's eyes were wide, her mind buzzing with a sudden thought and the words of Jim Sullivan. "Cold as a snowman's arse . . ."

"Cold as a what?" Toni laughed. "What are you talking about, Agatha?"

"Snakes and bastards!" Agatha breathed. "It's all starting to make sense! Yes!"

Toni and Patrick glanced at each other, then watched Agatha rubbing her temples as though massaging life into her thoughts. They remained silent. They both knew better than to say anything that might interrupt Agatha's cogitation.

"They froze him! The sisters froze Antonio!" Agatha slapped her hands on the desk.

"Why would they do that?" asked Toni.

"To give them time—but their plan didn't work!" Agatha leapt to her feet, fired with triumph, then rummaged in one of her voluminous desk drawers, eventually retrieving a large-scale map of the area. She spread it out on the desk. "This is where the Lone Warrior is," she said, planting a finger on the map.

"And this is where we first saw Edward." Toni traced her finger along the road.

"But there are tracks here, and here," Agatha indicated the positions, "on either side of the woods surrounding the Lone Warrior with lots of paths criss-crossing the place.

"What I'm saying is that the sisters bashed Antonio over the head and murdered him at the ice-cream company office. He was due to leave for Spain with Theresa last week but he never got close to leaving for Spain or Italy or anywhere else. They killed him there and then they stuck his body in one of the freezers. Freezing the body would give them time to create an alibi or, as John Glass put it, "an alibi for just about any time you can think of."

"Then they took the frozen body up to the woods on Saturday, probably stuffed into the freezer in one of their ice-cream vans. Yes, they'd have needed help, and I think Sullivan would have provided it. They parked in one of these lanes." Agatha tapped the roads to the side

177

of the woods. "Then they got the body out of the van and took it along one of the paths to the Lone Warrior."

"That would be difficult," Patrick noted. "Carrying the body along an overgrown path would be a struggle, even for a big bloke like Sullivan."

"We saw a tyre mark," Agatha drummed her fingers on the desk, thinking hard, "but only one. . . ."

"A motorbike?" Toni asked, then frowned, as though scolding herself. "That wouldn't help really, would it? And Edward would have heard the engine. And it would probably leave two tyre marks anyway. And . . ."

"A wheelbarrow," said Patrick. "If the body was hunched up like Edward described and frozen solid, they could have pushed it along the path in a wheelbarrow."

"Exactly!" Agatha agreed. "Then it just had to be lifted out and positioned on the Lone Warrior. That explains the little wet patch we saw on the stone. Antonio was starting to melt."

"But why put it there at all?" Toni asked.

"They placed the body on the stone," Agatha said, with a smug look, "because they wanted it to be discovered."

"But Edward says that the members hardly ever go all the way down the woods," Toni argued, circling an area on the map with her finger. "They've no reason to. Everything they need is here, in the garden area and by the pool and tennis court."

"The sisters knew that people at the club's barbecue on Sunday probably *would* come to take a look at the Lone Warrior," Agatha explained, "because Jasper said that it was to play a part in the grand finale of the angels and demons game. They put the body there on Saturday, frozen solid, but by Sunday it would have defrosted. That would certainly confuse the actual time of death. It would look like Antonio was killed at the Lone Warrior on Sunday, and they would have alibis set up to cover themselves.

"It would be no problem for them to hang some of Antonio's clothes in the 'Wizards'' changing room, and make it look like he had shown up at the club early on Sunday. The police would assume he was murdered there."

"But he was killed by a head wound that would have bled a lot," Patrick said. "There would be no blood at the Lone Warrior, so the police would know he wasn't killed there."

"Who's to say the sisters didn't have some of his blood to splash around as well?" Toni suggested.

"They must have thought they had plenty of time to stage the murder scene," Agatha said, "but then Edward showed up. The sisters didn't know that the barbecue was being brought forward by a day. Edward had sent out his 'phone chain' message to let everyone know. The sisters were both members. One of them had a phone that rang when the chain reached her."

"That's what Edward heard!" Toni was nodding vigorously. "They must have seen him coming and hid, watching him, but they didn't have time to hide the body. Then he heard the phone ring, realised there was a murderer lurking in the trees and ran in the opposite direction from the ringtone."

"So they must have been hiding here," Agatha said,

pointing to an area on the opposite side of the Lone War- rior to the lane where they had picked up Edward. "We can take a look, but they've had more than enough time to make sure that they left no trace. When Edward ran off, they must have retrieved the body, wheeled it back to the ice-cream van and taken it back to the deep freeze at the office."

"It all makes sense," Patrick agreed, folding his arms, "but where's our evidence?"

"The autopsy is bound to show something," Agatha argued. "The body must surely show signs of having been frozen. The pathologist will pick up on that."

"Maybe," Toni said, "but the body was subsequently dumped in Mircester Lake . . ."

"After having been badly re-dressed in a hurry," Ag- atha quickly added.

". . . and the lake is shallow water," Toni went on. "It's quite warm at this time of year. That might help to disguise any effects of the freezing."

"Then we need to talk to the pathologist," Agatha de- cided. "John should be able to help us with that."

Agatha worked through the rest of the morning with one eye on her phone, which she kept sitting within half a ring's snatching distance, waiting for Giovanni to call. She knew that he had a busy day ahead, but she was sure he would find a moment to have just a brief word to say how much he had enjoyed the previous evening, or even simply to ask if she had been able to deal with the work problem that had snatched her away from him so early in the morning. Maybe she should phone him to apologise for that. No—if he had any decency at all, he would phone her. But still the phone didn't ring.

"I've just had a call from Paula," Patrick said, popping his head round the door. "She's making friends with the other girls—now has a couple that she hangs out with regularly. No sign of any drugs yet. Sarah was out to dinner with her father last night. Paula's not too keen on her. Says she's a bit full of herself—acts like the whole college revolves around her and whatever she's doing."

"Girls that age are strange creatures," Agatha said. "They're either leaders or followers. The ones that giggle and whisper follow the ones that are full of bravado. For the leaders, that false confidence is all that stops them from being one of the followers."

"You seem to know a lot about teenaged girls," Patrick noted. "How come?"

"Patrick, I was one."

"Ah," he nodded, sagely, "and were you a giggling whisperer or full of bravado?"

"Neither," Agatha replied. "I was different—the exception to the rule. One of a kind."

"And you still are," Patrick said, letting one of his rare smiles escape as he returned to his desk.

News from Martinbrook encouraged Agatha to think about what she should say in her talk the following afternoon. She wanted to be entertaining enough to hold the girls' interest, yet also informative and do it all with the authority of someone who really knows what she's talking about. Was that really her? As Kathleen Partridge had discovered, she was actually just a girl from a rundown high-rise in Birmingham. One of her greatest dreads was that one day, when she was in a stressful situation surrounded by people with posh accents, the broad Birmingham twang she had spent so many years suppressing would come flooding out. On the other hand, would that really matter?

Yes, of course it would! She banged her fist on the desk. This sort of thinking is all down to bloody Giovanni not having phoned, she told herself. He's got me starting to think that I'm not worthy of his attention, that I'm not good enough. Well, bollocks to him! I'm Agatha Raisin. I'm a successful businesswoman and a first-rate detective and anyone who thinks I'm not up to scratch can go shove his Barolo up his Rusticana!

Agatha marched out of the office, her heels beating an angry tattoo across the floor. Simon looked up, feeling her shock of fury electrifying the room. He and Toni exchanged a look and Toni shrugged. Helen and Patrick kept their heads down. There was a hammering of footsteps down the stairs and the street door slammed. Agatha Raisin had left the building.

Sitting on a bench in the cathedral square in the shade of an ash tree with her hands in her lap, Agatha stared up at the branches, looking for all the world like she was counting the leaves.

"Mrs. Raisin—fancy bumping into you here!"

Agatha focused on the person now standing by her side and, for a moment, failed to recognise Margaret Bloxby.

"Mrs. Bloxby! Sorry, you caught me a little off guard."

"I can tell," Mrs. Bloxby said, taking a seat next to Agatha. "It's always a challenge when you see someone you know, but not in the place you're used to seeing them, isn't it?"

"Yes, it is. What brings you to Mircester?"

"I had a few errands to run. When I come into town, I always like to visit this spot. It's beautifully peaceful."

"That's why I like it. It gives you space to think."

"Problems with your murder investigation?"

"These things are never straightforward, but I think we're making progress. I just wish I didn't have other things bugging me."

"Sometimes, when you're in the thick of it, it can seem like there's no getting over a big problem."

"It's not a big problem. At least, it shouldn't be a problem . . . It's just . . . I think I've made a complete fool of myself."

"We all do that from time to time."

"Not like this you don't."

"Ah . . . man problems. James? Charles?"

"None of the usual suspects. Someone new. You know him, actually."

Mrs. Bloxby looked Agatha straight in the eye. "Giovanni . . ." she said slowly. "Well, you're not the first to fall for his charms."

"I realise that," Agatha said. "I just thought that he would care a bit more than he seems to."

"For men like Giovanni, the thrill is all in the chase and, dare I say . . . the conquest?"

"You dare," Agatha sighed.

"I suppose if you enjoyed your time with him, that's something you'll always have."

"True," Agatha agreed, "and maybe I was wrong to expect more. I just don't want to be seen as the latest in a list of conquests."

"Maybe you should look at it the other way round," Mrs. Bloxby suggested. "Regard him as merely the latest in your list of conquests."

Agatha laughed. "I'm sure my list is significantly shorter than his, but you're right. Why should I let myself feel like I've been used by Giovanni when I did exactly the same to him? If he can't find the time to spare a thought for me, then why should I bother about him? I have far more important things going on in my life."

Agatha said goodbye to her friend and marched back to the office, ready to take on the world again. No sooner had she sat down at her desk than her phone rang. Despite having pushed him out of her mind, her first thought was that it must be Giovanni and, despite her discussion with Mrs. Bloxby, she still felt a tingle of excitement. She tried not to sound disappointed when she answered and heard John's voice.

"John," she said in a flat voice. She then tried to sound a little more perky. "I was thinking about calling you, but I thought you'd be asleep by now."

"I'm just about to get my head down," he said. "Has young Mr. Black recovered from his time in the cells?"

"He's fine. I've got him working on his report."

"What was he up to at the brewery at that time of night?"

"I can't really say, John—client confidentiality and all that, you know."

"I know, but I can't help being curious."

"Actually, I'm a bit curious, too—about the autopsy on Antonio. Do you know if the pathologist found any sign of the body having been frozen?"

"Frozen? Why would it have been frozen?"

"It's a long story."

"I don't think there was anything in the report about that, but I can check. In return, you have to let me take you to dinner on Saturday. Then you can tell me the long story."

"Saturday? Well, I . . ." Agatha had a mental image of the naturist club and Jasper by the pool, then Giovanni sitting up in bed. Be honest, she told herself, he's never going to call and going out to dinner with John will give you an excuse to leave the club at a reasonable time. "All right, it's a deal."

"Great!" John sounded genuinely delighted. "I'll book a table at the Feathers in Ancombe and pick you up at seven."

The following afternoon, Toni accompanied Agatha to Martinbrook. High hedges shielded the college from the road and, on driving through the gates, they could see that most of what at one time must have been a lawned garden was now a car park. The building itself was brick built, rather than Cotswold stone, and there were pleasing flourishes of Victorian excess where geometric patterns had been created in the brickwork.

185

Inside, there was little trace of the college's Victorian heritage. The décor was modern, clean and stylish, white walls and blonde wood giving the place an almost Scandinavian feel. Mrs. Carling was waiting for them and took them to her office.

"The young lady you have working for you is exceptionally bright, according to her teachers," Mrs. Carling said.

"We'll ask her to dial that down a bit," Agatha replied. "We don't want anyone suspecting that she's anything other than an ordinary teenager."

"I'll take you to the staffroom shortly," Mrs. Carling said. "You'll be able to meet the teachers there but I want to stress how delicate this situation is. I don't want any of the staff to feel they are under suspicion."

"We'll be very discreet, Mrs. Carling. We won't be asking too many questions, just chatting to get a feel for who your teachers are."

"Very well," Mrs. Carling said, checking her watch. "It's almost time for the afternoon break, so we can make our way to the staffroom."

The staffroom was a large lounge with a variety of mismatched sofas and armchairs. There was a small kitchenette at one end and some of the staff were gathered outside it, being served cups of tea. As more teachers filed in, Mrs. Carling introduced Agatha and Toni, reminding them that Agatha was here to address the business studies group and asking the staff to make them feel welcome.

Agatha and Toni circulated, chatting, and Agatha was struck by the fact that there were no young people among the teachers. Most were women and they ap-

peared to be in their forties or fifties. Of the twenty or
so people in the room, Agatha could see only three men,
and they looked older than the women. She judged one
to be at least in his seventies. They were all conserva-
tively dressed, polite and friendly.

"They seem like a nice bunch," Toni said quietly
when she and Agatha came together in the middle of the
room. "None of them strike me as being a drug dealer."

"I agree. This lot are more into tweed than weed," Agatha said, looking round the room, "but I didn't expect to
find anyone here who looked like a street dealer."

"There will be others—ground staff, caretakers, that
sort of thing."

"We may get a chance to meet some of them later.
Mrs. Carling will give us a tour of the college. Right
now, I need to get ready for my little lecture."

The lecture theatre was in a modern extension to the
rear of the building and comprised a well-lit stage facing banked rows of seats. Around half of the seats were
occupied by girls who appeared to span the college age
range, all wearing identical light blue uniform blouses
and dark blue skirts.

Having been introduced to her audience by Mrs.
Carling as "a self-made woman who built her own successful PR agency in a highly competitive business envi-
ronment," Agatha took her place at the lectern on stage
and delivered her speech. She talked about marketing,
client liaison, the importance of understanding the finan-
cial side of the business, and threw in a few anecdotes, all
the time examining the girls in the audience. She picked
out Paula, looking like one of the youngest. Paula gave

187

no hint that she knew Agatha and was not one of those who raised a hand to ask a question at the end of Agatha's talk.

"Did you work with anyone famous?" The question came from a blonde girl sitting in the middle of the audience, surrounded by a handful of others who were clearly all friends. Agatha rattled off the names of a few celebrities, taking the opportunity to tell a story about one actress who missed an entire party being held in her honour when she managed to lock herself in the ladies' loo. The story was received with a ripple of polite laughter.

"Yes, but those people you just mentioned," the blonde girl spoke up again, a sly smirk on her face, "they're all a bit 'last century,' aren't they?"

The girl's friends giggled. Agatha glowered at her, but kept her temper in check.

"You might think of them like that," Agatha said, "but that sort of attitude would never win you any clients in the PR business."

One of the girl's friends handed her a smartphone. She looked at the screen and laughed.

"I knew I recognised you!" she said. "You were the one who got gassed on live TV by a farting donkey!"

The entire audience bust out laughing. Agatha gripped the lectern, fuming. The incident had not been her finest hour. Wizz-Wazz the donkey had made her look a fool at that press conference but she had put it behind her. She was about to say something about how you have to be resilient in business and bounce back from adversity, but the blonde girl's mocking grin was too much. Agatha blinked, then froze the girl with an ice-cold stare. The lecture theatre fell into silence.

"Wizz-Wazz and I became good friends," Agatha snarled, "but you're too much of a snivelling child to know what a real friend is—and I'd far rather be friends with a flatulent donkey than a snotty little stuck-up cow like you!"

"And that's where we have to leave it for today," said Mrs. Carling, swiftly replacing Agatha at the lectern. "Thank you so much, Mrs. Raisin."

She led the girls in a round of applause and Agatha walked off the stage. Toni met her outside the lecture theatre.

"I thought that went well," Toni said.

"You're not funny," Agatha said, still seething.

"No, I mean it," Toni said. "You gave a really good talk. I couldn't do that. I'd be far too nervous to stand there in front of those girls and give a lecture."

"Miss Gilmour is right, Mrs. Raisin," said Mrs. Carling, joining them. "That was an excellent talk—and it ended on a good, lively note!"

"Really?" Agatha was taken aback. "You're not upset with me about that?"

"Forget it." Mrs. Carling gave Agatha an impish smile. "That one really is a snotty little cow and it's about time somebody told her so! Come, I'll show you round the rest of the college."

Mrs. Carling's tour of the science labs, the gym, the pool, the sports pitches and the girls' accommodation left Agatha and Toni no closer to discovering who might be smuggling drugs into the school, although they both ended up with a far better idea of how the school was laid out and how it operated. After Mrs. Carling bade them farewell, they were on their way out to the car park when Toni realised she had left her jacket in the staffroom. She dashed off to fetch it and Agatha walked out to her car.

"That's her, Dad!" she heard a voice yell. "That's the one who called me a stuck-up cow!"

Agatha looked round to see the blonde girl from the lecture hall standing beside a black Mercedes and tugging at the sleeve of a broad-shouldered man. When he turned to face her, she immediately recognised Jim Sullivan.

"Mr. Sullivan," she said. "I didn't expect to see you here today."

"You again!" he spat, then advanced towards her. "I warned you what would happen if you didn't keep your nose out—"

"Agatha!" Toni emerged from the building, carrying her jacket. "Is everything okay?"

Sullivan looked from Agatha to Toni and back again, then pointed a chunky finger at Agatha's face. Agatha stood her ground.

"School's out for the weekend," he growled, "but you've still got a lesson to learn."

"Somehow, I don't think there's much you can teach me," Agatha replied.

"We'll see about that," Sullivan said. "I'm late. I have to deliver my daughter to her mother's house, so I don't have time for you now, but this ain't over!"

With another menacing glance towards Toni, he returned to his car and drove off with his daughter.

"That was the girl from the theatre," said Toni.

"It was," Agatha said through gritted teeth. "And that was Jim Sullivan. It's the second time I've met him. I don't think it will be the last."

Chapter Nine

Agatha began Saturday morning worrying about what to wear that afternoon but soon came to the conclusion that how she looked when she was dressed really made no difference. It was how she looked without her clothes that mattered.

She then spent an hour in front of the full-length mirror in her bedroom, naked, bending, stretching and twisting to examine as much of herself as she could to find any imperfections. She found plenty, but eventually decided there was nothing that could be done about them. Nobody was perfect after all, were they?

She rummaged in the drawer where she kept her holiday swimwear, found her favourite bikini and tried it on. She still looked good in it, and if she looked good in such a skimpy little item, she'd look good without it. In fact, she told herself, you'll look even better. With no bikini, there's nowhere for any flesh to bulge over the cloth. Yes, she decided, you will look just as good as any of those other nudies, and a lot better than most. Today, Agatha, you are baring all in public and you will look magnificent!

The doorbell rang. She looked at her bedside clock. Too early for Jasper. Crossing to the window, she stood to one side and peeked out from behind the curtain. Charles's Range Rover was parked outside. What on earth did he want? She pulled on the sundress she intended to wear later and hurried downstairs.

"Good morning, Aggie!" he said cheerily. "I was just passing and thought I'd ask how that business with Antonio was coming along."

Agatha folded her arms and looked at him, her head cocked slightly to one side. Carsely was not a place you could ever be "just passing." It was somewhere you had to have set out to get to; otherwise, you were lost.

"You'd best come in," she said. "We can have a coffee in the garden."

They chatted while Agatha prepared the coffee, then settled on garden chairs at a small table in the sunshine on the lawn.

"This is nice," he said, sipping his coffee. "Just like old times."

"It's nice that you stopped by, Charles, but it's not like old times."

"You're right. Back then I didn't have to ring the doorbell. I had my own keys. I miss all that. We used to have fun. I enjoyed it."

"I used to enjoy cigarettes," Agatha said, "but I kicked that habit."

"Are you saying I was a bad habit?"

"You certainly had bad habits—running around with other women, for example."

"I regret a lot of things that I did, but not being with you. You know that I'm always here for you—if you need my help with this murder case, for example. Or if you just need me."

"Thank you, Charles." She smiled. "We can't turn the clock back, but it's good to know that I can call on you. How are things at Barfield?"

"Well, the vineyard plans are progressing. I have a few investors on board. I suppose I could do it all with my own money, but I can spread the risk if others are involved. I'm still looking for other things to invest in myself, but running the estate keeps me pretty busy."

Charles asked about the case and Agatha explained her theory about the frozen body.

"I was given a tour of Antonio's," she said. "They have a couple of large freezer rooms there. That's where they must have frozen him."

"Gruesome. You need to be careful."

"I will be. Now, you'd best be on your way. Jasper is picking me up for an afternoon by the pool at the naturist place."

"You don't mean that you're going to . . ."

"I do," she smiled, enjoying the flicker of jealousy in his eyes, "but it's all part of the investigation, really. All in the line of duty. I'm going undercover."

"Except you're not!" Charles laughed. "You'll be completely *un*-covered!"

"It will be a new experience," she said, and ushered him back through the house to the front door.

When Jasper arrived, Agatha was ready to go. She had a small hold-all in which she had packed a beach towel, sunscreen, shampoo and other essentials along with a pair of flip-flops. They would be useful around the pool area but they weren't the sort of footwear Agatha could bear to wear anywhere else. She regarded a heel of some description as vital as the right shade of lipstick.

"There's a lot going on at the club today," he said, as they climbed into the car, "but that's generally the case at the weekend. They'll be decorating the bar area for a birthday party this evening and we have a team preparing the area near the Lone Warrior for our Grand Finale on Wednesday."

"Isn't Wednesday a strange night for such a big party?" Agatha asked.

"The game nights have always been on Wednesdays," he explained. "Not all of the members are involved and it wouldn't be fair to those who don't participate if we took over the club at the weekend when there are always functions like tonight's party. Wednesday has always been our night."

"That makes sense," Agatha said, fidgeting with the house keys that she was trying to put into her handbag. She felt a tightness in her stomach that was making her slightly breathless. She was nervous. Why should she be nervous? She hadn't felt at all nervous when she stood on stage in front of all those teenagers yesterday. Why should she feel nervous now? Because, she told herself with a heavy sigh, you weren't naked in front of the college girls.

"I'm guessing you're a bit apprehensive right now," Jasper said, pulling out of Lilac Lane into Carsely High Street. "That's perfectly natural. Once we're there, you'll settle down in no time. I'll have to take a little time to check on things at the Lone Warrior with Edward, but everyone else will make you very welcome. And you'll have Toni to chat to, of course. You've nothing to worry about at all."

Agatha winced and turned to look out of the window so that Jasper couldn't see the look of dread on her face. She had completely forgotten Toni would be there! Going starkers in front of a bunch of people she didn't know was one thing, but Toni was different. She'd be seeing Toni again in the office on Monday morning when they were both back in the real world, where people wore clothes.

"I'm not worried," Agatha lied, "and it will be good to see Toni. If she can do this, then so can I!"

Jasper looked across at her, a little surprised by Agatha's sharp tone, then smiled when he saw the expression of bold determination on her face.

"That's the spirit," he said, "but I promise you'll feel fine once you're there and we'll all enjoy a lovely afternoon."

At the club, Jasper directed Agatha to the "Witches" locker room before disappearing into "Wizards." Agatha undressed, put on her flip-flops and wrapped her beach towel around her. When she emerged back into the hall, Jasper was waiting. He was completely naked, carrying a towel over his arm.

"You can wear your towel like that if you like," he said. "No one will mind. It's your first time."

"Well," she said, taking a deep breath, "I suppose if I'm going to do this, I should do it properly." She plucked at the edge of the towel where she had tucked it in to hold it in place and pulled it free. She stood with the towel draped over her arm and caught sight of herself in the hall mirror. She held her head high and her shoulders back, just as she had done when Bert Simpson had spotted her in the garden.

"Agatha, you have nothing to worry about," Jasper said. "You look fantastic."

They strolled out into the sunshine by the pool area where a number of people were relaxing on sun loungers or standing chatting both in and out of the pool. Jasper knew everyone there and introduced Agatha in a relaxed manner that left her smiling and chatting as though she was at a garden party with old friends. Except, she told herself, they're not actually old friends, and everyone is starkers! After a few minutes, however, that didn't seem to matter and her smile switched from the professional version to one of genuine pleasure. Something began to happen that she really hadn't been expecting—she was enjoying herself.

She spotted Toni lying on a lounger at the far end of the pool reading a magazine. There was an empty sunbed beside her, so Agatha walked over and draped her towel over it.

"Surprise!" she said brightly.

Toni looked up from her magazine, pushed her sunglasses up onto her head, then froze for an instant with a look of absolute horror before instinctively attempting to cover herself with the magazine.

"Agatha! What are you doing here? You didn't tell me you were planning to . . ."

"Well, Jasper persuaded me to give it a go," Agatha said, lowering herself onto the lounger with as much elegance as she could manage, "and we all need to try something new from time to time, don't we?"

"This is just too weird," Toni said, shaking her head and laughing. She set the magazine aside and sat up. "I'm not sure I can cope with this without a drink. I'm off to the bar. How about a gin and tonic?"

"Perfect," Agatha said, lying back in the sun and closing her eyes. "I thought you'd never ask."

The warm sunshine, the faint splashes from swimmers in the pool and the burble of conversation left Agatha feeling, as Jasper had promised, more relaxed than she had done in a long while. The effect was soothingly soporific and when she opened her eyes slightly to see Toni returning from the bar, she got to her feet.

"I was in danger of falling asleep just then," she said. "You don't mind standing, do you? There's something vaguely vulgar about drinking lying down."

"I know," Toni agreed. "I get dribbles down my chin. It's not as if I'm going to get stains on a favourite blouse or anything, though, is it?"

They laughed and clinked glasses.

"Cheers," said Toni.

"Bottoms up!" said Agatha.

They were chatting about the weather, the club and how Toni had been promised a role in Wednesday evening's Grand Finale event when Ulrika and Ursula approached. Agatha was struck once again by how alike they were—both petite, both with long, slightly greying, brown hair. Ursula's face was a little rounder than her sister's but they both had the same disturbing expression and the same intense look in their green eyes.

"Mrs. Raisin," Ursula said. "Have you decided to join the society?"

"I've not quite made my mind up about that yet, Mrs. Danieli, but Toni loves it here and Jasper persuaded me to give it a try."

"Jasper . . ." Ulrika nodded and the women exchanged a slow look.

"Actually, I saw another mutual friend this morning," Agatha said. "Sir Charles Fraith popped in for a chat. He asked about your receptionist, Theresa." That was a lie. "I think she's caught his eye." That probably wasn't.

"Sir Charles will be disappointed," Ursula said.

"I doubt we'll be seeing Theresa again," Ulrika added.

"Really? Why might that be?" Agatha asked.

"We had an email from her," Ursula explained. "She's got another job, down in London. Says she won't be back."

"That's a bit odd," Toni said. "Didn't she have to work out a notice period?"

"She was on holiday. She said that covered her notice," Ulrika said.

"Not that it would have made any difference," Ursula went on. "We've closed down the business for now. As you've probably guessed, Mrs. Raisin, now that Antonio's gone, we're selling up."

The sisters wished Agatha and Toni an enjoyable afternoon, then drifted off together in the direction of the pavilion.

"They were lying," Agatha said. "Theresa didn't send them any email. If they have one, I'm betting they faked it—or they're about to fake it. Theresa was frightened. She didn't want to be in contact with them. She wanted to get as far away from those two as possible. She wouldn't have bothered sending a formal resignation to the people who murdered her lover."

"Anyone taking over the business would want to know about the staff they might be taking on," Toni reasoned. "They'd want to see some sort of resignation letter in Theresa's file. That might be why they'd forge an email."

"Maybe," Agatha mused. "Hopefully, Theresa is safely in hiding down south somewhere."

"I think we can count this as another first," Toni said.

"What do you mean?" Agatha asked.

"Well, we've never interviewed our prime suspects naked before!"

The rest of the afternoon passed quickly. Agatha chatted with Jasper for a while, got to know a few of the others round the pool and eventually decided, with only a few wispy clouds appearing to temper the heat of the sun, to take a dip. She lowered herself gracefully into the pool, with a slight gasp when the cold water reached her midriff, and swam a few lengths.

Agatha was a confident swimmer and had long since mastered the art of swimming the breaststroke while keeping her head out of the water, thus preserving her make-up and avoiding getting chlorine in her hair. She and Toni then had a discussion about how much easier it was to dry off without a swimming costume, and she ordered a cab to take her home.

She showered and dressed, and was waiting for the cab outside the front of the pavilion when Jasper appeared, draped in his black-and-gold robe.

"I was hoping that, you know . . . we might . . . go on somewhere afterwards," he said hesitantly.

Agatha smiled at the apparent shyness of a man who enjoyed wandering around naked in front of people.

"Some other time, perhaps," she said and, as the cab pulled up, she reached forward to give him a friendly peck on the cheek, the feeling of his facial hair brushing her chin immediately reminding her why she hated beards so much.

John picked Agatha up promptly in a cab and they drove the couple of miles to Ancombe. It had always been Agatha's idea of the perfect Cotswold village. Carsely and Ancombe had much in common—including a church at one end of town and a pub at the other. Unlike Carsely, however, where the houses and shops were strung out along the main street, Ancombe's pretty, thatched cottages with their neat, colourful gardens were more tightly gathered near its famous mineral spring.

Were there to be a beauty contest for villages, Ancombe would rank way above Carsely, and Agatha thought that a good reason for not living there. Ancombe was simply too pretty. It was becoming known as a "hidden gem" of the Cotswolds, a nascent tourist trap of the kind that Carsely would never be.

Also unlike Carsely, where the Red Lion served food that was edible but unremarkable, Ancombe's pub, the Feathers, was renowned for its cuisine. Having eaten very little all day, Agatha was looking forward to a delicious dinner. She surprised John by deciding on *terrine de campagne* followed by lamb shank without looking at the menu.

"Obviously you've eaten here before," he said with a grin.

"I love it here." Agatha smiled. "I wouldn't want to live in Ancombe, but I love coming here to eat. You couldn't have chosen better."

They sipped Aperol spritz cocktails while John studied the menu and Agatha perused the wine list. He asked her how her day had been and she explained about her nudist experience.

"So you went all-out starkers?" John broke into a wide grin. "I *so* wish I had been there."

"Now, now," said Agatha, delivering a genial scolding with a smile and a wag of her finger, "you're making that sound a little sordid. It's not a sexual thing. It's just a bunch of people hanging around relaxing in the buff."

"If you say so," John said, "but I'm still devastated at having missed out."

"Before you let your imagination run away with you, you should know that I was working while we were there. I interviewed our prime suspects. This is probably when I should tell you that long story. . . ."

Agatha explained her frozen corpse theory and how she was now more concerned than ever about Theresa's safety.

"I can try to check if she had reported in to a station in London," John said, "but I can't do much more than that without turning it into a missing persons enquiry, and Wilkes won't sanction that. She said she was going to London, and she's gone."

"But she also said she would keep in touch to let me know she was safe," Agatha pointed out, "and she hasn't called."

"All right, I'll put in a few calls," John said. "I've got a few mates down in London who can start asking around."

"What about the autopsy?" Agatha asked. "Any sign of Antonio having been frozen?"

"None, but the pathologist might have missed any signs. I'm told that if a body has been frozen, it can take days for it to thaw out. Rush the process and the outside starts to decompose while internal organs are still frozen. The pathologist would have noticed frozen organs."

"Toni suggested that's why he was dumped in the lake—to help everything thaw out."

"That might be possible but I doubt that Wilkes will want the pathologist to go back and take another look. At the moment, he has an autopsy that suits his robbery theory. He won't want to do anything that might give credence to an Agatha Raisin theory."

"We might not have the evidence we need yet, but you have to admit that Ursula's behaviour isn't that of a recently bereaved widow," Agatha said. "There hasn't even been a funeral yet and she was at the nudist place today carrying on as if nothing had happened—and what about her planning to sell the business? Surely she can't do that so soon?"

"If she owns part of the business, she can sell her share any time she likes," John said. "If Antonio owns the place, she can't sell any of it until his estate is settled, even if he left a proper will. She can plan to do it, but she can't go through with it. Of course, if she turns out to be the murderer, she can't inherit the business anyway. You can't be convicted of murdering someone and still inherit from them."

"They don't have any children," Agatha said. "I guess Antonio's family in Italy would inherit."

"That would take a lot of sorting out—could be months, maybe years."

"Oh, let's not talk about it any more tonight," Agatha said, shaking her head as if to rid it of all thoughts of the murder. "I want to enjoy our meal—and we've lots of other things to talk about. For example, you never explained why it is that a clodhopping great police inspector is such a good dancer."

To Agatha's surprise, neither the conversation nor her thoughts ever again returned to the subject of the murder. John was funny and entertaining, yet modest and reluctant to boast of his own achievements. It took Agatha some time to discover that he had been a competitive ballroom dancer as a youngster.

"I used to love it," he said, "but the guys I played football with didn't understand. Some of them could be quite nasty about it—especially when they saw the gorgeous girls who were my dance partners."

"That's jealousy for you," Agatha said. "It can make people do horrible things."

"I freely admit to being very jealous of everyone else at that club this afternoon," he said, laughing, "but I promise not to be horrible about it."

The evening evaporated far more quickly than Agatha realised and it was almost midnight by the time they arrived back in Lilac Lane, John stepping out of the cab to say goodnight.

"Here we are again," he said, "outside your front gate, and a taxi with the meter running."

"Then you'd best get back in it," Agatha said, but before he could move, she flung her arms around his neck. "I've had a lovely time this evening."

She kissed him and he held her close.

"Me, too," he said, and kissed her again.

"But I'm not ready for anything more at the moment. Things are complicated. You do understand, don't you?"

"I understand," he said, smiling, "but don't expect me to give up on you any time soon."

She watched him pull away in the cab and strolled up her garden path to the front door. Clouds had closed in from the west and a few spots of warm rain began to fall. She hurried inside to be greeted, as always, by Boswell and Hodge.

"What was I saying out there?" she asked the cats. "What was I thinking of? How can I not be ready for 'anything more' when I was with Giovanni?"

She sat at the bottom of the stairs, stroking the cats who both nuzzled against her, competing to see who could purr loudest, vying for her affection.

"Is it because Giovanni was just a flash in the pan? A moment of madness? He'll have forgotten about me already. John wouldn't do that, would he? Is that why I'm not ready for 'anything more' with him? Am I scared that 'anything more' might turn into 'something serious'?"

Agatha trudged upstairs to bed, feeling unusually tired. But then, it had been a very unusual day.

When she woke the next morning, steady rain was falling, although the brightness of the sky betrayed the fact that a summer sun was still lurking somewhere in the sky, waiting for the rain to wash itself out.

Agatha rose late, spent some time pampering herself, then grabbed an umbrella to walk through the rain to the Red Lion with the papers for Sunday lunch. She furled the umbrella and shook the water off at the pub door, then looked round to see Bert Simpson at the bar with a small bunch of regulars. They all gave Agatha big smiles of welcome. A few wiggled their eyebrows. Clearly they'd had little to talk about all week except what the window cleaner saw. She beamed a huge smile at them, walked up to the bar and put a hand on Bert's shoulder.

"I just want you all to know," she announced, still smiling, "that if Bert here has been telling you he saw me naked in the sunshine in the garden, then he was telling the absolute truth. It's my garden and I'll do what I bloody well like in it."

There was a burst of laughter, then one of the regulars said, "Good for you, Mrs. Raisin," and bought her a gin and tonic.

Agatha was browsing one of the newspaper supplements, waiting for the roast beef and Yorkshire pudding she had ordered, when Doris Simpson appeared, warning Bert that if he didn't come home to eat straight away, there would be trouble. Then she accepted a small glass of white wine as a reward for braving the wet weather. She chatted with the others for a while, then spotted Agatha sitting in the corner.

"Mrs. Raisin," she said, joining Agatha. "I didn't see you there. I've been meaning to have a word with you."

"Hello, Doris. What do you want to talk to me about?"

"Well, you see . . . it's this business of you sunbathing in your garden. I mean, it's none of my affair what you get up to in your own place . . ."

"I agree with you so far," Agatha said, beginning to feel slightly tetchy.

". . . but my Bert's been on at me all week to go running

around the garden with him in the nude! So I just wanted to say . . . keep it up." She winked and went back to join the others.

By the time Agatha was heading back to Lilac Lane, the shower had eased to a persistent drizzle just heavy enough to prevent the rain-stooped heads of the roses and geraniums in the gardens she passed from drying out and straightening up.

Back at her cottage, the cats looked at her like she was mad to have gone out in the rain, then demanded to be fed, yowling at the kitchen cupboard where they knew the cat food was kept.

Agatha dealt with a few chores, then settled in her favourite armchair in her living room to finish with the Sunday paper. She started reading an article about a series of murders in Italy, but after a few paragraphs found her mind wandering back to the murder of Antonio Danieli.

She was convinced that the sisters were behind it. They, or at least Ursula, had the strongest motive. Antonio had been cheating on Ursula and, with him out of the way, they stood to make a fortune from selling the business. For that to happen, though, the murder had to look like it had nothing to do with them. Theresa thought differently, but where was she now? Why hadn't she called? Could she also have become a victim of Jasper's two weird handmaidens?

Agatha contemplated how often pairs of women had cropped up over the past few days. There were two women with Giovanni, vying for the same role in *Ca-valleria Rusticana*; there were Lola and Santuzza in the opera; there were two witches in the tale of the Lone Warrior; and then there were Ulrika and Ursula. What was it going to take for her to be able to nail that pair?

Her phone rang and she reached to pick it up from a side table. Could it be Theresa? She congratulated herself on not immediately hoping it might be Giovanni, realising that he no longer mattered. In fact, it was John.

"I wanted to say again how much I enjoyed last night," he said.

"I did, too, John. It was lovely."

"I don't want you to think I'm being too pushy. I know you're maybe not in a good place right now but I want you to know that I'd like us to . . . carry on."

"Good," Agatha said. "I'd like that, too. Let's see how things pan out at work next week and we can plan another dinner date."

It wasn't until she put the phone down that she realised James would be back in a week. What was she going to do about James? They'd been talking about rebuilding their lives together but, by the way he had departed from the wedding, it didn't seem like there was much of their relationship left to salvage. Yet she missed him. Even now, thinking of his cottage standing empty next door, she missed him. That surely wasn't enough of a foundation for any kind of relationship, was it? She missed having frozen lasagne in the freezer when she'd run out, but she didn't want to marry one.

Was marriage something that she should even consider? And should she consider it with James? Should she consider it with anyone? She thought of the men who had featured in her life recently. Could she see herself marrying any of them?

Jasper, even though he had given her slight palpitations when they first met, was a non-starter, although he probably didn't think so. Let's face it, it was the beard.

Giovanni was dead and buried as far as she was concerned.

Charles wasn't quite dead and buried, more like dead in the water. She couldn't see that ever changing but she was clearly still special to him and, although she had vowed never to get involved with him again, if she was honest, he was still special to her as well.

James was a problem. She had once thought of him as the love of her life and they obviously both believed that they *should* be together. Could they ever make it work? Maybe the fact that she had to ask that question was an answer in itself. Yet if they could clear the hurdles that they knew existed . . . James was still a problem.

John was different. He was something new. He was interesting and fun and he seemed to understand her. She liked him, but for the time being, John was a definite "wait-and-see."

Having disposed of the men in her head, she decided on an early night, locked up and went to bed where the two sisters, the witches and a wailing soprano spun round in her head until she fell asleep.

She woke with a start. She'd heard a noise. An old house like hers made many different noises as roof beams and floorboards cooled and settled after a warm day, but those were the kind of familiar noises that her sleeping brain filtered out. A noise that could wake her was something alien.

Then came a hissing and yowling. The cats chasing each other around? No, there was the rumble of a man's voice and a dull thud followed by a series of heavy footsteps. Snakes and bastards! There was someone in the house! She tiptoed over to her bedroom door, slipping on a dressing gown that hung there, and peeked out. She could see nothing and ventured out onto the landing, glancing round a corner down into the hall where she saw torch beams sweeping the darkness and heard two male voices.

She flitted back into the bedroom and crossed the floor, carefully stepping over the floorboard she knew would creak. There were now footsteps on the stairs and she knew she had no choice. There were at least two men. She couldn't take them on—she had to hide. She snatched up her phone and went to the built-in wardrobe near the window, opened the door and quickly swept aside the long dresses and coats hanging there. Down by the floor was a small, triangular door which, like the wardrobe, followed the line of the roof slope. That door gave access to the eaves where there was a small crawl space.

Stepping into the wardrobe, she wriggled into the pitch-black crawl space backwards and reached out to swing the wardrobe door closed. She then did her best to drag the coats and dresses back into place before closing the little triangular door just as she heard footsteps enter the room. The creaky floorboard complained under the weight of one of the men.

"She ain't here," the voice was as heavy as the footsteps and loaded with anger. "What happened to them bloody cats? One of them near took my eye out!"

"They legged it out the back door," came a second man's voice. "Did you check that cupboard?"

Agatha heard the wardrobe door being wrenched open and torchlight squeezed through the crack at the base of the triangular door. She held her breath.

"Nothing here." The torchlight receded.

"Bed's still warm," came the second voice and Agatha shuddered at the thought of him touching the sheet on which she had been lying. "Window's open, though. Could she have gone out there?"

"She must have heard you tripping over them cats! She's gone, mate."

"Right, so we do a number on the place and shove off."

There then came the sound of furniture being overturned, bedding being slashed and glass being broken before the men moved to the bathroom, then the spare room and continued their orgy of destruction.

Agatha's fear had now turned to anger and she lay in the darkness, rigid with fury. When the men moved downstairs, they made even more noise and Agatha risked shuffling in the darkness to bring her phone up to where she could see it. She pressed a speed-dial number.

"John, it's me," she whispered, her voice trembling more with the rage of helplessness than fear of being

212

found. "There are two men in my house. They're wreck-ing everything!"

"Where are you now?" John asked.

"Hiding in the eaves."

"Stay where you are. I'm coming straight there. I'll phone this in. Don't move, okay? Keep yourself hid-den."

"I will. Please hurry!"

"We gotta go!" one of the men grunted to the other above the sound of demolition.

"I say we torch the place."

"Yeah, that thatched roof will burn nicely!"

"No!" Agatha panted, tears streaming down her face. "They're not going to burn my house!"

She pushed at the triangular door but it wouldn't move. She tried again, struggling in the cramped space to bring as much weight to bear on it as she could, but it was stuck fast.

She was trapped in a house that was about to be burned to the ground.

Chapter Ten

"Pile it in the middle of the room," one of the men downstairs ordered, his voice accompanied by the sound of breaking wood. "We can use it all to set the fire."

The sound of the men building their bonfire covered Agatha's increasingly frantic pummelling of the door to the eaves. It still wouldn't budge. She reached for her phone again and called John.

"John, I can't get out of the eaves," she said, surprised that her voice sounded so breathless. It was then that she realised she was breathing heavily. "I'm suffocating in here! And they're going to set the place on fire!"

"Try to stay calm, Agatha," he said. "Control your breathing and don't move about. I'm on my way. Stay still and stay on the line."

It was then that Agatha heard the siren. Was it over

the phone, from John's car? No, it was from outside, somewhere up the hill. It was both—he was that close.

"Hear that?" one of the voices blurted. "It's the cops!"

"Get out of here," said the other one. "Move it!"

There was a drum of footsteps followed by a silence that, for Agatha, was punctured only by the sound of her increasingly laboured breathing and the siren drawing ever closer.

"Hurry, John . . ." she gasped. "They're getting away."

"Never mind them," he said. "Let's concentrate on you. Keep your breathing slow and calm. Try not to panic, that will use up your air."

The next thing Agatha knew there was a commotion of noise and a splintering of wood. The small door was wrenched open and the crawl space was flooded with light. Strong hands reached in to grab her, dragging her out into the room.

"Is she there? Have you got her?" Agatha heard John's voice and the pounding of his feet on the stairs.

"We've got her, sir! She's passed out!"

"No I haven't!" Agatha wheezed, looking up through half-open eyes into the face of the police constable who had dragged her out of the eaves. She pushed herself out of his arms and lunged towards the open window, sticking her head outside to suck in great lungfuls of fresh air.

"Take it easy, Agatha," John said, soothingly, his arm round her shoulders. "A paramedic's on the way to check you over."

"I don't need a paramedic!" Agatha coughed, forcing

herself to her feet. "I need to see what those bastards have done to my house!"

She looked around her bedroom. The bed was over-turned and broken, the mattress slashed and the bedding torn to shreds. Her full-length mirror was shattered. Glass, clothes and shoes littered the floor. She picked a pair of sneakers from a pile of footwear and under-wear and put them on. Practicality, in this instance, tri-umphed over style. She needed to walk across the room and there was too much broken glass for bare feet.

The rest of her lovely cottage looked like it had been torn apart by a tornado. Everything that could be smashed or broken had been destroyed. She followed John into the living room where the burglars had been building their bonfire out of her ruined furniture.

"John!" she croaked, horrified. "What's that?"

She pointed to dark red splatter marks slashed across the wall. John examined the red marks, leaning close to sniff them.

"Oh, my God!" Agatha sobbed. "Boswell and Hodge . . ."

"Not here," John said touching his finger on some red goo and licking it. "This is ketchup."

The cats then appeared, wide-eyed and appalled, whimpering meows and cowering at Agatha's feet. She sat on a broken sofa arm, swept the cats into her arms and cried her heart out.

Lilac Lane was very quickly blocked by the arrival of the paramedics in an ambulance and a fire crew in their fire truck, joining the police cars to light the lane in flashing blue. John ordered the blue lights switched off but the headlights of the vehicles still lit up the night. The fire crew, having checked that the building was sound and no fire had actually been started or was likely to break out, departed first.

The paramedics, after checking Agatha as thoroughly as she could tolerate, were next to go. The police officers, although fewer in number as the night wore on, were still there at dawn. A fingerprint team added to the chaos by spreading black dust here and there, but they were sceptical about the possibility of finding any prints. They were convinced the intruders wore gloves.

John stayed with Agatha throughout the night. They reconstructed the kitchen enough to make coffee and, once she had given a statement to the constable who had hauled her out of the eaves, John sat with her, talking through it all.

"You have first-rate locks on the doors and windows," he said. "Whoever broke in knew exactly what they were doing."

"I've had break-ins before," Agatha said. "I got the best locks available, and an alarm system. They must have known how to disable that, too."

The commotion during the hours of darkness had attracted a handful of curious villagers, Agatha and James having relatively few neighbours in Lilac Lane, but more locals began to take an interest once it grew light and the village was starting to go about the business of Monday. By then only John's car was still outside, so there was less of a circus for any hopeful spectators.

John was helping Agatha try to make her bedroom habitable when she heard a voice calling from downstairs. It was Margaret Bloxby. Agatha hurried down, her friend gave her a comforting hug and Agatha burst into tears again.

"I've got to stop doing this," she said, mopping her eyes. "It's not helping to get things done."

"Sometimes it's the only thing that helps," Margaret said. "You must be exhausted, and you can't stay here. Come back with me to the vicarage. We have a spare room."

"That's so kind," Agatha thanked her, "but I won't impose. There's a place I can stay while I get my house back in order."

A little later that morning, Agatha phoned Charles and explained what had happened.

"Good grief, Aggie!" he said. "If you need somewhere to stay, you know you can come here. Barfield House is yours for as long as you need it. Can I come and pick you up?"

"No, thank you, Charles," she replied. "I'll pack what I can—find the things I need—and be there as soon as I'm ready."

"Whenever you like, old girl—we'll be waiting for you."

Agatha drove to Barfield House with Boswell and Hodge on the back seat in cat baskets. One was held together with tape, a casualty of the wrecking spree, but it still served its purpose. Her own essentials were stuffed into an old suitcase and any other bags or hold-alls she could lay her hands on.

From where she parked outside the house, she could see the terrace and the French doors to the library standing open. Rather than go to the front door, she walked round to the terrace, leaving the cats in the car. Charles was at his desk when she presented herself in the open doorway.

"Aggie, come in, my darling!" Charles rushed over and threw his arms around her before ushering her to an armchair. "You must be shattered. Can I get you anything? Coffee? Something to eat?"

"No thank you, Charles. I'd just like to take a moment and—"

"Charles, sweetie!" A woman's voice called from the hall before she appeared at the library door. She was in her late twenties, tall and slim with long legs and long dark hair. She was carrying half a dozen freshly ironed shirts on hangers. "Gustav wants to pack all of these shirts for you, but we're only going for two days and . . . oh. Who's this?"

"This is Agatha." Charles made the introduction. "Agatha, this is Penelope, the friend I told you about in Cumbria."

Agatha eyed Penelope and Penelope stared back with a pensive pout. Even when pulling such a face, there was no denying that she was beautiful. Agatha stood and walked towards the French doors.

"I think I had best leave, Charles," she said, and

strode past him. She heard Charles mumble something to the lovely Penelope, then he caught up with her by the car.

"Aggie, my dear, whatever's wrong?"

"Penelope is what's wrong, Charles. You didn't tell me about Penelope!"

"Don't you like her? Do you think she's too young for me?"

"Too young? When has that ever bothered you? She's not too young for you, Charles—she's too *tall* for you."

"Look, we're packing for a couple of days down in Cornwall. I don't really have time to get into all of this now."

"I don't have the time either, Charles," Agatha said, getting into her car. "Life is just too short—and so are you."

Agatha drove straight back to Carsely and parked outside the vicarage. She stood on the doorstep with a cat basket in each hand until Mrs. Bloxby opened the door and welcomed her with open arms.

Rather than waste time doing as she was told, resting and recuperating, Agatha spent most of the rest of the day organising workmen to come and clear her house before booking interior designers and decorators to come the following day. Everyone, of course, was far too busy to fit her in the very next day but somehow they managed to find the time when she offered them fees they couldn't refuse.

On Tuesday afternoon, she was standing in her living room with her fabric man looking at swatches for curtains that would match the new furniture she had chosen, when Simon phoned.

"Still clearing up after your visitors, boss?" he asked.

"I'm getting there," Agatha assured him. "It just takes a little organisation."

"Well, I have some interesting news for you. Patrick roped me in to help on the Martinbrook case. Paula came up trumps. There's a girl some of the others are wary of. Patrick and I got some photos off-site and Paula took some video in the school using her phone. I need to send it to you."

"My laptop survived the raid, so I can look at anything you send. I'll call you back once I've seen it."

Agatha looked through the photographs and the video, then phoned Simon back.

"Pass on my congratulations to Patrick and Paula," she said. "These visuals have made my day. Leave it with me now. I'll let Patrick know once I've decided what to do."

Taking a break from the refurbishment plans an hour later, Agatha put in a call to Mrs. Carling at Martinbrook.

"I have some news for you, Mrs. Carling," she said. "I think we need to call a very special parent–teacher meeting. Thursday afternoon would be good. Here's what's happened. . . ."

"But it's simply intolerable, Margaret!" Alf Bloxby, vicar of St. Jude's, had run out of patience, not that he had ever had much patience with Agatha to begin with. He had always resented the amount of time that his wife spent with "that dreadful woman," so having her move in—with two cats, no less!—was stretching his tolerance to the limit. "How long does she intend to stay? I have a great deal of work to do, and it's made all the more difficult when one of the cats decides to shred my notes for Sunday's sermon! She's got to go, Margaret!"

"That's not very Christian of you, Alf," Mrs. Bloxby pointed out. "It's only Wednesday morning. Agatha's barely been here for two days. Knowing her, she will have her own place habitable in no time."

Mrs. Bloxby was right. At that very moment, Agatha was supervising what she had come to call her "renovation team" and aimed to have a functioning kitchen and bathroom as well as a usable bedroom by that afternoon. That was all she needed. She called the office.

"Good morning, Helen," she said when the phone was answered promptly after just three rings. "I'm still tied up at the house, so can you scan any paperwork that I need to see and email it to me, please? Anything else can be signed off by Toni. Is she in yet? I need to talk to her about the Grand Finale event this evening."

"We haven't seen her yet this morning, Mrs. Raisin," Helen replied. "I will ask her to call you as soon as she appears."

By late morning Agatha had heard nothing and tried calling Toni's mobile. It appeared to be switched off. Agatha was concerned. Hadn't they agreed that they would keep their phones at the ready—keep in touch and stay safe? She decided to leave it a while longer, in case Toni was in a meeting about the Grand Finale where she didn't want to be disturbed.

By mid-afternoon, Agatha had still heard nothing from Toni and was getting worried. She left the renovation team hard at work and, wearing the T-shirt, jeans and sneakers that were her workwear, she drove to Toni's flat. There was no answer and no sign of anyone being home. A neighbour said she had seen Toni leave with Edward that morning. Agatha tried Edward's phone, but got no response. Neither did she have any luck when she visited his flat.

Given that the Grand Finale was that evening and both Edward and Toni were to be involved in some way, she decided to drive out to the naturist club to see if they were there. The route from Edward's flat to the club took Agatha close to Antonio's. The office, if Ursula was to be believed, would be closed. She took a slight detour to cruise past and look for anything suspicious. As she expected, Antonio's looked closed and quiet. From her car, she could even see a message in the front window saying that the premises were closed until further notice.

Then, when she turned into the street that ran up the side of the building, she saw that one of the gates to the yard was standing slightly ajar. That didn't look right. She decided to take a look and parked her car. Carrying only her handbag, she pushed the gate further open and poked her head inside, calling out: "Hello! Is anyone here?"

All was quiet as the grave, so she crept inside. The vans were parked in neat rows and she skirted past them. She tried the door that led into the office kitchen and it opened easily. Treading lightly, listening all the time for signs of anyone in the building, she headed for Ulrika's office.

She pushed open the door and was stunned to see Ursula sitting at her desk, looking straight at her.

"Come in, Mrs. Raisin," Ursula said, "we've been waiting for you."

"I . . . I thought something might be wrong . . ." Agatha said. "The gate . . ."

"You were snooping, Mrs. Raisin." Ulrika walked into view. "Looking for your young friend Toni, no doubt."

"Where is she?" Agatha demanded, stepping into the room. "What have you done with her?"

"She is being prepared for her role in the Grand Finale," Ursula answered, and the door slammed shut at Agatha's back. Jasper now stood behind her.

"Jasper, what's going on here?" He stood smiling at her but said nothing, his eyes watery and barely focused. "Jasper?"

"He obeys and responds only to us when he's like this, Mrs. Raisin," Ulrika said. "Now take a seat. Jasper—make her sit."

Jasper grasped Agatha's upper arms tight enough to bruise, making Agatha squeal, and propelled her towards a vacant office chair. Agatha made a show of stumbling, sprawling on the floor and spilling the contents of her handbag. She scrabbled as if to retrieve the contents, secretly palming her mobile phone and swiftly shoving it up her T-shirt, tucking it into her bra below her armpit.

"Leave all that, Mrs. Raisin—you won't be needing any of it," Ursula said. "Now, sit down."

Agatha did as she was told, glowering defiantly at the sisters as Jasper stood guard.

"What's wrong with him?" she asked, nodding at Jasper.

"Jasper is rather too fond of the Devil's Delight," Ulrika explained. "He can't resist it. The chilli spices mask the taste of a little extra flavouring we use. It's made from the *Datura*, or devil's trumpet, plants that I grow in my greenhouse. It has an effect similar to scopolamine. When he's dosed up, he does whatever we tell him. Afterwards, he remembers nothing about it. He may have a few strange hallucinations, but otherwise he's fine."

"So it was Jasper who helped you move Antonio's body," Agatha surmised.

"It was," Ursula admitted. "I see you've worked out our little plan."

"You did the same to Ulrika's husband, didn't you?" asked Agatha.

"Cheating husbands, Mrs. Raisin, get what they deserve," said Ulrika. "Your interference is putting everything at risk. Once we sell this place, we will have enough money to keep us in luxury for the rest of our lives. We can't let you carry on messing things up."

"We're running late now. Jasper, you know what to do with her," Ursula said, and Jasper yanked Agatha out of the chair. He wrapped his arms around her and lifted her off her feet. She screamed, kicking her legs, trying to free her arms to claw at him and flinging her head back to try to hit him in the face, but he was too strong for her.

He carried her from the office out into the yard, Agatha fighting with all her strength to break free. After crossing the yard, the sisters caught up with them and Ursula opened the door to the freezer. Jasper carried her inside, then flung her into a corner against a wall of choc-ice boxes.

"Calm down, Mrs. Raisin," Ulrika advised. "You'll soon be as cool as your friend over there."

Agatha looked to her left where the frozen body of Theresa stared back at her with lifeless eyes.

"Snakes and bastards!" Agatha howled. "You can't leave me in here!"

The sisters turned their backs, and Jasper slammed the door closed, locking it from the outside. The main light went out and Agatha snatched the phone from her armpit. She was about to dial a number, then thought better of it and turned the phone off. The main light flicked on again and she quickly jammed the phone between two choc-ice boxes.

The door opened and Agatha charged forward, hoping to batter her way past her three adversaries, but Jasper was too quick for her, engulfing her in another bear hug.

"Where is your phone?" Ursula asked, holding up Agatha's handbag.

"On my kitchen table," Agatha said, "out of charge."

Ulrika frisked Agatha and, finding no phone, plucked Jasper's phone from his back pocket. She keyed a few buttons to call Agatha's number.

"There's no answer," she reported. "It's dead."

"Leave her," Ursula instructed Jasper. "Then lock everything up." The door was locked once more and Agatha was plunged into darkness.

Agatha cursed and fought back the urge to burst into tears. She had almost died when she had been locked in a freezer once before while on the trail of a drugs gang. She had been lucky then, but this time she had more than luck to rely on. She felt her way back to the choc-ice boxes and found her phone. Switching it on, she could immediately see on the illuminated screen that she had no signal. Having been overheating trying to free herself from Jasper's grip, she was now cooling down fast, starting to shiver.

The light from the screen gave enough illumination for her to find her way to the four corners of the freezer and she climbed on boxes, turning her phone this way and that trying to find a signal. All the while, she grew colder and was shivering uncontrollably. Eventually, having climbed into a high corner of the freezer, her phone registered a signal and she called John. When he answered, she struggled to respond.

"Agatha?" she heard him ask. "Agatha, is that you? Are you okay?"

"C-cold," was all she managed to say. "S-so cold in here . . ."

Then the signal died.

She spent the next few minutes moving around, frantically trying to find a signal again and desperately struggling to keep warm. She tried jumping up and down, running on the spot and waving her arms and legs around but the only thing that felt like it was doing any good was when she wrapped her arms around herself and curled up in a ball in an attempt to seal in her body heat. By now she was feeling exhausted and her eyes slowly closed. Surely, she thought, I can't be falling asleep . . .

Suddenly the main freezer light was on again and she looked up to see the door open. She saw a man's legs step towards her and felt warm arms encircle her.

"Let's get you out of here," she heard a voice say, and realised it was John.

He carried her out of the freezer and into the office kitchen where he sat her in a chair and switched on the cooker. Agatha immediately felt the heat reaching out to her. John was rubbing her hands and her bare arms, while examining her face.

"No white spots—no sign of frostbite," he informed her. "How are you feeling?"

"Warming up," she said. "Tingling."

"I'll make you some hot tea," he said, draping his jacket over her shoulders, "and we'll call you an ambulance. You must have been seconds away from serious hypothermia."

"No," she insisted. "No ambulance. I'm warming up nicely."

She explained what had happened while sipping her tea.

"It was a trap," she said, angrily, "and I walked right into it. We need to get after the sisters. They'll be at the naturist place for the Grand Finale."

"When does it begin?" John asked.

"There's stuff going on all evening, but the main

event isn't happening until it starts to get dark—better for the fireworks."

"I'll get some uniforms up there right now," John said, reaching for his phone.

"No, don't!" Agatha warned him. "Your lot will scare them off. They'll make a run for it and we may never find them again—and that means we might never find Toni."

"At least we know she's not in there," John said, nodding towards the freezers, "but poor Theresa is. I need to call this in, Agatha."

"If you do that, we'll both be stuck here giving statements and answering endless questions," Agatha argued, "and Theresa's not going anywhere, is she? We can just lock up and leave."

"Lock up," John repeated. "How come the place was left open like this? I was able to walk straight in."

"They told Jasper to lock up," Agatha said. "I doubt he's capable of complicated tasks when they've got him in that state."

Agatha insisted on being allowed to move about and, when she did, she reported no ill effects. She walked into Ursula's office, found her handbag and, rifling through the desk drawers, produced one of Jasper's ceremonial daggers. She tested the blade and it collapsed smoothly into the handle. The other dagger was nowhere to be found.

"John, we need to get to the club," she said. "I've a feeling something awful is about to happen!"

The car park at the club was almost full and John made no real attempt to park, abandoning the car at the entrance before they rushed inside. The hall and the clubhouse was empty, but they could see through to where a procession of naked people carrying flaming torches was making its way down the lawn towards the woods and the Lone Warrior.

"Let's go," said John, stepping forward.

"Not so fast," Agatha said. "We'll be spotted straight away if we go out there like this. And those two witches will vanish. If we're going to find Toni, we don't want to attract attention."

"Oh, you don't mean . . . ?"

"Yes—don't be such a prude. Leave your stuff in the Wizards locker room."

When Agatha emerged from the locker room, John was standing in the hall. He was holding a towel in front of him, folded over his arm, but was wearing nothing at all except his black leather Oxford shoes. Agatha stared at them.

"I can't walk about outside in bare feet," he said, trying not to stare at her nakedness and failing completely. "The soles of my feet can't stand it."

"All right, come on," she said, snatching his towel and flinging it into a corner. "You won't be needing that."

They followed the group of players into the woods. Some were wearing elaborate costumes that made Jasper's black-and-gold robe look very ordinary. There were sequinned capes bearing strange symbols, the significance of which only the game players could have understood. There were men and women wearing nothing but what appeared to be chainmail tunics, and any number of participants who wore nothing bar a few exotic and mystic symbols painted on their flesh. Everyone was chatting, laughing and enjoying themselves. Agatha nudged John, ordering him to cheer up.

Making their way through the throng, they came in sight of the Lone Warrior and Agatha took John to one side, where they could watch for the sisters unobserved. Drum music was playing from large loudspeakers and the flaming torches held by the game players cast pools of flickering light that made the shadows in the trees dance to the beat.

The glade in which the Lone Warrior stood had been cleared of undergrowth and brush to provide space for the assembled game players and either side of the Lone Warrior blazed two large bonfires. Behind the stone, a platform had been erected and a throne draped in black velvet stood waiting.

Suddenly there was a massive explosion in the sky, the blast strong enough to take Agatha's breath away, and a shower of white stars marked the beginning of an impressive fireworks display. The pyrotechnics ended as they had begun, with a huge bang, and when the last echoes had died away, the drum music began again.

There was a murmur in the audience and the crowd parted, allowing a figure to pass. It was Edward. He wore a red cape and, lying prone in his arms, he carried Toni, who was draped in a wispy white sarong. Edward walked forward with her to the Lone Warrior and laid her on the stone before retiring a few paces. Agatha stared hard at Toni's slender form. She could see that

Toni was breathing but she couldn't tell whether she was unconscious or play acting.

"We need to get her down from there," Agatha said and made to move towards the stone, but John stopped her.

"Look over there," he said, pointing.

Jasper entered the glade, clad only in his black-and-gold robe, and accompanied by Ulrika and Ursula as naked torch bearers. Agatha peered at him through the firelight. He had the same smile she had seen on his face in the office, and his eyes still had the glazed look that identified him as being under the influence of the Devil's Delight. He took his place on the throne and his handmaidens knelt beside Edward. The music stopped, and Jasper rose and approached the stone where Toni lay, unmoving.

"Friends!" he called, holding his hands aloft and allowing his robe to fall open. "We are gathered here to celebrate the end of the game. The angels failed to complete their final challenge and have lost. They are required, therefore, to forfeit one of their number."

He passed his hands through the air above Toni's body and when he raised both arms aloft he was holding the dagger high above her.

"Snakes and bastards—Jasper, no!" Agatha screamed, rushing forward.

Jasper looked at her with a confused expression, then down at the stone. He saw the earth heave and churn and then a hand claw its way out of the ground. The earth then burst open and the figure of a man in armour climbed out from beneath the stone. A red glow blossomed behind the eye slits in his helmet, then seemed to crystallise into two fiery eyes. At first unfocused, the eyes became more animated and struck Jasper with terror when they looked directly into his with terrifying intelligence and a purpose of which he was in no doubt.

"The Lone Warrior!" he screamed.

The figure clasped Jasper's hands in his armoured gauntlets. With one swift movement, he turned the dagger towards Jasper and plunged the blade into his chest.

"What the hell happened there?" asked John, rushing past Agatha to where Jasper lay. "He's dead! He killed himself!"

Toni sat up, rubbing her eyes, as though waking from a long sleep.

"Are you all right, Toni?" Agatha asked.

"Sure," Toni said, looking round, mystified. "What's going on?"

"I think Jasper was seeing things we weren't," Agatha suggested. "Hallucinations, I'd say. You were about to be sacrificed, then he screamed something about the Lone Warrior and stabbed himself in the chest—he's dead."

Agatha turned to the audience, who were spellbound. Some of them began to applaud. Agatha blinked. They think this is all part of the show, she told herself. Then she saw the handmaidens getting to their feet, preparing to leave.

"Friends!" she yelled, holding her arms in the air. "These two witches cast a spell on the demon master. They must not escape. The . . . um . . . Sword of Turiddu

233

and all the Treasures of Santuzza await those who cap-
ture them!"

The sisters dashed for the cover of the trees but the
crowd let out a mighty cheer and raced after them. Ulrika and Ursula were dragged back towards the Lone
Warrior, each held firmly by two painted women. John
stepped forward.

"The game's over," he said. "I am a police officer . . ."
He reached for his warrant card in his pocket, but felt
only his bare chest. "I really am a police officer—you
can tell from my shoes. These two women are under arrest for murder. Bring them to the pavilion while I fetch
the cuffs from my car . . ."

Within half an hour the Mircester Naturist Society premises were crawling with police officers and
John, relieved to be back in his clothes, was directing
the crime scene. The formalities of taking statements
and questioning witnesses went on long into the night.
When Agatha finally made it home and dropped onto
her brand-new bed, she was asleep as soon as her head
hit the pillow.

The next morning, she knew she had one last thing to
do in order to close the file on Antonio's murder. She
phoned Charles. Given the way their previous conversation had gone, there was a little awkwardness at first,
which Agatha schmoozed her way past using all of the
skills she had acquired during her years in the PR business.

"So what can I do for you, sweetie?" he asked.

"Charles," she gritted her teeth and ignored the "sweetie," "I need you to get on the first available flight to Rome. . . ."

On Thursday afternoon at Martinbrook Sixth Form College, Jim Sullivan and Kathleen Partridge sat either side of their daughter in Mrs. Carling's office, with the headmistress facing them across the desk. There were two empty seats to one side of the desk. Mrs. Carling was peering over her glasses at some paperwork.

"So what's all this about?" Sullivan demanded. "I ain't been up in front of the headmistress since I was a nipper and it ain't my idea of fun."

"I have two guests I need you to meet, Mr. Sullivan," said Mrs. Carling, tapping her papers into a neat pile. "Ah . . . here they are now."

Agatha walked into the room with Patrick.

"What's she doing here?" Sullivan growled.

"I'm doing my job, Mr. Sullivan," Agatha said, taking one of the spare seats, "and sticking my nose into your affairs."

"You need a proper slap, you snooty bitch!" Sullivan spat, starting to rise from his seat.

"As you were, sunshine," Patrick said, pointing to the corner of the room where a camera near the ceiling was covering the scene. "You're on camera here, so you need to be on your best behaviour."

"Like I give a shit about some camera," said Sullivan, pushing back his chair.

Agatha held a small device in her hand and pressed

a red button on top. Two very large young men wearing black T-shirts stretched tight over tattooed muscles were in the room in less than an eye-blink.

"Patrick's days of taking down bruisers like you are long gone," she said, smiling sweetly. Patrick shrugged and nodded in agreement. "So, I brought along Ron and Dave. I'd rather they waited outside so we can keep all of this to ourselves, but . . ."

"Sit down, Jim," Mrs. Partridge said forcefully. "You'll only make a fool of yourself."

Ron and Dave left the room.

"Let's not waste any more time, Mr. Sullivan," Agatha said. "We are here because Mrs. Carling and Mrs. Partridge commissioned Raisin Investigations to look into how quantities of Class A and Class B drugs were getting into the college."

Agatha opened her briefcase and set up a touchscreen tablet on the desk. She tapped it to wake it up, then swiped through a series of photographs.

"These photos were taken when you went out to dinner with your daughter yesterday evening," Agatha explained. "You can clearly see you handing a package across the table to Sarah."

Sarah groaned and hid her face in her hands.

"We have a video here," Agatha went on, "taken in one of the college common rooms. Here you can see Sarah opening the package, distributing smaller packets to a group of girls and accepting cash in exchange."

"Jim!" Mrs. Partridge howled. "How could you? You gave Sarah drugs to sell in school!"

"It wasn't much." Sullivan dismissed the accusation

with a wave of his meaty hand. "Just enough for her to earn some pocket money and learn a bit about business. . . ."

"Business?" Mrs. Partridge was furious. "The drugs business! You make me sick! And as for you," she turned to her daughter, "I never thought I'd be ashamed to say I was your mother, but I am—I'm ashamed! Don't you realise that what you were doing was dangerous—and completely illegal?"

"Very much illegal," Agatha said gravely. "If Sarah was to be convicted, because she is under eighteen she would spend any custodial time in a juvenile secure unit. Mr. Sullivan, on the other hand, could face anything up to life in prison for supplying Class A—the cocaine—and up to fourteen years for supplying Class B—the cannabis."

"However," said Mrs. Carling, "I know that the board of governors here at Martinbrook is keen to avoid such unpleasantness. I have to tell you, Sarah, that you are suspended from the college with immediate effect. The board will decide whether that suspension is extended to a permanent expulsion. Mr. Sullivan—you are banned from ever setting foot on college property again."

"And you can forget about seeing Sarah!" Mrs. Partridge yelled at her ex-husband.

"I have a right to see my own daughter!" he roared in reply.

"Not after what you've done! You stay away from her or I'll make sure all of that evidence goes straight to the police!"

Grabbing her daughter by the arm, she marched her

out of the room. Sullivan gave Agatha a look of utter malice, eyes blazing with fury. Agatha met his stare, eyes wide with mock innocence. She pressed the button to summon Ron and Dave.

"I think we need you in here now, boys," she said. "Mr. Sullivan will have to be escorted off the premises once we have finished our little discussion."

"Feel free to use my office as long as you need, Mrs. Raisin," said Mrs. Carling, standing to leave.

"We have another matter to discuss," Agatha said once Mrs. Carling had gone.

"I got nothing to say to you!" Sullivan snarled, jabbing his finger in her direction. "Except that this ain't over!"

"You've said that before," Agatha reminded him, calmly, "but this time I agree with you. You see, I really don't like being threatened. You threatened me. Then you sent two thugs to trash my house. Had they succeeded in setting it on fire, I would have died in there. I can't prove that was down to you, but you and I both know it was."

"Maybe you won't be so lucky next time!"

"There won't be a next time," Agatha assured him. "In fact, you'd best pray that nothing bad ever happens to me because we have multiple copies of those photographs and that video, and if I'm ever harmed, neither your ex-wife nor Mrs. Carling will be able to stop my people taking copies to our friends at Mircester police station.

"And just so you know not to cross me again," she leant forward and pointed a warning finger at him, while briefly checking her watch, "two things are happening right now that will make life a little uncomfortable for you. Food hygiene inspectors from your local authority have just arrived at your ice-cream plant. I hope you have everything spic-and-span there, Mr. Sullivan, because they're itching to shut you down.

"Also around now, a good friend of mine is arriving in Italy for discussions with Antonio's family. Antonio owned the whole business, Mr. Sullivan. None of it belonged to Ursula and, because she's going down for his murder, she can't inherit any of it. Antonio's family in Italy will inherit and want to get the business up and running again as soon as possible, but they need a partner in the UK. My friend has the finances in place to make it all happen, so you can kiss goodbye to any plans to take over Antonio's.

"What was it you told me, Mr. Sullivan? 'You need to move fast in this business—no point in hanging around.' I think you'd best not hang around. You need to get back to work and pacify those hygiene inspectors."

She asked Ron and Dave to see Mr. Sullivan out and they took an arm each, leading him to the door where he turned and looked back over his shoulder. He opened his mouth to speak but Agatha beat him to it.

"I know, I know—'this ain't over,'" she said, sounding a little bored. She waved the tablet at him. "I decide when it's all over for you, Mr. Sullivan."

Agatha arrived home to find James standing in his front garden, looking across into Agatha's cottage where the decorators had started stripping the torn and ketchup-stained wallpaper.

"Remodelling?" he asked, when she called to him from his garden gate.

"Let me fill you in on a few things," she said, and he invited her in.

They sat together drinking tea in James's back garden and Agatha ran through everything that had happened.

"I've been gone for less than two weeks," he said when she'd finished. "I can't believe that you've put yourself in so much danger."

"I didn't choose to have people try to kill me, James," she said, cross that he should attach any blame to her.

"No, no, I know that, my dear," he said, recognising the way the Raisin temper fuse was starting to smoulder and appealing for calm. "It's just that I'm appalled that you might have come to harm and I wasn't here to help you. I would be devastated if anything happened to you."

"You would?"

"Without a doubt. On that cruise I was surrounded by people most of the time, yet I don't think I've ever felt so lonely. Oh . . . look . . . you know I'm not good at talking about this sort of thing but . . . I missed you."

"James, believe me, I missed you, too."

"Come on, then—the sun's past the yard arm so let's have a glass of wine to celebrate my homecoming."

"And my survival."

"Yes, yes, of course. The most important thing is that you came through it all unscathed, so to speak. Maybe you can also show me what you're doing with the new décor."

James poured two glasses of Malbec and they strolled down his front path and up Agatha's where she showed him the extent of the damage and the plans for refurbishment. They paused in the kitchen where he picked two tickets off the work surface.

"*Cavalleria Rusticana*," he said. "I haven't heard that performed for years."

"Mrs. Bloxby dropped them by," Agatha explained. "It's just the local choir. I doubt it will be very good."

"We should go along anyway—show our support. It might be better than you expect."

So it was that Agatha and James came to be sitting in St. Jude's church hall listening to a recital of Mascagni's opera with Giovanni, in a white tuxedo, conducting a selection of professional musicians and the plucky amateurs of the Carsely Choral Society. She stared at his face when he addressed the audience at the beginning of the performance and was immediately aware of what it was that she, and presumably other women, found so beguiling. He was like a magnet. He first attracted your eyes and then seemed to draw you irresistibly towards him.

His eyes scanned the audience as he spoke, then he stopped, looking directly at her. He had picked her out of all the faces in the audience. He smiled, raised an eyebrow and, in that instant, she knew that he hadn't forgotten her. The connection was still there.

When the performance began, she watched his back

and his arms moving, urging the choristers to infuse their singing with the passion that the music demanded. Some of them made a commendable effort. One of them, the glamorous soprano playing Santuzza, whom Giovanni had brought in from another choir, was exceptional.

When the final notes had died away and the enthusiastic applause petered out, Agatha watched Giovanni mix with the choir, praising them for having done so well while also graciously accepting congratulations from members of the audience.

"I thought that was really rather good," James said, before excusing himself, heading for the gents' lavatory.

Agatha took the opportunity to make a beeline for Giovanni, then saw his soprano get there first. She slipped a hand round his waist and he responded in kind, his hand drifting from her waist to her bottom. She reached across and kissed him. Those were not the actions of a man and woman who were simply friends. It was obvious to anyone who had seen what had just happened that they were lovers.

The woman made for the ladies' lavatory and Agatha followed. She joined the soprano at the washbasins, and made a pretence of reapplying her lipstick.

"You were good," Agatha said.

"Thank you," the woman replied.

"The Barolo at the Royal Oak is very nice," Agatha said, casually.

"Pardon?" The woman looked at her suspiciously.

"Be a good girl and tell Giovanni that I lost an earring

in his room last week," Agatha said with a broad smile. "I'd love to have it back some time."

Agatha walked out, found James and set off for home.

"You know," James said, as they walked down the high street, "all that tale of love and romance tonight got me thinking about us."

"Really?" said Agatha, who had mainly been thinking that there was no way she would ever put up with Giovanni treating her like his little Santuzza. He really was dead to her now.

"Yes . . . we really should be together, you know. Our marriage was . . ."

"Yes," said Agatha firmly. "If that's heading towards a proposal, James, then the answer's yes!"

"Well, I . . . splendid. Jolly good."

Agatha tucked her arm in his and they turned into Lilac Lane.

"So will you sell your house?" James asked.

"What do you mean sell my house?" Agatha asked. "I've spent a fortune doing it up. I'm not selling it."

"But it makes no sense to have two houses side by side."

"Well, you sell yours then and move in with me."

"I don't know about that, Agatha. Your new décor isn't really to my taste."

"What do you mean? What's wrong with my new look?"

"If you look at it properly, it's all a bit feminine, that's all."

"I like it!" Agatha snapped. "If you don't, then that's your problem!"

"My problem," James corrected her, "is that you are so damned intolerant!"

"If that's what you think," Agatha said as they reached their garden gates, "then maybe we shouldn't rush back into a marriage that we were both so keen to rush out of!"

"Perhaps not!" barked James, and they each stomped up to their own front door.

Maybe I'm destined never to maintain a stable relationship with any man, Agatha thought as she plodded up the stairs to bed. On the other hand, maybe I just haven't tried it with the right man yet. After all, there's always John, and he did look good without his clothes . . . apart from those shoes!

Read on for an excerpt from

DEAD ON TARGET—

the next Agatha Raisin novel by
M. C. Beaton and R. W. Green,
coming soon in hardcover
from Minotaur Books!

Chapter One

"I'll kill him! I swear I will! We can't let him get away with this!"

The woman was furious, storming past the refreshments-tent queue with a man in her wake. He reached out to grab her by the arm and she spun to face him, her long blonde hair a swirling mane.

"Just wait!" he pleaded. She was a few years younger than him and for a moment he stood over her, as though he were about to chastise a child, but he quickly relented, attempting to reason with her. "It's not too late to get him to change his mind. I'll have another word with him . . ."

"Why bother?" she snapped. "He doesn't listen to you. He doesn't give a damn what we think! The time for talking is past. We have to *do* something! Understand? We have to do something about him!"

"Listen to me . . ." The man looked round, suddenly aware that those waiting in the queue had abandoned their own conversations and the half-finished text messages on their phones to be entertained by the unexpected drama. One woman in particular caught his attention. She had a smooth bob of glossy brown hair and an expression of intense curiosity. He glowered at her. Agatha Raisin stared back at him, her bear-like eyes unflinching.

"Let's talk in the car, my love," he said as the blonde woman shook her arm free. He urged her towards the nearby car park. "Too many eavesdroppers around here."

"Such excitement so early in the morning, Mrs. Raisin," came a voice from behind Agatha, catching her by surprise.

"I was thinking exactly the same thing, Mrs. Bloxby," Agatha replied, turning to greet her friend. It amused them to address each other in public with the customary formality of the Carsely Ladies Society, while in private, over a glass of wine or a schooner of sherry, they were Agatha and Margaret. "We don't usually see such theatrics at the Carsely Village Fete until well after the beer tent has opened."

Agatha nodded towards a marquee where staff from the local Red Lion pub were unpacking glasses, stocking shelves with bottles and exchanging friendly banter with a growing huddle of local men waiting patiently in the sunshine, all eagerly anticipating their first pint of the day.

"I hope you didn't take what was being said literally," said Mrs. Bloxby, smiling. "I'm sure Stephanie isn't about to kill anyone. That's just something people say when they're upset."

"I know," Agatha said, "and something was certainly upsetting both of them. I take it you know them?"

"Yes, Stephanie and Gerald were married here." Mrs. Bloxby looked to the edge of the field in which they were standing, where the steeple of the Church of St. Jude poked its spire above the trees. Agatha had never been a particularly religious person, but she had always found the fourteenth-century church, with its stained-glass windows set in mellow Cotswold stone, a gently comforting presence in the village. It helped, of course, that she knew Margaret Bloxby would generally be waiting with a warm welcome in the rectory next door. Her husband, Alf, was the vicar at St. Jude's.

"Gerald's father, Sir Godfrey Pride, owns Carseworth Manor, the big house in the woods over there." Mrs. Bloxby pointed to the trees beyond the field in which they were standing. "His family donated this land to the church for the benefit of the local people. That's why the fete is now held here each year."

Agatha gazed out over the colourful collection of tents arranged in neat rows around an open arena in the middle of the field. Jolly, candy-striped canvas structures stood shoulder-to-shoulder with sun-bleached white bell tents and traditional ridge tents while tall teepees and elaborate marquees mingled with family campers and basic garden gazebos. Most had trestle tables set up outside displaying a variety of goods from homemade cakes and home-grown fruit and vegetables to children's toys, second-hand tools and flowering plants.

Some tables and tents were overwhelmed with myriad articles that some liked to call bric-a-brac but Agatha called crap. Who really wanted to buy mismatched, discoloured crockery, chipped china ornaments, dull crystal decanters or plastic Buddhas? She could well imagine why people would want to rid their homes of such junk, but how on earth could anyone take delight in buying someone else's junk?

"We seem to have rather a lot of pre-loved treasures for you to browse this year," said Mrs. Bloxby, watching Agatha disdainfully appraising the closest of the bric-a-brac tables.

Agatha gave her friend a sideways glance, aware that she was sporting a mischievous smile. Margaret Bloxby was petite and neat with plain brown hair laced with occasional wispy strands of silver-grey and a kind face well-practised in forming expressions of sympathy and compassion. The impish smile was reserved for teasing Agatha. Although she would never normally tolerate anyone poking fun at her, the slightest spark of provocation easily igniting her infamously short fuse, Agatha could never be angry with Mrs. Bloxby. On so many occasions she had provided Agatha with a warm welcome, a patient ear, a shoulder to cry on and sage advice. She had always been a good friend.

Yet what had always impressed Agatha most about Mrs. Bloxby was not her gentle, caring nature, which she greatly respected, but her stalwart fortitude, which she hugely admired. She had a heart of gold and a back-bone of steel. Was that, Agatha mused, too much metal in one person? No matter—Mrs. Bloxby's unflinching cour-age had saved her more than once. She remembered the time when she had been punched by a man whom Mrs. Bloxby had immediately smacked over the head with a jar of homemade chutney. Then there was the gun-man who would surely have killed them both had Mrs. Bloxby not wrestled the weapon from him and shot him in the chest. He had survived, but Agatha often won-dered how Margaret Bloxby would have fared had he not. She had been distraught at the thought of having al-most taken another's life. Perhaps sometimes there was an overwhelmingly discordant clash of gold and steel.

"You know how much I hate all that stuff." Agatha laughed, waving a hand at the bric-a-brac, dismissing the junk along with the disturbing memories. "Still, I suppose all of this goes towards helping good causes."

"It does indeed," Mrs. Bloxby agreed. "One of them this year is the restoration of our old graveyard."

"I hope you're not going to set all the old gravestones straight. They wouldn't look right in tidy rows. They should stay as they are, all higgledy-piggledy, like a bunch of best pals growing old together, not soldiers on parade."

"I agree. The restoration work's all about rebuilding the graveyard wall and the paths. Besides, some of the stones are so fragile that they'd fall apart if anyone tried to move them."

Having reached the front of the queue, Agatha insisted

on paying for their coffees and was handing one of the recyclable paper cups to Mrs. Bloxby when she heard a jingle like sleigh bells. A middle-aged man walked past wearing a tall black hat, a red neckerchief and a white shirt with white trousers. His hat was decorated with a garland of flowers while red sashes fastened with rosettes crisscrossed his chest. The jingling bells were clustered on straps tied just below his knees.

"Ah, the morris men." Mrs. Bloxby gave the man a cheery "Good morning!" and a generous smile. "I've always loved the morris men, haven't you? We should really call them morris dancers now, of course—they're no longer men-only groups."

Agatha spotted the rest of the dancers in the distance, all similarly attired, approaching from the car park. She squinted at one of the figures. There was something familiar about the way he moved, the way he held his shoulders. It couldn't be, could it?

"Quickly!" she breathed, holding her coffee cup out to Mrs. Bloxby. "Take this!"

In what appeared to be one swift movement, she produced a compact mirror from her handbag, smoothed her hair, checked her lipstick and straightened her dress. She felt a wave of relief that she had chosen that particular dress. The white flower pattern on a black background wasn't too frivolously summery and the skirt reached well below the knee, but the neckline still dropped low enough to provide a certain . . . allure. A white rope belt cinched it neatly at the waist. An instant later, the compact was back in her handbag and she was retrieving her coffee.

"Slick." Margaret Bloxby nodded her approval. "What was that in aid of?"

"John!" Agatha called to one of the approaching morris dancers, waving madly.

A tall, well-built man looked towards her and grinned. He removed his hat and pretended to hide behind it as he drew nearer, feigning embarrassment at having been exposed as a morris dancer.

"You never told me you were involved in this!" Agatha chided, wagging her finger in mock rebuke.

"I can explain!" He laughed, stooping to kiss her cheek. "One of the lads was injured and they asked me to stand in. I might be a bit rusty—I haven't done this for years."

"Mrs. Bloxby," Agatha said, sweeping a hand towards her in introduction, "this is my friend John Glass."

Mrs. Bloxby watched Agatha and John exchange a glance and caught a twinkle in Agatha's dark eyes.

"Pleased to meet you, Mr. Glass," she said, shaking John's hand. "I'm so looking forward to seeing the morris . . ."

She was interrupted by a rapid popping noise followed by a dull boom from the PA system's loudspeakers.

"Good morning, everyone . . ." came a man's voice.

Pop! Boom!

". . . is this thing working . . . ?"

Pop-pop! Boom!

"Well . . . welcome to the Carsely Village . . ."

Pop! Boom! Pop!

"Oh, dear," sighed Mrs. Bloxby. "Alf's making the announcements. He's quite at home delivering one of his

Sunday sermons from the pulpit, but this is well outside his comfort zone."

The Reverend Bloxby, dressed in a short-sleeved black shirt and black trousers that made him look even smaller and thinner than ever, struggled on, gripping his microphone with knuckles as white as his dog collar. Agatha could see his lips moving as he stood in front of the administration tent, reading from a sheet of paper, but now no sound was coming from the speakers at all. She was surprised at how flustered he seemed. Normally he came across as quite confident and self-assured, almost arrogant. Suddenly his voice came blasting out.

". . . so we'll have everything from archery and morris dancing to shin kicking and dwile flonking . . . wait . . . what? That can't be right . . ."

The PA system let out a banshee screech.

"Oh, bloody hell!" wailed the reverend.

"I think I'd better go lend a hand," said Mrs. Bloxby, handing Agatha her coffee and hurrying over to her husband.

"Fancy a coffee?" Agatha asked, offering John Mrs. Bloxby's cup. "Margaret didn't touch it and it'll be cold by the time she gets back."

"Thanks," John said. "I wasn't sure if you'd be here today."

"Nor I you," Agatha replied. "I thought you were working."

"I managed to swap to a late shift in order to help out the lads."

"Is that a privilege of rank in the police force, Inspector Glass?"

"Not really. You usually need a bit of luck on your side to swing it."

"I see—so how did you become a morris dancer?"

"Quite by chance, really. Years ago, a couple of friends met a bunch of morris men in the pub and they persuaded us to give it a go. I gave it up when work started taking over."

"So who was it that was injured? What happened to him?"

"So many questions!" He laughed. "If I didn't know you were a private detective, I could probably have guessed. My old pal Wayne mistimed a move, slipped and got one of these in the face."

John held up a stout, smooth stick.

"I take it you don't normally whack each other with batons?"

"Some of the dances involve clashing sticks together. They say ash or hazel make the best sound. It's all part of the fun."

"Speaking of fun, when are you going to take me out dancing again?"

"I checked with Strangley's. They're having another ballroom night in two weeks. I've already booked."

Agatha had first met John when they danced together at the wedding of their mutual friends, Alice and Bill Wong, also both police officers. It was the first time in years that she could remember having danced the night away in the arms of a man who neither stood on her toes nor tripped over his own feet. She regarded herself as an accomplished dancer but John, whom she learned had danced competitively when he was a youngster, was impressively elegant and graceful.

Less than a week ago, John had surprised her with dinner at Strangley's, a spa hotel between Mircester and Chipping Camden. Agatha had previously only ever thought of the hotel as the sort of place for hen parties and golfing weekends, neither of which held much interest for her, but John had discovered their special dinner-dance events. The evening had spun on late into the night and she had woken the next morning in her cottage bedroom, lying in John's arms.

"You're an angel," she said, craning her neck to kiss him on the cheek, and he slipped his arm around her shoulder. "Steady, tiger," she added, removing his arm. "Remember . . ."

"I know . . ." he said, with a resigned sigh, fully aware that Agatha regarded too many displays of public affection as being undignified, slightly vulgar and really only for teenagers, ". . . there's a time and a place for everything."

"Speaking of which," Agatha said, "why do we have morris dancers here today? We're well into autumn and I thought it was something that happened in the spring. Isn't it all to do with fertility rites and suchlike?"

"Not entirely. Cotswold dances traditionally tended to focus on Whitsun, which is at the beginning of summer, but morris dancers have always been out and about on Boxing Day, at New Year—pretty much any time, really. The dances have been performed for centuries. Working men, farm labourers, builders and all sorts got involved because they were paid in cash, food and ale. Nowadays we do it for charity—and the ale!"

"So what was all that about shin kicking and . . . vile thonking?"

"Dwile flonking," John corrected her and she raised a suspicious eyebrow, half convinced that he was about to try to hoodwink her with some dubious shaggy-dog story.

"They're both real things, honestly." He grinned. "Shin kicking's been part of the Cotswold Olimpicks since . . ."

"The Cotswold Olimpicks?" Agatha folded her arms, her head cocked slightly to the right, challenging John to prove that he wasn't simply pulling her leg.

"I kid you not," John defended himself, smiling. "The Cotswold Olimpicks are held every year just outside Chipping Camden around the spring bank holiday. The games were first staged in the seventeenth century, long before the modern Olympic Games. There have always been lots of traditional contests—tug-of-war, running races and suchlike—but shin kicking has been part of the games since they began. It's a kind of wrestling. Two competitors face each other, grab each other by the collar and take swipes at each other's shins. You have to try to force your opponent to the ground or get him to surrender."

"And dwile flonking? Is that also an Olimpick sport?"

"It is nowadays. It involves a group holding hands

and dancing round in a circle. The person in the middle of the circle is the flonker and has to dip a stick like this . . ." he held up his morris dancing stave, ". . . into a bucket of ale. The flonker then fishes out a cloth soaked in ale, the dwile, and flings, or flonks, it at the dancers. A dancer who's hit has to drink from the bucket and . . ."

"Don't tell me." Agatha shook her head with a resigned smile. "The flonker drinks the ale if no one is hit. It's a drinking game, isn't it? How do you know who's won?"

"No one can ever remember."

"I take great pride in being able to tell when men are lying to me," Agatha said, laughing, "and that's all too ridiculous not to be true."

"No shin kicking or dwile flonking for me, though," John said with, Agatha thought, a hint of regret. "I'm on that late shift tonight and I don't want any injuries before our next ballroom date!" He struck a dance pose, as though holding an invisible partner in his arms, and waltzed off towards the other morris dancers, explaining that he had to "go through some of the dances with the lads," then he turned, pausing for a second to blow her a kiss.

Agatha watched him join the huddle of white-clad dancers. John seemed very relaxed—far more so than when they had first met. He had always been charming and good company but as they had come to know each other better, she had started to see a man far younger than his fifty-four years begin to emerge. That, she told herself, never one to dim the sparkle of her own personality beneath a cloak of modesty, is entirely down to me—Agatha Raisin. I have made a difference to that man's life. He . . .

"He really rather likes you, doesn't he?" The cultured drawl of Sir Charles Fraith came from over Agatha's left shoulder. She turned to face him.

"I wish people would stop sneaking up on me!" she snapped, suddenly furious at having her thoughts interrupted, especially since Charles seemed somehow to be reading her mind. "You're the second one today. What happened to a simple 'Hello' or 'Good morning' to attract someone's attention rather than just blundering up and disturbing them?"

"Sorry, Aggie, I . . ."

"And don't call me that!" Agatha had tolerated the pet name when she and Charles had been close, when they had been lovers, but saw no reason to do so now that they were, at best, uneasy friends.

"Agatha . . ." Charles took a deep breath and a smile etched lines in his perfectly shaved face, the tiniest of wrinkles appearing at the corners of his eyes. There were no such creases on his crisply pressed shirt, his blue sports jacket or his cream trousers. Sir Charles Fraith was, as always, immaculately turned out, with scarcely a lock of his fine, fair hair ever out of place. Even when he was stark naked, Agatha knew from past experience that he was an utterly crumple-free zone. "Good morning. I apologise for catching you off guard."

"Feisty little filly, ain't she, Fraith?" said an older man accompanying Charles.

"Feisty little . . . ?" Agatha glowered at the man. He

was far older than Charles, old enough to be his father, and taller, although most men were, with a voice that had the same upper-class tone. His was tinged with an added croak where decades of cigarettes and whisky had dulled its refinement. "Who the hell are you?"

"Agatha, this is Sir Godfrey Pride," Charles explained. "We are what you might call neighbours."

"No," Agatha said firmly, "you are not what I might call neighbours. It would take a day to walk from where you live at Barfield House to where he lives. Your house is surrounded by over a thousand acres, Charles, so you're never going to have a cup of tea and a chat over the garden fence like what I might call neighbours."

Neither did they seem the likeliest of chums. Sir Godfrey had a shock of wild grey hair, a ruddy face and bleary eyes peering out from behind dark, shaggy eyebrows. His tweed jacket was scuffed and threadbare at the cuffs and his voluminous, rumpled corduroy trousers had badly worn areas that were faded pink, yet were alarmingly red elsewhere, a bit like the boozy face of the old man himself. He reached out, offering Agatha his hand. She made no move to shake it.

"I am not a filly," she said coldly. "I am a business-woman."

"Meant nothing untoward by it, my dear," he said, by way of apology, "and it's your business skills that I'm interested in. I hear you're very good at what you do."

"The best," Agatha confirmed, finally accepting his handshake. "I understand that this field is part of your land."

"It was once," he said, nodding, "but everything changes. Only old dinosaurs like me, set in our ways, remain the same. Pride's the name, don't y'know, and pride is the enemy of progress."

"Sir Godfrey has a problem he'd like to discuss with you," said Charles.

"Yes, but I won't trouble you with that now," Sir Godfrey said, smiling softly at Agatha. "You should enjoy the fete and this lovely weather. The dark days of winter will be upon us soon enough."

"If there's something I can help you with, then we should arrange to meet," Agatha said, handing him her business card. "You can reach me on this number on Monday morning."

"Thank you, my dear. I shall look forward to talking to you again then. In the meantime, I can see something that needs my urgent attention." He was looking towards the Red Lion tent, now open for business. "Care to join me, young Fraith?"

"It's a tad early for me, old chap," said Charles, "but I may catch up with you again later."

Sir Godfrey stuffed his hands in his jacket pockets and bumbled off towards the beer tent.

"What was that all about?" asked Agatha once the old man was out of earshot.

"No idea," Charles said, shrugging. "I bumped into him on the way here. Haven't seen the old devil in years, but he asked me to introduce him to you. He needs help with something but doesn't know who to trust. Said he wanted to see if you were the right sort."

"The right sort?" Agatha felt a wave of exasperation

261

turning to another rising tide of anger. "Honestly, you people never cease to amaze me. Do you mean the 'hunting, shooting and fishing' sort, or the 'loyal, obedient servant' sort?"

"His words, not mine," Charles said, defensively. "All I think he meant was that he was looking for someone trustworthy."

"And did I pass the test?" Agatha folded her arms, a look of defiance on her face.

"I should say so!" Charles laughed. "You stood your ground, demanded respect. You couldn't have been too upset by him, though. You still gave him your card."

"Business is business," Agatha said, letting her arms drop and the tension drain from her shoulders. "How are things going with your new enterprises?"

"Rather well, actually. The new vineyard looks fantastic and the winery is under construction. By this time next year we will be producing our first wine. It's all damned expensive, though. A lot of investment."

"I thought you'd found business partners to help with that?"

"I've had lots of interest, but most of them want to see things up and running before they commit."

"Oh, Charles," Agatha sighed. "You haven't staked everything on this business, have you?"

Agatha recalled the lean years prior to Charles inheriting a fortune from the family of his deceased wife following their short marriage. He had been what is often referred to as "land rich but cash poor," after a series of increasingly desperate, utterly disastrous investment schemes.

"Not at all," Charles assured her, with what Agatha saw as forced nonchalance. "I've had to spend a bit on essential maintenance around the estate, too, but there's still plenty left in the pot . . . enough to take you out to dinner perhaps?"

"Charles, I . . ." She glanced over to where John was in animated discussion with the other dancers.

"Ah, yes." Charles nodded. "Your morris man. I noticed the way you were looking at him."

"I like him a lot. He's a good friend."

"We were good friends once. Practically inseparable. I miss that . . ."

"A lot of water has flowed under the bridge since then, Charles. There's no going back. That will never happen."

"Never say never." He smiled. "Who knows what the future holds, after all? How is James?"

"I haven't seen or spoken to him in quite a while," Agatha said. Her last conversation with James Lacey, her ex-husband and next-door neighbour, had been a short, high-volume exchange that had ended with the slamming of their respective front doors. "I think he must be off on his travels again, writing articles about Bolivia, or Outer Mongolia, or somewhere."

"Really? I heard that . . ." Charles paused, running a hand through his hair, a sure sign, Agatha knew, that he felt he was on shaky ground.

"You heard what?" she prompted him. "Come on, Charles, spit it out."

"No, it's nothing," he said, quickly. Then, realising that he had his catch on the line, he decided to reel her

263

in. "Idle gossip, I'd say. Let me find out if there's any truth in it and I can tell you all about it over dinner . . . Monday evening?"

"Dinner," Agatha said, fully aware that she was being played but peeved that Charles might have heard something about James that she had not. What was it? Another woman? Was he moving out of Carsely? She shook her head, trying to persuade herself that she couldn't care less, but she had to know. "Dinner only. Call me."

She marched off, leaving Charles in no doubt that the conversation was over by taking a sudden and avid interest in the nearest bric-a-brac stall.

The events at the fete were soon in full swing and Agatha enjoyed watching the first of the morris dances, which involved energetic hopping and handkerchief waving in time with music provided by an enthusiastic fiddle player and a tiny, white-bearded old man who was almost hidden behind a giant accordion. Despite his misgivings, John never put a foot wrong, as far as Agatha could tell.

There followed an archery demonstration by the Ancombe Archers Club. Six archers—three men and three women—using modern, high-tech bows stood at shooting positions near the middle of the arena, aiming at targets around fifty metres away. There were no spectators anywhere near the targets, and the area behind the targets was a tangle of shrubs and bushes that marked the edge of some woodland. The circular targets had a white outer ring, with a black ring inside it, then a smaller blue ring, a red ring and a gold centre circle. They staged the demonstration as a competition, each archer firing six arrows and the one with the lowest score dropping out until there was just one winner, one of the women. Agatha applauded each stage of the contest along with the rest of the spectators. She was impressed that not one arrow missed the target and amazed at how many of them struck gold. The Ancombe Archers were deadly accurate.

When the archery was finished, Mrs. Bloxby could be heard once more on the PA system announcing that anyone interested in archery should join the archers down by the targets for a brief lecture, while the top end of the arena would now host the dog show.

"There will be awards," she informed everyone, "for the cutest puppy, the most beautiful female, the most handsome male, and the dog who looks most like its owner. Last year that one was won by Stan the bulldog and his owner, also called Stan. Stan's wife told me that Stan didn't snore as loudly as Stan, but Stan definitely drooled more than Stan—and I never worked out which Stan was the snorer and which was the drooler . . ."

Agatha had never considered herself a "pet person" until she had been given her two cats, Boswell and Hodge. At first, she had been wary of looking after the animals, but once she realised how independent they could be, which took some of the worry out of having them in the house, and how affectionate they were, which had both surprised and delighted her, she had come to adore them. Dogs, on the other hand, were too much of a burden. She found herself smiling, however, when she saw the gaggle of puppies on leads being walked into the arena. Some trotted along, tails wagging, some bounced around, and some leaped on others, rolling and wrestling in a tangle of leads. Any reprimands from their owners were met with lolling tongues, wide, bright eyes and more tail wagging. They're cute, Agatha admitted to herself, but the archers are really impressive. Those bows could kill—an almost silent murder weapon—and that makes them far more interesting than a bunch of smelly little puppies!

Agatha strolled over to where a small crowd had gathered around the group of archers. Barriers had been put in place and the spectators were encouraged to stand behind them as two of the archers, one male and one female, set up a target about ten metres from where a bearded man with a cloud of snowy white hair stood holding his bow. Agatha guessed he was in his late seventies, but he stood tall and straight and, once those setting up the target were well clear, he selected an arrow, drew back his bowstring and shot the arrow straight into the centre of the gold circle.

"Good morning, everyone!" the old man said, lowering his bow and turning to the spectators. "My name's Robin Hood . . ." A ripple of polite laughter flowed from the crowd. "That always gets a bit of a laugh," the man continued, grinning, "but my name really is

Robin Hood. You're probably all now thinking, 'Poor sod—how could his parents do that to him?' Well, Hood's my father's family name and his first date with my mum was a trip to see the old nineteen thirty-eight Robin Hood movie, so I've always been quite grateful they didn't call me Errol Flynn Hood! In fact, if they'd met a couple of years later, I could have been Pinocchio!"

There was more laughter from the crowd and Agatha smiled. Public speaking was something she'd had to do many times in the past when she had run her own London public relations agency. She had given speeches to gatherings of sophisticated, highly influential businesspeople and had always prepared rigorously beforehand in order to conquer her nervousness. She'd been spurred on by a horrendous recurring dream where she was addressing an audience only to hear her voice slowly revert from the acceptably cultured accent she had worked so hard to perfect, to the Birmingham twang that betrayed her roots in a council tower block. Mr. Robin Hood, on the other hand, had a natural, relaxed manner that easily charmed his audience.

"So, with a name like Robin Hood, what other sport could I possibly take up than archery?" Robin Hood laughed. "Now, who would like to give it a go? How about you, young lady?"

It took Agatha an instant to realise that he was looking at her.

"Come along, don't be shy—give her a round of applause, everyone. What's your name, young lady?"

With the eyes of the crowd now upon her and the applause ringing in her ears, Agatha gave Robin her name, taking a tentative step forward to be met by one of the female archers who asked if she was right- or left-handed. On being informed that she was right-handed, she asked for Agatha's left arm and, once Agatha had set her handbag on the ground at her feet, she helped her to strap a leather protector over her inside forearm.

"My Maid Marion will help you with the kit," said Robin, standing close to the spectators, a few metres to Agatha's right. "Actually, her name's Petula but none of Robin Hood's rogues were ever called Petula, were they?"

The woman laughed. She was the winner of the archery contest, slender, dark-haired, and Agatha judged her to be in her early forties. She helped Agatha fit a kind of three-fingered glove on her right hand.

"The arm protection stops the bowstring from doing any damage when it's released, Agatha," Robin explained, addressing the spectators as much as he was Agatha, "and the finger guards do likewise when you draw back and release. Spider will now show you the bow. He's called Spider because of that spider's web tattoo on his left elbow. For goodness' sake nobody ask him where the spider is—he might show you!"

Spider was a skinny, scruffy individual in his late twenties and only a little taller than Agatha. He showed her how to fit the bow's hand grip in the "V" between the thumb and forefinger of her left hand.

"The grip allows you to balance the bow there without clutching it too tightly," Robin explained. "Then, standing sideways with your shoulders aligned with the target, you can raise your hand to shoulder level, keeping your arm straight."

Robin demonstrated raising the bow and Spider, standing much closer behind Agatha than she would have liked, gently lifted her wrist until her hand was at shoulder height. As Robin outlined the importance of adopting a "square stance" with your feet parallel to the target, Spider released Agatha's wrist. His fingers traced a path up her arm, drifting gently down to linger lightly around the side of her left breast. Agatha froze. She could scarcely believe it. Had she really just been secretly groped in front of a crowd of people? She turned her head to glower at him only to see a sly leer on his face.

"Keep your distance and keep your hands to yourself, Spider!" she hissed. "Or I'll crush you like a bug!"

Undaunted, he remained standing close behind her. Robin was now demonstrating, without actually drawing the bowstring, how the thumb on the right hand should come back to a point just below the jaw.

"You need to keep your body straight," he said, "so that your arms are level across your shoulders, forming a 'T' shape with your torso . . ."

"Like this?" Agatha asked, bringing her elbow up and flinging it back. She caught Spider just below the nose. He yelped and doubled over, cupping his hands over his face. Some of the spectators winced, others simply burst out laughing.

"Whoops!" Robin called. "Gently does it, Agatha. You'd best take a step back there, Spider!"

Spider retreated, rummaging in the pocket of his jeans to retrieve a crumpled tissue and stem a faint trickle of blood from his nose.

"Maid Marion, would you take over with Agatha, and give her an arrow, please?" Robin motioned Petula forward.

"He deserved that," Petula said quietly, lending Agatha a hand to fit the groove or "nock" at the base of the arrow to the bowstring. "He's such a creep. Somebody needs to teach him a lesson."

Agatha looked Petula in the eye, the younger woman returning her gaze from beneath a furrowed brow. With that brief exchange, a moment of dark understanding passed between them. Petula had also suffered from Spider's unwelcome attention. Petula stepped back, Robin calling out instructions.

"Keep the arrow pointing down the range at the target, Agatha," he called. "Now, with your index finger above the nock point, your middle finger and ring finger below, raise the bow. Keep that left arm straight and bend your right arm to draw back the bowstring, thumb below your jaw."

Agatha did as instructed, looking down her left arm to where the arrow rested on the grip's "shelf," lining the arrow up with the round target. Then her eyes flicked left, distracted by a yellow shape that had popped into view near the bushes just beyond the target. A young Labrador dog gazed back at her. To her horror, she realised that she was now looking down the arrow, directly at the puppy, and she could feel the bowstring starting to slip on the leather finger guards.

"Oh, please, no!" she breathed, but it was too late. She felt the string release and shut her eyes tight as the arrow took flight.